ROB THOMAS

Rob Thomas is the creator of the television series *Veronica Mars* and *iZombie* and the co-creator of the television series *Party Down*. He lives in Austin with his wife and two children. He has finally recovered from Ray Allen's three-pointer in Game 6 of the 2013 NBA Finals.

JENNIFER GRAHAM

Jennifer Graham graduated from Reed College and received her MFA from the University of Texas at Austin. Her short stories have appeared in *The Seattle Review* and *Zahir*. She currently lives in Austin with her husband.

MR. KISS AND TELL

veronica
MARS

MR. KISS AND TELL

Rob Thomas

and

Jennifer Graham

Based on characters from the series *Veronica Mars*, by Rob Thomas

Vintage Books
A Division of Random House LLC | New York

A VINTAGE ORIGINAL, JANUARY 2015

Produced by Alloy Entertainment
1700 Broadway, New York, NY 10019
www.alloyentertainment.com

Based on characters from the series *Veronica Mars*, by Rob Thomas.

The Library of Congress Cataloging-in-Publication Data
has been applied for.

Vintage Books Trade Paperback ISBN: 978-0-8041-7072-7
eBook ISBN: 978-0-8041-7073-4

Thomas author photograph © Eric Doggett
Graham author photograph © Jennifer Grandin Le
Book design by Claudia Martinez
Cover design by Mark Abrams
Cover photographs: key © Ragnar Schmuck/Corbis;
woman © moodboard/Alamy; image of "Veronica Mars"
based on a photography by Robert Voets 2014 WBEI

www.vintagebooks.com

Printed in the United States of America
10 9 8 7 6 5 4 3 2 1

veronica
MARS

MR. KISS AND TELL

PROLOGUE

It was raining in Neptune. That was rare, even for early March; the little SoCal city usually boasted blue skies year-round. But the clouds had rolled in off the ocean, and now raindrops pattered across the houses of rich and poor alike, the one great equalizer in a town without a middle class.

A grimy white van trolled slowly through the east edge of town, where Zen landscaping gave way to weed-strewn lots. There were no millionaires' homes here—no boutiques, no surf shops, no post-op resorts for wealthy nip/tuck patients. Out here were prefab houses propped on cinderblocks, biker bars, chop shops. The buildings were all sun-bleached and dingy, the roads speckled with potholes that sent the van bucking on its worn-out shocks.

Frank Kozlowski was a junk dealer, just like his old man had been. His late wife always liked to say he was in "antiques," but ninety percent of what he found was well and truly junk—broken appliances he stripped for parts, scrap metal he recycled at a buck a pound. But every so often he found something really good. In a town like Neptune, where the wealthy always had more than they knew what to do with, a guy with wheels and initiative could make out like a bandit. High-end furniture that just needed reupholstery or refinishing; designer clothes with minor stains and tears. Paint-by-numbers art, antique road signs, and metal lunch boxes with '70s-era cartoon characters on the front. He salvaged the best of it and resold it from his garage, mostly to young, Tyrolean-hatted guys and buzz-cut girls in resale mom jeans who used words like "naive" and "authentic" to describe his wares. Kozlowski didn't mind—or in most cases even notice—the affectation. These kids kept the mortgage paid and the fridge stocked with beer.

He drove slowly through the rain, alert for any kind of glimmer from the underbrush. A rosary swayed back and forth from his rearview mirror, almost in time with the wipers. In the passenger seat, his little wire-haired mutt, Gus, sat at attention, ears pricked forward. It was just after seven a.m. and he'd already been out here for two hours. So far all he'd found was a stack of warped two-by-fours, a brass drawer pull, and a molded plastic chair pocked with cigarette-burn stigmata.

But the business was like that. Some mornings were a bust. Other mornings, the junk fairy lit a path at your feet and led you to something special. That's what really got him out of bed at four in the dark, cold-ass morning. Not so much the promise of cash as that into-the-red spike of adrenaline, the thrill of the next big find. The way a single magic discovery could vindicate a hundred shitty, wasted trips. He'd never been able to explain that to Nell. She always groaned when he came back with rusted, filthy roadside dross. "Jesus, Frank, why can't you just hit up estate sales like everyone else? Flea markets. Thrift shops. This stuff is worthless."

Worthless. The word—the very idea—left him dumbstruck. Nothing was worthless. Not if you knew who needed it. Not if you knew how to salvage it. She'd never really appreciated that.

Still, that road went both ways. He'd been startled by the silence in the house in the year since she'd died (emphysema; she'd never been able to give up the fucking cigarettes), startled by how hard it was to sleep without her cold feet on his calves all night. They'd never had any kids. Now it was just him and Gus and a restless, edgy energy that sent him pacing from room to room and woke him in the pre-dawn chill, hounding him out of the house and into the junkyards and abandoned buildings fringing Neptune. He never thought to call the feeling grief.

Now, cruising along the empty road, his mind drifted. He thought about the donuts he always picked up on the way home, and the hot shower he'd take after unloading the shit from his van. Gus would need a bath too, after the rain and mud. He'd just about decided to throw in the towel and head home when he saw it.

There.

He eased his van onto the shoulder and killed the engine. The road banked sharply downward toward a lot fringed with buckwheat and sumac, a scraggly patch of land with a faded FOR SALE sign nailed to a post. The sign had been there at least a decade. This wasn't exactly prime real estate, situated on the edge of town in the empty miles between a ramshackle trailer park and the Balboa County Youth Correctional Compound. Half of Neptune seemed to use it as a cost-effective dumping ground, making it a regular stop on Kozlowski's circuit. He'd found some good stuff in that lot over the years. A box of dog-eared *Playboys*. A six-foot fiberglass cheeseburger from a long-defunct drive-through. The front half of a '68 Buick Skylark that he'd sold to a restoration company. And now he'd caught a glimpse of something through the gloom—something that might just be worth stumbling down that bank for.

Gus jumped lightly out of the van and took off running, his tail flailing right and left. He loved the hunt as much as Kozlowski, sensing his master's excitement and feeding off it. Kozlowski stepped out after the dog, slamming the door behind him. Icy needles of rain stung his cheeks and neck. He hunched his shoulders against the cold, his boots sinking down in the mud. For a moment he couldn't see anything, and he wondered if he'd imagined it. But then he found it again—a dirty pink shape, half hidden in the sedge. A dress form, perhaps a mannequin? His heart gave the familiar little stutter that almost always meant a good score.

The man knelt alongside Gus and patted the dog's trembling rump. "What do you think? Worth getting wet for?"

Gus whipped around in a tight, fast little circle. That was good enough for Kozlowski.

The incline was steep and slippery. He edged his way down, leaning back to keep from going ass-over-teakettle. Gus scampered ahead of him and then paused at the base of the hill, shaking water from his coat. Kozlowski's eyes locked in on the thing in the field. Definitely a mannequin—he could see the arms and legs splayed out in the mud. Cleaned up and restored it might get him a C-note from a vintage shop or a tailor. And there was the outside chance it was worth real money. He'd heard of antique mannequins going for seven, eight hundred a pop, sometimes more if it was a rare model in good condition.

But even from fifty feet away, this one was looking pretty rough. Its wig was so tangled and dirty he couldn't guess what the original color might have been. The left arm crooked out at a strange angle to the rest of the body, probably busted. Dark streaks of mud wreathed the pale figure. Gus darted ahead across the field toward the thing, running in wild circles around it for a moment as Kozlowski approached.

He was a few yards away when the hair on the back of his neck suddenly shot up. Something felt wrong about the whole scene. The mannequin's skintight dress was hiked up around its waist, its sculpted buttocks bare to the sky. Another time he might have thought it was funny, trying to imagine why the hell the manufacturers had designed a dress-store dummy with a realistic ass. But here in the rain, splayed out in the mud, it looked so sad—so sick—he felt a creeping unease that crowded out the dollar signs he'd imagined.

Gus was pawing at the thing's torso, a thin whine coming up from his throat. Through the sound of the rain, Kozlowski could hear the distant croak of a raven from the tree line around the lot. He stepped closer, barely noticing the dull throb in his knee or the cold weight of his soaked denim jacket, kneeling down next to the shattered form in the gorse.

Two things happened at once.

The first was that Kozlowski's eyes confirmed what some part of his gut already suspected: that the pale peach color was not fiberglass but flesh. That the dress was torn almost to shreds. That the black grime caking the skin was laced with streaks of dark red.

The second was that the woman's left hand—jutting at a grotesque angle from the rest of her body—slowly clenched, fingers curling down into the dirt.

She was still alive.

CHAPTER ONE

The mid-July heat in Courtroom Three was stifling. Spectators packed into the gallery had removed their jackets and loosened their collars, shirts and blouses sheer with sweat. Makeshift paper fans, folded from crime-prevention handout flyers, fluttered throughout the room. The AC in this wing of the Balboa County Courthouse was out. And because the criminal justice institutions of Neptune, California, thought Eli "Weevil" Navarro's conviction was a foregone conclusion, they hadn't seen fit to move the proceedings to a cooler part of the building. It figured to be a quick day's work proving that an inked-up *ese* with a rap sheet dating back to grade school had returned to his old ways.

Generally a safe call around here, thought Veronica Mars, sitting near the back of the courtroom next to her father. *Neptune's finest seldom collar anyone who can afford a long trial. If you're poor or nonwhite, our wheels of justice run fast, but not necessarily true.*

She opened the collar of her shirt and gave it a few quick tugs, trying to accomplish what the dead AC couldn't. *But say this for us: When we railroad 'em, we do it in classic Hollywood style. Sweltering courtroom . . . fluttering paper fans . . . court reporter blotting her cleavage. All we lack are the bailiffs in Colonel Sanders suits and the gallery full of saturnine black folks in overalls.*

"In the past week, you've heard the evidence against my client fall apart piece by piece." Cliff McCormack stood in front of the courtroom, his dark hair plastered to his forehead. He was fiftyish, six-three, and angular, dressed in a gray suit and a *Jungle Jewels* green tie that was one part razzle-dazzle and two parts JC Penney clearance rack. His voice was deep and whiskey-dry as he addressed the jury.

"The so-called witness who claimed to have sold the gun to Mr. Navarro rescinded his statement in the weeks after the incident. The recording of the roadside-assistance call Celeste Kane made to the Beacon Corporation just before the incident also contradicts much of her story—including her claim that Mr. Navarro threatened her verbally."

Is it me or did someone put extra sambal *in Cliff McCormack's pad thai? The old warhorse is bringing it hard for Weevil.* Veronica had known the public defender for most of her life; he and her father were old friends. He had a sardonic, often self-deprecating manner—he referred to himself as the Kmart of the legal system—but Veronica knew better. Cliff worked hard to try to get his clients a fair shake. It was quixotic work in a town like Neptune, with justice for sale to the highest bidder, but he was one of the good guys. "The prosecution has gone out of its way to paint a picture of a hardened criminal returning to his old ways. But what are we to make of the *five years* between his last conviction and the events that took place the night of January twenty-fifth? Five years in which Eli Navarro has proven himself a responsible and law-abiding citizen, time and time again. You've heard from dozens of character witnesses—friends, coworkers, clergy—who say my client is a hard worker, a loving father and husband—in all respects a model of reform."

Hmm . . . laying it on a bit thick there, Cliffy, Veronica thought. Sure, until six, seven months ago, Weevil Navarro *had* seemed like a changed man—a far cry, at least, from the high school crime kingpin Veronica had known a decade earlier. Back then, Weevil was the alpha head cracker of the local bike gang. His photo was a staple in *BUST*ed!*, the local police mug shot tabloid. But when she'd seen him at their high school reunion less than a year earlier, it seemed he'd finally settled down. He was happily married, a doting father, a small business owner.

That had all changed when he'd tried to help Celeste Kane after her car had broken down in one of the more "colorful" parts of town. Weevil had woken up in the hospital with a hole in his shoulder and a stack of criminal charges on his head, including attempted theft, attempted assault, and brandishing a deadly weapon. Celeste claimed he'd threatened her. According to the cops, he'd been clutching a stolen Glock in his hand when they'd arrived on the scene. According to Weevil, he hadn't touched a gun in years.

Since then, his once-successful auto repair shop had folded. None of Neptune's wealthy wanted their Bentleys and McLarens being cased by a guy who'd allegedly pulled a gun on one of their own. He'd been putting in a few hours at his uncle's body shop, but he was barely scraping by. Small wonder, then, that he'd backslid into some of his old habits with his old crew of biker reprobates. Weevil took care not to tell her more than he thought she, a detective and the daughter of a former sheriff, needed to know. But his new-found discretion made it, if anything, even clearer that he was extralegally supplementing his income.

"In the end," Cliff said, "the prosecution's case is a house of cards, collapsing from the weight of unanswered questions and flatly bizarre assumptions. Remember, the alleged attack took place just *sixteen minutes* after he'd taken his babysitter home." He paused to let this fact sink in.

From her seat, all Veronica could see of Weevil was the back of his head. It was close-shaven, shiny with sweat. The fading Gothic letters of a tattoo were just visible, creeping up his neck right above his collar. Behind him, Navarro siblings, cousins, aunts, and uncles crowded into the gallery, tense and silent. She recognized Chardo, the cousin who'd once let Weevil take the rap for his own credit card fraud. Apparently that was water under the bridge now.

A few chairs down from Chardo, Weevil's wife, Jade, sat with her shoulders rigid, her gaze fixed on the jury box. The pretty, doe-eyed woman looked more haggard every time Veronica saw her—dark semicircles under her eyes, collarbone showing through her top with alarming sharpness. Between the garage's closure, the medical bills, the criminal charges, and Weevil getting back with his boon companions in the PCH gang, Jade was under a lot of falling dominoes. And now the last one was teetering and ready to fall one way or the other.

"According to Ms. Ortiz, Mr. Navarro was sober, lucid, and cheerful when he dropped her off. So are we supposed to believe he spent the evening of his ten-year high school reunion scheming to slip in a quick assault and robbery before picking up diapers and going home to his wife and child? It doesn't make any sense. Why would a success-

ful small businessman with a family to support risk everything to carjack one of Neptune's best-known citizens? Why
would a man who has worked tirelessly to escape a life of
crime and poverty just wake up one day and decide to throw
it all away?"

Cliff was, indisputably, killing it. Yet Veronica knew
these weren't the questions he really wanted to ask. While
preparing Weevil's defense he'd had Keith look into the
accusations of planted evidence against the Sheriff's Department that had popped up in the past few years. Keith had
found dozens of people who claimed to be victims. They
were all predictably easy targets—the poor with priors, most
of whom pleaded out in order not to suffer long trials and
trumped-up charges. They'd planned to use the claims of
falsified evidence to show a pattern of corruption and help
clear Weevil's name, but all that testimony had been thrown
out before the trial. Judge Oglesbee had deemed it "irrel-
evant."

Veronica had seen Cliff take some hard knocks over
the years, but that one was egregiously painful. Cliff paced
a few steps away from the jury, then turned again to face
them. One of Veronica's law professors at Columbia used
to swear he could call any verdict based solely on the jurors'
expressions during closing arguments. Based on the twelve
blank faces she could make out in the jury box, she had to
conclude respectfully, Professor, that that was a steaming
load.

"Ladies and gentlemen of the jury, as you deliberate, we
ask you to consider: Has the prosecution answered *any* of
these questions? Have they accounted for the holes in the
evidence, the flaws in the timeline, the lack of credible moti-

vation? If they haven't, Eli Navarro should go free. Thank you very much."

Murmurs rolled through the courtroom. The judge pounded his gavel in two brisk strokes.

"We'll now adjourn for deliberations. Bailiff, please show the jury to the chamber."

Veronica and Keith exchanged glances. All around them, chairs scraped the ground, people clambered to their feet.

All they could do now was wait.

CHAPTER TWO

"How can you do that right now?"

Two hours and change after the jury withdrew, Keith Mars sat with his daughter in a booth at Miki's, a surf-themed greasy spoon across the street from the courthouse. Keith had frequented the place since his days as sheriff, and the diner had barely changed since then. Sure, there were a few more duct-taped tears in the vinyl seats, a few new dings in the fiberglass surfboards lining the walls, but the bacon was still crisp and pancakes were available twenty-four hours a day, the way the good Lord intended.

He looked up from the crossword puzzle he was filling in to see Veronica, her French toast untouched in a congealed pool of syrup, her fingertips anxiously tapping her coffee mug.

"I don't know if you realize this, but your old man is pret-ty sharp." He held up the newspaper to reveal a smear of blue ink, almost illegible in the puzzle's neat black grid. "How many people do you know have the *guts* to work in pen?"

"Got it, Steve McQueen; you laugh at danger and break all the rules."

"Honey, I'm that cold-blooded dude in Tiananmen

Square. And this puzzle's the tank—frantically zigging and zagging to escape humiliation!" Keith smirked, nodded with exaggerated slowness, and filled in another long word.

Veronica rolled her eyes. "Bit more work on that Yeezy chin thrust and you could have a nice gig entertaining his 'second string bitches.'" She sighed, drumming her fingers more urgently against the mug. "How much longer do you think they'll take?"

She reached for the mug's handle, but Keith intercepted the saucer, pulling it a few inches away. "Maybe it's time to lay off the coffee. You've had four cups since we got here."

"Okay, you're right. Good thing we decided not to wait in the bar. By now I'd be standing on my chair, trying to start a 'Livin' on a Prayer' sing-along." She rested her chin on her hand and sighed. "I just can't stop obsessing over Cliff's case. Trying to figure out which way the jury will go so I'll be braced for it. I mean, his argument was really solid. Discrediting all the evidence, making the prosecution's story sound ridiculous . . ."

"Look at you," he said. "It's almost like you went to law school." Veronica had turned down a job at a top law firm in New York to come back to Neptune, a choice Keith was still struggling to get on board with even nine months later. Following in his footsteps as a PI had never been what he wanted for his daughter.

"Would that I really had 'almost gone.'" Veronica rolled her eyes. "Anyway, I feel like it could go either way. If they'd let us use the planted-evidence testimonies . . ."

"I know, but they didn't. We can't keep dwelling on it." Keith reached across the table and patted her hand. "Look, Cliff was inspired. He did a fantastic job considering what he had to work with. All we can do is wait and hope the jury agrees. We've got to accept that some things are just out of our control."

Veronica paused, weighing her words. "Permission to speak freely?"

"Of course."

"Dad, what you just said—it's one of those serenity prayers that old folks share on Facebook, not a Keith Mars response to getting hosed. You did all that legwork on the planted evidence, and now we can't even use it. Plus, Lamb's about to get away with it again, even if Weevil gets off." She gave him a sidelong look. "Not to mention the car crash. You should be way more bitter about this."

Keith pretended to mull over his crossword puzzle again. Veronica had been fishing for information about the accident for months now and he wasn't about to rise to her bait this late in the game. He knew she suspected the truth— that he'd been meeting with Deputy Jerry Sacks about the planted evidence. That Sacks had been about to turn whistle-blower on the department when someone in a delivery truck T-boned their car, then circled back and rammed it again. Sacks had died and Keith had come close.

Keith had been investigating the crash for six months with little to show for the effort. The official story was that Sacks had been on the take and his relationship with one of his underworld contacts had gone south. But Keith hadn't found any evidence that Jerry Sacks was dirty. And while he couldn't prove that the truck driver had been operating on Sheriff Dan Lamb's orders, he believed it with bone-deep certainty.

Which was why Veronica wasn't going to be involved.

Lamb and Company had already proved they were willing to kill to keep their secrets. He wasn't about to put her at risk too—no matter how badly he wanted to expose the department's corruption.

"Why do I need to be bitter? You're bitter enough for both of us." Keith smiled faintly and jotted down "RAMIS" in twelve across: *Bespectacled ghost exterminator.* "At this point I'm just hoping Eli doesn't get prison time. If we can clear him, I'll consider that a success."

Veronica sighed and looked down, but she didn't argue. She had to know he was right. Neptune had always been dirty, and it would be for a long time to come, with or without Lamb. If Eli went free, they'd have at least prevented him from becoming the town's latest victim.

But Veronica never had been good at picking her battles, a clearly hereditary trait. After all, Keith had been filling his laptop with information on Lamb for months, interviewing dozens of people who claimed the Sheriff's Department had planted evidence to gain a conviction, or used excessive force, or taken property under some yanked-from-their-asses interpretation of search and seizure law.

Aside from the victims in the planted-evidence cases, Keith had finally pieced together a clear picture of the corruption within the department. Lamb had a racket functionally identical to that of an organized crime ring. Local businesses that paid up got protection; the ones that didn't ran the risk of theft, arson, even assault on their premises. The money trails were labyrinthine and nearly impossible to follow. But Keith knew Lamb shouldn't have been able to afford the beach house he'd just purchased, never mind the annual Tahoe ski trip, the brand-new Escalade, or the floor-side seats he got, five or six times a season, to see the Lakers.

Time was, Veronica would've followed all these developments in real time after snooping around his desk and figuring out his safe code. She'd done it before. Maybe Keith should have stopped her, that night eleven years ago when he'd realized that she was looking through the Lilly Kane files. But for some reason he still didn't fully understand, he couldn't bring himself to shut her out. She'd gone after Lilly's murderer with a single-minded fury, and Aaron Echolls had almost killed her—and then Keith—for her trouble. The memory of flames licking at his legs, of knowing that Veronica was trapped behind them, still made him flinch involuntarily.

But that had been a long time ago. They were partners now. She was almost twenty-nine; she had her own caseload, her own life. As far as he knew, she'd respected his decision to keep her at arm's length on the planted-evidence investigation.

The waitress stopped by their table to freshen their coffee. Veronica tugged her mug back across the table, and started her compulsive drink-doctoring ritual. Keith watched in silent amusement as she shook the sugar packet—four times, as always—ripped off the end, and dumped the contents into her coffee, followed by a generous slosh of cream. She dinged the spoon three times against the mug and placed it on a neatly folded napkin.

"What'll it mean for Lamb if Weevil gets off?"

The question tumbled out of her abruptly. Keith put the crossword puzzle down next to his empty plate.

"Well, there might be an inquiry into the stolen Glock.

Knowing Lamb, he'll find a way to shake it off. You know, pin it on a couple of low-ranking deputies, fire them, and proclaim the whole department squeaky clean."

She grimaced. "At least it'll generate some bad press. That could hurt him in the election."

"Well, he's running uncontested, so it's hard to see Weevil's case driving the outcome. For that you'd need a scandal outrageous enough to totally invalidate him as a candidate." Keith gestured to the front page of the paper, which showed a grinning Lamb shaking hands with the mayor at some awards ceremony.

"I'm beginning to view democracy as the Siri of political systems. *So* much better in theory." Veronica put her elbow on the table and rested her cheek in her hand. "But I keep hoping for Lamb to deliver an eleventh-hour Hail Mary. Public livestock-shagging, instituting Sharia law, Tasering a cappuccino-skinned movie star he didn't recognize. Something so appalling people just can't ignore it anymore."

"There's my girl, always praying for someone's downfall!" Keith glanced back at his puzzle. "Now help me out with this. I need a nine-letter word for 'anatomical name for Achilles.' Starts with 'C'—unless 'CAROL CHANNING' is wrong for thirteen down, but I don't think . . ."

He was interrupted when both their phones chimed at the same time. He glanced down at the screen.

It was from Cliff.

> Jury's back. Ten minutes until they announce.

Their eyes met over the table. In spite of all his feigned calm, Keith's heart gave an uneven lurch in his chest.

"Ready?" he asked.

"Yeah, I'm ready." She grabbed her bag and slid her jacket back on over her shoulders. "By the way, it's 'calcaneal.' You know . . . the tendon behind your shin. Achilles' downfall."

"Okay, smarty." Keith punched her lightly in the arm. "Let's go find out if we've got anything to celebrate."

CHAPTER THREE

"Congratulations!"

Cindy "Mac" Mackenzie met them at the door of Mars Investigations, her elfin face stretched in a smile.

Veronica threw her purse down on an end table. "Free man, coming through. Stand back, everybody!"

Behind her, Keith and Cliff filed in. Weevil brought up the rear, looking dazed.

The Mars Investigations office was dim and cool, a relief from the sweltering heat outside. Dust motes glittered in the bars of light falling through the blinds. The rented space looked and felt industrial, more in terms of its original function—brewing enormous vats of lager—than any conscious design mode. It had twenty-foot ceilings and stained concrete floors. The rooms were so big they were hard to light, and deep shadows pooled in the corners. The one part of the room you might call "sleek and modern" was Mac's desk, laden with computer equipment. Some clients wondered why a receptionist needed five different monitors. More observant ones realized Mac probably wasn't just answering phones.

"Cleared of *all* charges?" Mac asked now, looking at Weevil.

"Every last one." Weevil grinned. He shed his suit coat and unbuttoned his pressed blue button-down, revealing a white tank top underneath.

From the far side of the room, Cliff's two-fingered newsie whistle silenced the crowd. "Attention, please!" he shouted. "If I could just have everyone's attention. The bar is officially open. And for this special occasion I brought the *middle-*shelf Scotch. None of that rotgut swill we usually drink." Cliff held the bottle aloft.

"Today, we are victors, and to the victors goes the John-nie Walker Red Label." Keith went to the kitchenette in the corner and started pulling down glasses.

"Cliff seems pretty jazzed," Mac said to Veronica.

"He should be. Mr. McCormack was great," Veronica said, raising her voice so Cliff could hear. "By the time he finished proving reasonable doubt I wasn't even sure Weevil actually existed."

"Thank you, Veronica," Cliff said. "Coming from an almost-lawyer, that praise means a lot to me." He accepted a glass from Keith. "Truth be told, we really lucked out. If that informant hadn't retracted his story, this could have been a whole different show."

Keith gave Veronica a knowing look. "Yeah. Lucky, that."

She pretended not to notice. Okay, so she'd been the one to tell Weevil about that snitch. It wasn't like she'd *encouraged* him to track the guy down and . . . do whatever he'd done to invoke his better angels.

She brushed the train of thought aside. It didn't matter now. The important thing was that Weevil's name was clear. Cliff was right; if that stoolie had still been willing to talk when they went to trial, the prosecution might have won and Weevil would be doing time for a crime he didn't commit.

Cliff held up his glass, half full of warm-amber liquid. "What should we drink to? The best defense lawyer taxpayer money can buy?"

"Hey!" Veronica frowned. Cliff, Keith, and Weevil all had cups. Keith hadn't brought one for her or Mac. "What is this, Sterling Cooper 1963? Where's mine?"

"What, you drink Scotch now?" Keith raised an eyebrow.

"I drink *victory* Scotch!" Veronica said over her shoulder as she ducked into the kitchen to fetch some glasses.

"For the record," Mac said, "I also drink Scotch. But I'm not picky. I'll take the victory Scotch, or the Scotch of defeat. Or the rotgut swill."

Veronica returned with two glasses. She thrust one at Mac, grabbed the bottle from Cliff, and poured a couple of Big Gulp–sized drinks, ignoring Keith's amused look.

"As I was saying," Cliff continued. "To . . . me. And to everyone else who helped a little bit too."

They all lifted their glasses, clinking them gently together.

Veronica took a small sip—the Scotch seared her throat, and she swallowed a mangled cough along with the booze. Mac smirked, taking a long pull from her own glass without flinching.

"Lamb didn't look happy, did he?" Cliff said, his eyes twinkling over the top of his glass.

"I watched the press conference before you got here," Mac said, sitting on the edge of her desk, legs crossed. "Lamb said he's doing 'a fine-tooth investigation in the department'; he's 'redoubling his efforts to find the stolen evidence.' *Blah, blah, blah*. The same brain-dead derp our local media normally feast on like starving goldfish. Only this time they didn't. They were, like, *grilling* the dude. Seriously. I thought he might cry when Martina Vasquez asked him if there was 'a fundamental problem with leadership in the Sheriff's Department.'"

As drink refills continued, the debriefing maintained a steady if increasingly ragged energy. The group kept up their Lamb-basting exercise a while longer, then moved on to Celeste Kane, the prosecuting attorney, and the population of Neptune at large. Keith and Cliff huddled, reminiscing about cases from their shared past, Cliff listing ever more to starboard as the Scotch supply dwindled. Mac leaned over her computer, futzing with a nineties rap playlist. Veronica watched Weevil for a moment as he stood looking out the window. Outside, people were heading toward their cars from the offices and warehouses up and down the street, clothed in the transitional neighborhood's mix of paint-spattered coveralls and business casual. She suddenly realized it wasn't the street life Weevil was watching; it was his own reflection, faint in the glass. She walked over to him and set her empty glass on the windowsill.

"So what's next for you, now that you've got your life back?" Veronica asked, trying to keep her voice cheerful.

Weevil glanced at her, then turned back to the window. "If this is getting my life back, we set the bar way too low." He studied the liquid in his glass, swirling it. "I mean, don't get me wrong. I'm thrilled not to be headed off to prison. But I lost my business. I'm only working half-time at the garage—and even if they wanted to offer me more hours I couldn't take them, because my rotator cuff is perma-fucked. I still got medical bills piling up, and still I gotta pay you guys and Cliff . . ."

"No, you don't," she said quickly. "We didn't really do anything."

Weevil shook his head. "Man, I know you guys tracked down all those poor chumps who got busted with planted evidence. You did the work, even if we didn't get to use it."

"Forget it." She waved a hand.

"I always pay my debts, V. You know that."

Veronica let it drop. She could argue with him, try to get him to let her work pro bono, but what was the point? She knew better. Because in some ways, she and Weevil were the same kind of animal. Prideful, independent, and prickly.

Weevil startled her with a rueful laugh. "Go ahead and say it, Veronica: 'Shut the fuck up, Navarro, at least your brown ass ain't headed to Chino next week.'"

Veronica smiled. "Consider it said. Seriously, your luck is way overdue for a turnaround. And for now, Jade must be thrilled. Where is she, anyway? I'd have expected her to be ready for a drink too."

His flinch was almost imperceptible, a downward flicker of his eyelashes. Veronica's stomach dropped.

"I, uh . . . I told her I'd meet up with her later." He sighed. "Truth is, me and Jade . . . we haven't been so good these last couple months. She's . . . uh . . . been living with her mom out in Pan Valley."

"Weevil . . ." Veronica murmured, thrown for a loop. Weevil's lips tightened.

"It just makes more sense, you know? Rita can watch Valentina during the day. I've been so busy with Cliff, gettin' ready for the trial and all, and Jade's had to pick up more hours since I lost the garage."

"Plus, I bet she's not so into you being back on the bike," Veronica said, sensing an apt time to broach this touchy subject. *Or into your boys dragging you out at all hours to do God knows what.*

"Yeah, well. There's a lot about my life—and about me—that she's not into these days." He ran his hand over the back of his head. "And I ain't saying I blame her. She grew up with someone looking out for her. She never had to make a choice between breaking the law or sleeping in a drainage ditch." He shrugged. "With any luck, neither will Valentina."

Her eyes narrowed. Before the night of the attack, she'd seen how happy he was—how he loved his wife and doted on his little girl. She'd seen pictures of him cradling Valentina as a baby, of the two of them playing on the beach, of trick-or-treating with her dressed as Little Red Riding Hood and him as the Big Bad Wolf. And now he was trying to tell her it was *okay* if he lost his family, that it was somehow for the best? She'd been left by a parent who couldn't take the heat. She'd been left, and it had taken over a decade to forgive her mom for what she'd done.

But before she could say anything, a dry male voice came from the doorway.

"Excuse me?"

They all looked up to see a man standing just inside the propped-open door. His suit was charcoal gray, and he held a black leather briefcase in one hand. He glanced around the room with an expression of mild irritation.

"Sorry to interrupt," he said, loud enough to cut through the Missy Elliott. "This *is* Mars Investigations, isn't it?"

The room was silent for a few lingering seconds. Mac cut the music, then Keith stood up from the sofa and stepped toward him, his hand outstretched. "Yes, it is. Please excuse the noise. We just wrapped on a case and we're taking a little time to celebrate. I'm Keith Mars."

The man took Keith's hand, giving it a perfunctory pump.

"My name is Joe Hickman. I'm a claims adjustor with the Preuss Insurance Company. We have a rather delicate problem I'd like to discuss. At your earliest convenience." His eyes swept around the room, taking in the shabby furniture, the tipsy lawyer on the sofa, and the tattooed biker by the window.

Keith gestured toward his open office door. "If you'd like to step into my office we can speak more privately . . ."

Hickman's expression didn't alter. "I'm sorry, Mr. Mars, I think there's been a misunderstanding. I was hoping to hire Veronica. Petra Landros from the Neptune Grand Hotel referred us to her."

The room was suddenly intensely quiet, all eyes turning toward Veronica. Mac gave her a helpless shrug. Veronica couldn't quite bring herself to look at her dad.

The tension was broken by the sound of pouring. Veronica looked to the sofa, where Cliff was refreshing his drink. He noticed everyone looking at him, and arched an eyebrow.

"What? Do you know how rarely I win criminal cases? I'm not done celebrating, even if things *did* just get awkward."

Veronica sprang into action, as much to escape the tense moment as to impress Hickman with her eagerness. She stepped past Keith and opened her office door.

"Please," she said. "This way."

Hickman followed her through to her inner office. Just before she shut the door behind him, she caught a glimpse of Cliff topping off her father's drink.

CHAPTER FOUR

Veronica had never imagined a moment like this—a client actually choosing her over her dad. Mars Investigations had always been a united front, even when she was technically just the receptionist. She and Keith had always worked *together*, parceling out cases for efficiency's sake but backing each other up whenever needed. It never occurred to her that, at some point, the model might breakdown. And she wasn't sure how she was supposed to feel about it.

For a moment, she faced the closed door, her hand still lingering on the knob. Then, pasting a cool, businesslike smile on her face, she turned around to face her potential client.

"So what exactly can I do for you?" she asked, moving briskly to her desk and taking her seat. She picked up the yellow legal pad from the blotter and clicked her ballpoint pen.

"I'm here to investigate a claim made against one of our clients," Hickman said. His posture was stiff and straight, his pale hands motionless in his lap, like a pair of gloves. "What do you know about hospitality insurance, Ms. Mars?"

"Hospitality? As in hotel coverage?"

"Exactly. We offer hotels and resorts protection in cases.

where an accident, or some kind of mismanagement, has left them liable for damages. As you can imagine, that's a big risk in the hospitality industry. Nearly three million people stay in US hotels every night. There are a lot of moving parts; a lot of opportunities for things to go wrong. And with $150 billion in sales per year, a lot of people—some less than scrupulous—are looking for a piece of the pie."

"So you cover the hotel when someone's feeling litigious," Veronica said.

Hickman gave an almost indignant snort.

"It's not quite that simple," he said. "We have to investigate the claim first. Determine if the hotel was at fault, and if so, to what extent. Then decide whether it's more cost-effective to fight it out in court or just settle."

Veronica put down her pen. "So what exactly do you need from me?" she asked.

The man shifted slightly in his seat. "A nineteen-year-old woman was found in an empty lot on the edge of town on the morning of March seventh of this year," he said. "She was . . . well, she was in terrible shape. She'd been . . . violated."

"Raped," Veronica said mechanically. She didn't have patience for euphemisms.

"Yes. Raped, and beaten half to death. The police found DNA evidence, but it doesn't match anyone in their database. Back in March she claimed she didn't remember anything. She couldn't provide a description of her attacker, and said she didn't know how she'd gotten to the lot. All she remembered was arriving at the Neptune Grand the night of the attack."

Veronica nodded. This was, of course why Petra Landros had recommended her. Petra owned the Grand, and in March the hotelier had hired Veronica on behalf of the Neptune Chamber of Commerce. Two girls had gone missing during Neptune's lucrative spring break season, and Neptune's local business owners had wanted Veronica to find them before the tourist dollars dried up.

"Was she a guest?"

Hickman shook her head. "She's a local. She was just drinking in the bar that night."

Veronica frowned. "I don't understand. The Neptune Grand is one of the most monitored locations in town. They've got security cameras at every entrance. If she left with her attacker, one of those cams would've caught it."

"Well, that's the problem," Hickman said. "The video cameras show her arriving. They show her sitting in the bar for about an hour. They show her disappearing into a stairwell at about eleven forty-five. And then she just vanishes."

"Vanishes?"

"She never shows up on camera again. She goes into the stairwell at eleven forty-five, and the next morning at seven o'clock she's found half naked in an empty lot miles away. No sign of what happened in between."

Veronica tried to bend her mind around this story. It was impossible to sneak out of the Grand. Or it should have been.

"Then a few weeks ago, the victim suddenly—some would say *conveniently*—got her memory back," Hickman said, an edge of exasperated scorn in his voice. "She gave a description of her attacker that perfectly matches that of Miguel Ramirez, a former laundry-room employee of the Neptune Grand. According to her lawyer, that explains how no one saw her leave. He says her attacker was able to smuggle her out using his knowledge of the hotel's layout."

"And your problem with that story is . . . ?"

"The problem is, her alleged attacker was deported last month after getting caught in an ICE bust. No one seems to know where he is now, so there's no way to get a DNA sample. And now the victim is suing the Grand for three million dollars. Her lawyer claims the hotel showed criminal negligence in hiring undocumented workers."

"So what am I being hired to do?" Veronica asked slowly.

"Well, either the victim is telling the truth and someone attacked her somewhere on hotel grounds and then snuck her off-site past the cameras," said Hickman. "Or she's lying, and she managed to leave undetected and was attacked elsewhere. We need you to find out how she left that hotel, and with whom."

Outside, night settled over the warehouse district. Sounds rose from the street: shouts, laughter, and car horns, window-buzzing dubstep. In a nearby live music club, mic checks and tune-up chords from electric guitars set off ragged cheers.

Hickman was making little effort to hide his skepticism about the girl's story. And Veronica understood why. The details—at least the ones he'd seen fit to share—didn't add up.

But her own memory tugged at the corners of her mind, insistent and furious. She'd been sixteen the day she'd staggered into the Balboa County Courthouse in a torn white dress. Shaking from head to foot, she'd sat across from then-Sheriff Don Lamb and had told her story. How she'd gone to Shelly Pomroy's party the night before. How she'd woken up

in a strange bed without her underwear, aching and humiliated. How she couldn't remember anything else.

She could still recall with cinematic clarity the conversation in Lamb's office. The way the sheriff leaned back in his
chair, leering across the desk. Her struggle to stay composed
as he repeated questions, trying to catch her in contradic-
tions. Lamb's voice, his tone of cold, unvarnished contempt:
*I've got not a shred of evidence to work with here but that
really doesn't matter to your family, now does it?*

She looked down at the open file folder on her desk, the
pictures of the girl's ravaged and broken body on top. Someone had done this to her. And so far, he'd gotten away with it.

"Okay," Veronica said steadily, holding out her hand. "I'll
do my best to find out what happened to this girl."

Hickman's soft, dry palm was in hers then, and they
shook.

"Excellent," he said.

CHAPTER FIVE

"So," Cliff said, flopping an arm around Keith's shoulder. "How you feeling, Papa Bear?"

Cliff's breath was hot and boozy on the side of Keith's face as he broke the silence. A few feet away, Mac was standing next to Veronica's door, trying to eavesdrop. Weevil stood at her side, also making periodic efforts to snoop but clearly finding more entertainment value in the Keith-Cliff conversation.

Keith raised his eyebrows. "Papa Bear? Is this a new thing we're doing, or only when you've had the better part of a bottle of Scotch?"

"You know what I mean," Cliff said. He glanced around the room as if waiting for someone else to chime in. "We all just saw that, right? Like a Mamet play. The new hotshot taking the tired old man's accounts?" He took Keith's glass out of his hand. "Scotch is for closers."

Keith smiled.

"We took the training wheels off Veronica a long time ago. She's had some high-profile cases and done brilliant work on them. I'm proud, not surprised."

Mac chose that moment to dive in. "Me too. And just getting it out there, I'm always totally up for supporting either of you guys, playing no favorites, regardless of which . . ."

Veronica's door suddenly opened and she emerged, speed-walking across the room and past the conversation group on her way to the reception desk.

". . . *Death Proof*—okay, whatever, pat yourself on the back," Mac improvised as Veronica opened a desk drawer and retrieved a folder. "But nowhere else can you say my boy's just 'making movies about movies.' It's more like a, a—what's that word?"

"Motif," Keith said.

"Yes! Thank you. A *motif* running through his body of work," Mac said, glancing up at Veronica, who'd paused by the sofa and was scanning the group with a baffled expression. "Oh hey, Veronica, just a little movie chat going on here."

"'kay. Sorry to interrupt." Veronica threw them a final quizzical side-eye before hustling back into her office and closing the door behind her.

Unflustered, Keith picked up the thread right where it had been dropped. He leaned back against the sofa and stretched his legs out in front of him. "Like I was saying: No, I don't resent any of the attention or responsibility Veronica's been getting. Frankly, she's welcome to it. I'm ready for a few weeks in my hammock."

"Like an old busted mule, out to pasture," Cliff said.

"Or maybe," Keith said, a slight edge to his voice, "like a guy who's *literally* been run over by a truck after spending months crawling through the open sewers of Neptune politics—and is about ready for a goddamn vacation."

He'd spent much of the last few months trying to verify

the claims of planted evidence that had sprung up during the nearly four years of Lamb's term. It hadn't been easy. The department picked its victims deliberately; many of them had priors and none could afford long legal battles. A few were people Keith had busted back in his old days as sheriff—petty criminals and bottom-echelon dealers. He'd haunted dive bars, dingy tenements, crusty punk camps, trying to earn the trust of people who had no good reason to trust anyone. Some had been eager to tell their stories and had heard that Keith Mars was one of the few people interested in helping people like them. But more than a few had been scared to talk—scared of what would happen to them or their families if they did. Keith couldn't exactly blame them. He still had a dull ache in his back from the accident that'd almost killed him. And every time he got in his car there was a moment—just a split second—when he felt his heart fall out of rhythm and flutter against his chest.

For the past few weeks, Keith had been feeling edgy and burned out, unfocused in a way he hadn't experienced since right after the accident. He'd been busting his hump in the ultimately wasted effort to gather evidence against Lamb. What he'd just said to Cliff wasn't just spin. He truly was ready to disengage from the madness and catch his breath.

So, fine. Veronica's star was rising. No surprise there; she'd gotten a lot of media coverage in the wake of the Dewalt-Scott case. Before that she'd solved the murder of one of the biggest pop stars in the country, resulting in a short profile about her in *Vanity Fair*. In his twelve years as a PI, he'd ridden similar waves a few times. No *VF* profiles though. He definitely was not an adorable twenty-nine-year-old blonde.

Veronica's door opened again. The suit emerged first, his mouth and eyebrows set in parallel lines across his face. Veronica followed, notepad in hand.

Hickman headed straight for the office's side exit, pausing in the doorway. "There are several boxes of evidence. We'll send them tomorrow morning," he said.

"Sounds good," Veronica said. "Thanks for coming by."

He gave her a brusque nod and closed the door.

Veronica latched the deadbolt, then turned and scanned the room, a wry smile on her lips. Keith couldn't help but notice she didn't meet his eyes.

"Wow, it's sure quiet out here. I hope all that eavesdropping didn't interrupt the party too much," she said.

"No one was *eavesdropping*," Mac said.

"Yeah," said Weevil. "We gave up when we realized the door was too thick."

Keith watched as Veronica made her way to the reception desk and perched on the edge. He had a killer poker face, affectless as an Area 51 alien's. It came in handy whenever he wanted to observe, to learn without overtly prying. His daughter knew better than to trust it, but at the moment she still wasn't looking at him.

"So are you going to tell us what that was about?" Mac asked, opening her hands wide in a shrug.

"It's no big deal. Petra Landros referred him to me because of the work I did on the Dewalt case," Veronica said. "Okay, so do you guys remember anything about a sexual assault back in March? A girl left for dead in a field on the edge of town? I don't remember it hitting the local news."

And there it was: The reason Keith didn't want her here, in spite of everything. Because imagining her anywhere near a case like that gave him a knee-jerk spasm of terror. He focused on breathing slowly and carefully, his fingers curling around the glass of Scotch.

It was Cliff who answered. "I remember that. It was in the blotter. That was the week before Hayley Dewalt went missing, so the story probably got lost in the circus." He leaned back into the sofa and looked up at Veronica. "I remember there being some question whether the cases were linked. The victim was the same age as Hayley and Aurora, but the cops ruled out any connection pretty fast. And then I didn't hear anything else about it."

"Well, the case is still open apparently," Veronica said. "They never figured out what happened. Or maybe they didn't try very hard. The version I got might have been . . . biased."

"Was that guy her lawyer?" Mac asked. "Are we going after the rapist?"

Veronica hesitated, and in that single beat of silence Keith saw her blush very slightly.

"He was an insurance adjustor. But he does want to find out who did it." Her eyes flickered toward Keith and away as quickly. "We're not being asked to determine liability, just help the hotel's legal staff do it. But, you know, there's a chance that finding the rapist could be a by-product of this noble mission."

"Well, that's—depressing," Mac said finally, her chin sinking heavily on her hand. "'Hey! Sorry the actual criminal justice system couldn't get the job done, but maybe if you threaten someone's bank account we'll be able to help you.'"

Weevil just smirked. "Congratulations, you live in Neptune."

Veronica grabbed the neck of one of the few remaining Scotch bottles with a couple of swigs left in it. "Excuse me for troubling your Capraesque lives with this first-ever note of moral unclarity." She poured a dram into her glass and set the bottle back down with a loud *clunk*.

Keith laughed. "Fair enough." There was always plenty of Monday-morning quarterbacking in their field, and he'd certainly had his share of successes, noble failures, and out-right fiascos. He drained the final mouthful of booze from his glass, put his feet up on an ottoman, and drifted back into his own thoughts.

Then, out of left field:

"'*But maybe if you threaten someone's bank account . . .*'"

"Say what?" Cliff said.

"Oh, just what Mac said a minute ago. It touched off something in my mind."

"About what Veronica's doing?" Cliff said, still scrambling.

"No, about us. And Lamb. Innovative cat-skinning solutions for a changing world."

Cliff's face lit up as understanding hit. "For a busted old mule, you're pretty fucking smart. What can I do to help?"

"Well, for starters, who do you know in civil?" Keith leaned forward to the edge of the couch, resting his elbows on his knees.

"Horowitz is good but he's got a full caseload these days." Cliff was pulling file folders and stacks of paperwork out of his briefcase. "Jarvis and Associates have a good team. Choi's an up-and-comer—I'm pretty sure she'd take it just for the publicity."

"What are you guys talking about?" asked Veronica. She

held her glass halfway to her lips, glancing back and forth between them.

Instead of answering, Keith and Cliff both turned to face Weevil.

"Eli," said Keith. "What do you think about bringing a lawsuit against the Balboa County Sheriff's Department?"

Weevil gave a little start, blinking rapidly.

"I don't know if you realize, but I just got *out* of a lawsuit with them. I'm kind of happy it's over, you know?"

"This would be different," Cliff said. "We'd be on the offense this time. We'd be looking to prove that the deputy who arrived on the scene planted that gun on you."

Veronica drew in a breath. "You could use all the evidence the judge threw out. All those other people who claim evidence was planted? You could publicly rake Lamb over the coals. If we do this right, the worst-case scenario is that his career is over."

"And what's the best case?" Weevil asked, smiling as he anticipated her reply.

"The civil case leads to a criminal one, and Dan Lamb goes to prison for five, maybe up to ten years."

The energy in the room surged. Keith let himself imagine the look on Lamb's face as he sat on the stand, proof of his own corruption on public display.

"This would help recoup at least some of what you've lost, Eli," Cliff said. "At risk of sounding like a daytime-TV commercial, you could claim medical costs, lost income, pain and suffering. And I wouldn't be shocked if it opened the door for other individual lawsuits. Your kid could grow up in a very different Neptune than you did."

Weevil leaned forward, resting his forearms on his knees.

He was starting to look excited. "You really think we'd have a shot?"

Keith grinned. "I've already done most of the dirty work. We've got almost thirty witnesses who claim the Sheriff's Department has planted evidence. Some of them might even get their records expunged if Lamb gets enough of a black eye on this."

"And the media is already hammering Lamb with questions about that disappearing Glock," Cliff added. "We just have to make sure they don't let it drop."

Eli looked down at his feet, motionless for a few long seconds. When he finally looked up, it was with a crooked grin.

"All right," he said. "I'm in."

CHAPTER SIX

Veronica, Keith, Weevil, Cliff, and Mac polished off the Scotch, discussing strategy for hours. It was agreed that Keith would take point on any further legwork, since, as he put it, "the resident big-shot has her *own* case to deal with." Veronica noted the wink with which her father delivered this jab. She smiled wanly, but she was grateful.

It was after ten when they finally dispersed. Keith and Cliff went off in search of greasy, gluten-rich food—they'd invited Veronica but she declined—and Mac was meeting with some old Sun Microsystems colleagues at a bar. Veronica was ready to go home. She'd spent the last week in knots of anxiety. Now, with Weevil exonerated, she just wanted to sleep.

The silver RAV4 she'd purchased after the Hayley Dewalt case was parked on the street below the office. She'd opted for the little crossover to help with surveillance. Dearly as she missed streaking up the coastal highway in Logan Echolls's BMW convertible, the SUV made it easier to see over and around traffic. She pulled away from the curb, still chewing over the details of the new case, and headed south.

Most of Neptune's sparkling shoreline belonged to the city's elite. Movie stars and captains of industry had man-sions looking out over the Pacific. Yacht clubs, private beaches, and five-star resorts took up the rest. But Dog Beach, a four-mile stretch of golden sand and crashing surf, had always belonged to the hoi polloi. It had long been home to the oddball assortment that gravitate to any public beach: surf bums, earth mothers, buskers, carnies, bikers, burnouts, and street artists, along with the rest of Neptune's trust-fund-impaired. And now it was home to Veronica. Once the doctors had finally given Keith a clean bill of health, she'd moved out of his little bungalow and into an apartment just a quarter-mile walk from the shoreline, in a fading beauty of a building with a Spanish tile roof and deep casement windows.

She parked her car and started up the open stairs. Moths batted stupidly at the porch lights as she passed. Behind one door she heard the low murmur of a TV. Faintly, she caught the sharp salt smell of the ocean from a few blocks away.

The air in her third-floor apartment was close and heavy as she opened the door. The little window-unit AC just blew dust through the rooms, so she usually didn't bother with it. When she was home she left the windows open wide for the Pacific coast breeze to move through. Now she turned on the ceiling fan and a lamp, stepping gratefully out of her heels and onto the hardwood floor.

The unit was small but cozy, decorated with a combination of secondhand finds and one or two things she'd pilfered from her dad's house. A gray-and-white striped sofa sat across from a low walnut bookcase, flanked by floor lamps with vintage-store shades. The walls were lined with reprints of WPA travel posters, advertising Yellowstone, the Grand Canyon, and Crater Lake in bright blocky colors. Half-melted candles sat on an end table, between a phrenological head and a framed photo of her half brother, Hunter.

When she'd been living in her father's house, it had been inevitable that she'd feel in some vague way like a teenager again, as if she'd been tugged backward in time toward everything she'd tried to walk away from. But here was the evidence that she'd *chosen* this town, this lifestyle, this career. It didn't hurt that the apartment was better than anything she could have afforded in New York. The entire Brooklyn studio she'd had through law school would have fit in the bedroom here.

The kitchen, tiled in white and cherry red, was visible on the other side of a high counter lined with stools. She opened the fridge and grabbed last night's take-out. She didn't even bother heating it. Grabbing a fork, she took it back to the bedroom. A single light shone under the door.

"You're still awake?" she said softly, pushing the door open.

Logan sat up against the headboard, bare chested, the blankets pulled up across his lap. The TV on the top of the dresser was tuned to *The Daily Show*. The sight of his military-grade biceps sent a flutter through her sternum.

Okay, what first? Binge-eat sesame chicken, change into pajamas, or jump straight into bed with the half-naked boyfriend? She compromised by taking a bite and then setting down the container to undress while she chewed. The half-naked boyfriend, after all, would be a lot more enjoyable if she took the time to get out of her suit.

"You're home late," Logan said, and she could feel his eyes on her as she wiggled out of her skirt and hung it carefully back on its hanger. "But I should have guessed. Your family throws the best after-acquittal parties."

"We still had some leftover balloons from yours, so we just reused them. Weevil didn't seem to mind." She turned around, still in her camisole and underwear. His eyes tracked her closely, but she picked up the take-out container and took another bite, standing just out of reach and feigning obliviousness to his gaze. "What'd you get up to tonight?"

"Not much. I got home late myself."

"*Another* homoerotic-beach-volleyball emergency?" She put a hand on her hip. He smirked.

"Whatever it takes to keep Am'urca safe," he said, saluting smartly.

"I thank you for your service."

The novelty of seeing him there in her bed still gave her a little thrill, even though he'd been more or less living with her since he'd returned from his naval tour in the Persian Gulf two months earlier. Before that, they'd been apart for six months. And that was nothing to the nine years they'd been apart before *that*. It was no wonder she was constantly startled by the simple, shocking pleasure of waking up to find him within arm's reach, of coming home to find him there. The domestic bliss was . . . well, blissful. Neither of them had been prepared for that, lifelong adrenaline junkies that they were.

Logan had been reassigned to San Diego for his shore rotation, where he flew F/A-18 Hornets for the Fleet Readiness Center, helping them run diagnostics. "Basically, I try to help them find out what's busted before it's too late to fix it," he'd told her. Veronica didn't love that job description, but it was definitely better than picturing him running missions over enemy territory. Definitely better than trying to grab snippets of conversation with him long distance, never knowing if the connection would be good enough, or if he'd be called away and unable to meet her online.

For a moment she almost blurted out the details of the new case—leaving them sketchy to keep the girl's privacy, of course, but filling him in on the basics. Instead, she set down the take-out box and went to the adjoining bathroom to brush her teeth. They had a no-cases-in-the-bedroom policy. Too often her jobs involved other peoples' infidelities—not the best pillow talk. But it became especially necessary in cases like these, when she was looking into something truly ugly. She already had a habit of carrying her work around with her, lodged in her mind. She wanted at least this boundary.

After she washed up, she went back into the bedroom. Logan had turned off the TV. He leaned back against the pillows, hands behind his head, watching as she crossed the room. She slid under the covers next to him.

"You could have joined us," she said.

"Sure. That wouldn't have been awkward at all." Logan slid his arm around Veronica and pulled her toward him. She caught a whiff of the cedar and sandalwood of his aftershave as she rested her head against his shoulder.

"Come on. They wouldn't have minded."

"Oh, yeah? Is Mac still calling me 'Not-Piz'?"

"That was just a joke. Besides, you and Weevil are cool, right? I thought you guys had some kind of edgy-outlaw-mutual-respect thing going on after all was said and done."

"Right . . ." Logan said. "That was his verbatim comment when I friended him on Facebook."

"I'll bet you favorite all his Tweets too," Veronica replied, propping herself up on her elbow and looking at him.

"*Favorite?* I retweet every word that man posts."

Their tone was light, but the conversation wasn't a new one. Veronica had no doubts about Logan's place in *her* life, but there was still so much awkwardness between him and the other people she cared about. He'd spent half his high school career as a cynical, entitled jackass, which hadn't endeared him to her father *or* her friends. Since she'd moved back to Neptune and gotten back together with Logan, everyone had made a sincere effort at acceptance. Logan and Veronica went to Keith's once a week for dinner, and Logan had taken them both to a Padres' game for Father's Day. Among her friends, there'd been some cordially awkward get-togethers. Everyone got an A for effort, but she still sometimes found herself wondering if it'd always be this hard—if Logan could ever sync smoothly with her other relationships.

He smiled, tracing the line of her cheek with a fingertip. She went quiet then, all thoughts of the case and her friends and her father, all the vague anxieties she had about making this relationship work, in spite of all the differences between them, banished. How could any of it matter, when he was *here*, when they were together? She leaned up and kissed him.

His arms tightened gently around her.

"Welcome home," he whispered.

CHAPTER SEVEN

Preuss's evidence had already arrived when Veronica got to the office at nine the next morning. It was crowded around her desk, a dozen cardboard bankers boxes labeled in black Sharpie. The sight made her feel slightly claustrophobic.

"They said a *few* boxes," she said incredulously.

Behind her, Mac stood cradling her coffee mug. She smirked knowingly.

"Please. Endless stacks of evidence and unsorted information to sift through? You're thrilled. This is Veronica Mars catnip."

"Yeah, better get your spray bottle at the ready in case I start rolling on a pile of carpet-fiber spectrographs," Veronica said with a mock scowl. "This is why you shouldn't hire your friends. It's all nice and professional until the insubordination starts." She sighed. "Well, you know where *I'll* be."

"I'll poke some food under the door at lunchtime," Mac said, giving a jaunty little wave.

Once she'd shut her office door, Veronica just stood for a moment, looking around the cramped office. One box was labeled MEDICAL in a barely legible scrawl; another said CRIME SCENE. Several others were unlabeled. A few seemed to be packed past capacity, bulging ominously.

One of the first lessons Keith Mars had taught his daughter about solving crimes was that their most important tool was organization. That didn't necessarily mean keeping an immaculate system of files and notes and evidence. Keith's own notepad was indecipherable and incomplete, his corkboard a fluttering mess of scrap paper. But his mind was a Euclidean engine of perfect order and universal recall. He had his way; she had hers. But both understood that, without some way of sorting and cataloging facts, there was no way to see patterns. No way to change scope from forest to trees and back again. Her first job was to get a sense of how the case hung together, piece by awful piece.

She pried the lid off a box and started to unpack.

The first few folders contained schematic maps and photos of the place where the victim had been discovered—a field halfway to Pan Valley, more than twelve miles from the Neptune Grand. It had been raining on the night of the attack, and dark puddles mottled the landscape in the pictures. The rain seemed to have washed any evidence away; the only boot prints they had found belonged to the man who found the victim, an antiques dealer named Frank Kozlowski. The cops had found a tire print fifty yards away, on the road above the empty lot, and had identified it as a Firestone belonging to a midsized car, but there was no way to know if that print was connected to the crime.

Behind that folder, Veronica found another file crammed with photos. At first, she couldn't quite tell what she was looking at: a bloodied mass of flesh; a shapeless form, black-and-blue and pink. Then the image resolved and she saw that it was a girl lying in a hospital bed.

She'd braced herself for the photos of the victim's

injuries—the insurance adjustor's circumspect language told her the attack had been brutal—but she still stiffened at what she was seeing. The girl's skin was a patchwork of contusions. Her nose was swollen, twice its normal size. Her eyes were blackened, lashes sticky with blood. One cheek was split jaggedly open. Her left arm was in a cast; her fingers were in splints. An ovoid pattern of bruises crisscrossed her throat.

Strangled, Veronica thought. She set the photos aside and picked up the medical report.

According to the medical examiner, the victim had suffered over twenty broken bones, including her nose, clavicle, three fingers, and the hyoid bone at the base of her neck. Her left shoulder had been dislocated. The cartilage in her throat had been torn and bruised, leaving her unable to speak for days after the attack. She had a severe concussion. On top of that, the examiner noted symptoms of cerebral hypoxia, meaning her attacker had choked her long enough to cut off her air supply. Semen evidence taken from her body had been entered into the DNA database, but had yielded no matches.

Veronica placed the ME's report next to the toxicology panel. The victim had tested negative for everything except evidence of moderate alcohol consumption and traces of Xanax, for which she had a prescription. There was no sign of anything recreational—no meth, no heroin, no Oxy, no E. Not even cannabis. No Rohypnol or GHB either, meaning her memory loss was likely a result of her brain injuries and her trauma.

Or an act, Veronica thought. Though for the girl to cover for her attacker after what he had subjected her to? Not impossible, but definitely implausible.

She worked slowly, spreading files out across her desk and labeling them, rearranging and collating as she went. There were more photos, some showing further details of the girl's injuries, others showing details of the field. One showed the dress she'd been wearing, filthy and torn, laid out on a metal exam table. A close-up of the tag revealed that it was Versace.

Finally, she found what she'd been looking for: the police report. It was dated March 9, two days after Grace had been found. Two deputies had signed it, a Tim Foss and a Jerrell Bundrick—neither familiar to her. In cramped type, they had detailed a living nightmare in flat, bureaucratic language.

Victim currently unable to speak as a result of her injuries, but was able to answer preliminary questions with pen and paper.

Victim arrived at Neptune Grand at approx. 10:30 p.m. on March 6, 2014. Victim claimed she was there to meet her boyfriend, but was unwilling to give his name. She waited for him in the rooftop bar, but according to victim he canceled their plans at 11:15; she stayed on and ordered more drinks. Victim says she remembers entering the stairwell, which she "always uses." Victim remembers receiving blows to her face, head, and torso, but cannot describe her attacker. She also remembers having her air cut off by someone

or something crushing her throat. She is
unsure where the attack took place, and
doesn't remember leaving the hotel. At
this time, victim is still disoriented and
confused—the medical examiner's official
report is pending but according to the
ICU doctor, memory loss and confusion are
normal in cases of strangulation.

Veronica read on and stray words registered—*blonde, shock, evidence.* Then her eyes fell on the victim's name. *Grace Elizabeth Manning.* Age nineteen.

It took a moment for the name to register.

Grace Elizabeth Manning.

It couldn't be the same Grace Manning. It just couldn't.

CHAPTER EIGHT

Even as Veronica fought the idea, she knew in her gut that it was true. The girl in the photos, beaten to the brink of death, was the same Grace Manning she'd last seen ten years ago, when she'd still been in high school. Their paths had crossed because of Veronica's friendship with Grace's older sister, Meg.

Meg had been an anomaly among the '09ers; she was pretty and popular but also genuinely kind. She'd been one of the few friends who stuck with Veronica after Lilly Kane's murder. The friendship lasted even after Meg started to date Veronica's ex-boyfriend, Duncan Kane, but hit the rocks hard when he got back with Veronica.

The intensity of Meg's spite had surprised even Veronica, who knew bitterness all too well. Then came the bus crash that killed eight of their classmates and severely injured Meg. Veronica soon learned the real reason for her hostility to Veronica and Duncan: She was pregnant with Duncan's child.

Meg died from her injuries, but her baby survived and the Mannings got sole custody. A few weeks later, Veronica broke into the Manning house to investigate hints of child abuse. There she found Grace Manning, nine years old and terrified, crouched in a tiny compartment behind the wall in her closet. She'd been shut in by her parents, religious fanatics who didn't believe in sparing the rod. Veronica and Duncan's next move was the only viable one they could see: Duncan had kidnapped the baby, and Veronica had master-minded an escape to a safe home far away from Neptune. She hadn't heard one word from Duncan since.

Veronica didn't know what had happened in Grace's life since that night. She didn't know what triumphs she might have celebrated, what hopes and dreams she'd pursued. All she knew was that it wasn't fucking fair. Sometimes light-ning struck twice; sometimes, one person got more than their share of suffering.

But none of that mattered now. There were still boxes and boxes of information to comb through, and a hundred unanswered questions about the attack. Veronica picked up the file and continued reading. Deputies Bundrick and Foss kept going back to the girl's bedside and asking the same questions, over and over. *They're trying to catch her in a lie,* Veronica realized, staring down at the fourth such interview. *She's lying there in a hospital bed, unable to speak, barely able to move, and they're trying to figure out how to get this case off their desk.* Their frustration was palpable. So was Grace's.

> BUNDRICK: So you remember going into the
> stairwell. Do you remember going into one
> of the rooms on the way down?
> VICTIM: No. I remember walking to the
> stairwell and starting down, but nothing's
> clear from there on. I don't know what
> happened.

BUNDRICK: But last time we were here you claimed to remember someone hitting you in the face.

VICTIM: I remember the sensation of someone hitting me in the face. I don't remember what he looked like, or where I was. But I remember how it felt. I remember falling down. I remember someone hitting me again and again.

BUNDRICK: But you don't actually remember being hit in the face, then. You remember getting hurt, but you don't actually remember how it happened. Is that right? Now, now, there's no need to cry, Miss Manning. We're on your side.

Foss, on the other hand, was obsessed with finding out the identity of Grace's boyfriend.

FOSS: Look, Grace, I'm going to be straight with you here. We can't move forward on this investigation until you tell us more about this man you're protecting. We really need to know more about him if we're going to rule anyone out.

VICTIM: But he wasn't even there that night.

FOSS: Grace, honey, you know who the perp is in 99.99 percent of cases like this? The boyfriend, that's who. Are you afraid of him? Because we can protect you.

```
    VICTIM: No! I'm not afraid of him. He
didn't do this to me—why would he do this
to me? I already told you. He's married.
He's got a reputation to protect. He'd lose
everything if anyone found out. I can't do
that to him. But he wasn't there that night.
    FOSS: We're going to find out who he is
anyway. Trust me, it'll be a lot better for
you and your case if you just cooperate
with us now.
```

By mid-April, there weren't any more transcripts or notes. It seemed the case had stalled or been shunted aside. But suddenly in June there was another flurry of paperwork. New memories had surfaced as Grace recovered from her physical injuries. Veronica found an amended police report dated June 4, signed off by Deputy Foss.

```
    Victim claims that she's retrieved more
memories of the night of March 6. She
now recalls the features and build of the
perpetrator and describes him as being
Hispanic, about 5'11" and 170 lbs, wearing a
red polo shirt with the Neptune Grand logo
on the breast. However she still admits to
no memory of the location of the attack, or
the aftermath.
```

A police sketch was attached to this report: it showed a brooding man with an aquiline nose and a close-shaven bristle of hair. Veronica placed it next to the mug shot of Miguel

Ramirez—the Neptune Grand laundry-room employee who'd been deported in late May. *Ninety percent chance it's the same guy in both images,* she thought.

She kept reading all through the morning, taking in bits of information, making notes, sorting through the mess. A familiar, almost mechanical feeling was taking over, her focus sharpening, her mind clicking into gear. By the time she started watching the hotel surveillance footage, she was ready to give Mac her due for the catnip crack. There *was* a deep, rhythmic gratification to be found in scanning and organizing evidence; it was as close to high as Veronica got.

A couple of hours passed almost unnoticed, then a soft knock came at her door.

"Yeah?" Veronica said, jarred to reenter the physical world.

Mac opened the door and poked her head in. "We're ordering sandwiches. You want one?"

"Would you come look at something for me?" Veronica asked, not even looking up from where she sat staring at her computer.

She sensed Mac move silently in behind her. "What's up?"

Veronica hit a key on her laptop. The Neptune Grand surveillance footage started to play.

"This is the night of the attack. The victim comes in through the main entrance of the hotel at ten twenty-seven." The camera showed a sleek young woman walking briskly through the doors. Her long blonde hair was twisted up at the nape of her neck. She wore a tight blue dress that showed off a double take–worthy figure. The shoes were expensive-looking silver stilettos.

The lobby was busy for a Thursday night. Grace passed a cluster of women in flamboyant red hats—some kind of social club, it looked like—clustered around the reception desk. She cut between four tall college-age boys in matching team jackets, all of whom checked her out as she passed. A family of five got out of the elevator as she clambered on, then made their way arguing toward the front door.

"A series of cameras track her across the lobby. Then she takes the elevator up to the rooftop bar." She clicked through different windows, marking the woman's path. The camera in the elevator gave a closer and sharper view of her features than those in the lobby. "Oh you kid! Opal blue eyes, heart-shaped face, bee-stung lips—insert 1930s *Variety* prose here."

Grace's makeup was flawless and made her look older than she was. It gave Veronica a slight pang, imagining the shy child she'd met a decade ago as this chic sophisticate—and then imagining her again as the savaged figure on the hospital bed.

"Okay, now our young Jean Harlow gets out at the Eagle's Nest." Veronica pulled up a different file, showing the Neptune Grand's rooftop bar. It wasn't exactly new—it'd been there since Petra Landros's renovations a few years ago—but it still gave Veronica a chill. The last time she'd been anywhere near the roof of the Neptune Grand, Cassidy Casablancas had been trying to force her to jump off of it at gunpoint.

Back then, the roof had just been a roof; now, it was a coolly lit pleasure garden with a view of the city below. Clusters of oversized chairs were arranged near the railings so patrons could take in the view. In the center of the rooftop a large open-flame fire pit flickered steadily, surrounded by low, curved benches. The clock in the corner of the screen registered the time as 10:31 p.m. when Grace Manning stepped out of the gleaming brass elevator.

"She hangs out at the bar for an hour or so," Veronica said, hitting Fast Forward. The image picked up speed, the bartender—a young woman in a cummerbund and bow tie—darting erratically, like an agitated squirrel, while a handful of patrons zipped in and out. No one talked to Grace except for the bartender. "She has three drinks. She chats a few times with the bartender. Then she gets up at eleven thirty-seven. But instead of going back to the elevator, she goes into the stairwell."

Mac leaned over her shoulder, frowning. "Why would she do that? It's, like, fourteen stories. She's wearing stilettos."

Veronica shook her head. "No idea. But here's the real question." She opened up all of the lobby camera files and hit Fast Forward again so they all started to run at once. "Where did she go?"

They watched the video in silence. The clock in the corner of each screen ran up, minutes slipping by. 11:40. 11:45. 11:50. At midnight, there was a shift change, with several housekeepers and clerks leaving through the service exit. The bar closed down and the handful of stragglers left. After that there was very little movement except for graveyard-shift clerks fidgeting to keep themselves awake, and one or two employees moving up and down the service corridor.

At just after 5:13 a.m., a parade of sleepy-looking college guys in matching red jackets traipsed through the lobby. Another camera, positioned in the passenger loading area, filmed them outside, climbing groggily onto a charter bus waiting in the valet lane. It was still dark, and drops of rain speckled the camera's lens. Veronica could just make out the letters on the backs of their coats: PSU BASKETBALL. After they left, no one else came through the lobby until the continental breakfast started up at six.

At no point did Grace reappear on the cameras.

She didn't come out through the stairwell on the ground floor. She didn't get on or off the elevator. She didn't pass through the glass double doors at the front, or the service exit in back, or the parking garage.

"I've watched it all the way through to seven a.m.," Veronica said, looking up at Mac. "That's when the junk guy found the victim in the empty lot ten miles away. But I don't see any sign of her leaving through any of the exits."

Reflected light from the monitor shone in Mac's eyes. She reached over Veronica's shoulder and grabbed the mouse, backing up the video and playing it again.

"There aren't cameras on the individual floors?"

"Nope. But the service corridors are all covered." Veronica opened up a window that showed the basement hallway. "Petra Landros likes to make sure she gets her money's worth out of the help. No sign of her there either. But there's the guy the victim accused." She pointed to a man in a red polo shirt, pushing a laundry bin up the hallway. The image was heavily pixelated, but she recognized him from the mug shot. Dark hair, broad shoulders.

Mac frowned. "Those laundry baskets are pretty big. Maybe he used one of them to move the victim?"

"That was my thought too. But the bins don't leave the hotel, at least not that I can see." She leaned back in her chair. "So we're left with the same question either way. How did *this* girl"—she touched the image of Grace on her screen as she disappeared once again into the dark, unmonitored stairwell—"end up *here*?" She gestured to the pile of photos on the desk next to her. Mac picked up the top one, an image of Grace's bruised and broken face, and blanched.

"If we can't get DNA from the guy she accused, there's no way to prove for sure he did it."

Veronica paused, staring for a moment at the photo in Mac's hands. Staring at the face of a woman who, all other points aside, had been raped, brutalized, and left for dead.

"And that means the asshole who did *that* might still be out there right now, digging into a big old sack of fried cheddar sticks at the ballgame."

Mac's eyes lingered on the photo for another moment before she looked up at Veronica. "So how are we going to stop him?"

Veronica sighed. "Well, the first order of business is going to be to talk to the victim. Fun! *Hey girl, I'm working for the suits who're trying to prove you're lying about your rape. Coffee? My treat?*'"

Mac winced. "Do you think she'll talk to you?"

"Wouldn't blame her if she didn't. But I've got to try." Veronica picked up her phone. "I need her side of the story. And she deserves a shot at telling it her way, on her own turf."

For a moment she considered going straight to Grace's apartment unannounced, seeing if she could catch her in person. With most witnesses, that was the go-to strategy. Catching people off guard often paid off in straight, unrehearsed answers. But she didn't want to ambush Grace—didn't want to blindside her with questions about what presumably was the most traumatic day of her life. So she punched in the phone number from one of the police forms and waited.

The voice that answered was a calm, even alto. "This is Grace."

Veronica jumped slightly. She'd half expected it to go to voice mail.

"Hi, Grace. My name is Veronica Mars." She didn't mention their connection. Either Grace would remember it herself, or she wouldn't. Given the context of the call, Veronica wasn't sure which she'd prefer. "I'm sorry to bother you. I'm calling because I'm doing some research for the insurance firm that covers the Neptune Grand." She paused, her mouth suddenly feeling dry. "First of all, I just wanted to tell you I'm sorry for everything you've already been through . . ."

"What's your question?" The girl's voice was still calm, but quicker than before, a bit impatient.

"Well, I was hoping I could meet with you in person and ask a few questions."

"Fine." The word came with no hesitation. "Are you free this afternoon? I'm in rehearsals for the summer show until five. You can meet me at Hearst. You know where the drama building is?"

"Um, yeah. I do. I can meet you there."

"I'll be on the main stage. I'm guessing you've already seen my picture. You'll know who I am."

And then, before Veronica could say anything else, Grace hung up.

CHAPTER NINE

A few hours later, Veronica stood in front of the Eloise Gant Theatre Building at the heart of Hearst College's verdant campus. The bell tower had just chimed five. The quad was almost deserted; very few students stuck around for summer. A single mole-like professor blinked and scurried toward the parking lot. Otherwise, the only movement was from the flock of pigeons strutting across the cobblestones.

A painful sense of déjà vu set in. Veronica had gone to Hearst for a year before she transferred to Stanford, and happy memories were pretty thin on the ground. In fact she'd spent most of her first year of school trying to stop the Hearst Rapist, the predator who managed to drug and rape at least four women before Veronica finally exposed him. One of the victims had been Mac's roommate—and Veronica had heard the assault as it happened. At the time she'd thought it was consensual; she'd heard a moan, a creak of bedsprings. It hadn't occurred to her to turn on the lights and investigate.

She'd never fully forgiven herself for that. Not even after she caught the rapist. If she'd just turned on the lights that night, if she'd just asked a simple question—*Hey, Parker, are you okay?*—she could have stopped him sooner.

And here we are again: same shit, different day. Questioning a girl who's already been through the details more times than anyone should ever have to.

She steeled herself as best she could and pushed in through the building's glass doors.

Hearst's main stage was a cavernous theater bounded by red velvet. Painted across its high ceiling was a dramatic, swirling mural of the constellations—Orion with his club, Ursa Major with its too-long tail, Pegasus with wings outstretched—dotted with pinprick lights that represented stars. She entered quietly, holding the door to keep it from shutting too hard. On the stage, a group of actors were clustered midscene. Veronica sat down in the back row of plush seats.

A man at stage right held his back strangely hunched, facing a woman at stage left. Behind her a small entourage waited. Everyone was in street clothes, and it appeared to be early in rehearsals. Some of the ensemble didn't seem to know where or how to stand yet, still experimenting with postures and blocking.

"Sweet saint, for charity, be not so curst," cooed the man, taking the woman's hand in his. She violently snatched it away.

"Foul devil, for God's sake, hence, and trouble us not."

Veronica recognized the voice before she recognized the speaker. It was the same buttery alto she'd heard just a few hours earlier on the phone. Now, though, it rang from the rafters.

"For thou hast made the happy earth thy hell, fill'd it with cursing cries and deep exclaims. If thou delight to view thy heinous deeds, behold this pattern of thy butcheries.

O, gentlemen, see, see! Dead Henry's wounds open their congeal'd mouths and bleed afresh!"

Grace was almost unrecognizable as the exquisitely coiffed creature Veronica had seen in the surveillance photos. Now she wore slouchy boyfriend-cut jeans, a plain white tank top, and sneakers. Her hair was in a sloppy ponytail, her face free of makeup. But as she moved, Veronica could see it: that same deliberate energy, the same poise that she'd shown crossing a lobby in Jimmy Choos. She projected the nuance and subtlety of the scene to the very back of the theater.

As the scene went on, Grace took a step toward the hunched man, her fingers clenching below her chin and then falling impotent at her sides. "O God, which this blood mad'st, revenge his death! O earth, which this blood drink'st revenge his death! Either heaven with lightning strike the murderer dead, or earth, gape open wide and eat him quick, as thou dost swallow up this good king's blood which his hell-govern'd arm hath butchered!"

She was good. No, not just good . . . she was remarkable. Grace Manning was far more than a lovely face—she was an actress. And every word, every movement, every flourish told a story.

After the cast broke, Veronica hung back as the actors dispersed. Grace picked up a red flannel shirt from a seat cushion and pulled it around her shoulders.

No haute couture duds, no makeup, no Mouawad handbags, thought Veronica. Either the way she'd dressed that night at the Grand was just a lark, or Grace had gone radically normcore in the months since the attack. Veronica knew it wasn't out of the ordinary for women to become self-conscious about their appearance after an assault. All part of the brain's profoundly unhelpful self-blaming tendency: *Harlot, cover thyself; had'st thou not drawn attention to thy body, thou would'st remain undefiled.*

"Grace? I'm Veronica." When Grace didn't take her hand, she let it drop. "The show looks like it's going to be amazing."

Grace smirked. "Sorry we didn't have time to get *Titus Andronicus* up for you. That's the one where they rape me and cut out my tongue. But maybe it's a little too on the nose."

How very theatrical, Veronica thought, but she kept her face carefully neutral. In a way, she was relieved. She'd feared a nerve-racking eggshell walk through the emotional ruin of rape—shame, grief, terror. But anger? That one was easy.

"Do you want to go somewhere more private to talk?"

"No, this is fine." Grace gestured around her. "Everyone's gone. And everyone knows what happened to me anyway." She crossed her arms over her chest. A faint white scar stretched from her cheekbone to her lip, zigzagging where her skin had torn under the force of the blows. "So you're here to find out if I'm lying?"

"I'm here to find out what happened to you, Grace."

"On behalf of people who don't want to take responsibility for what they did."

Veronica shook her head. "Look, I know you don't have any reason to trust me. But just so you know, I'm not making these guys a Pinterest scrapbook of custom-curated facts. The evidence I find is exactly what they're getting. All I want is to find out what happened that night." She paused, watching Grace's expression.

For the first time, a spark of emotion flickered in Grace's eyes. She blinked, looking down at her feet for a split second before sitting down carefully in one of the red velvet seats. Veronica sat too, keeping an empty seat between them to give the girl some room.

"What do you want to know?" Grace's voice was still steady, but softer. Maybe a shade less hostile.

Veronica took a slender notepad from her jacket pocket and flipped to a blank page. "Well, let's start with what you remember. Can you walk me through what happened that night?"

A faint crease formed across her forehead. She looked down at her lap, her hands flat against her thighs. "It's all come back in fits and starts—it's kind of hard to put in order."

"Just do your best," Veronica said.

Grace shrugged. "All right. I showed up at the bar to wait for my boyfriend. It was around eleven. I had a few martinis, sat and chatted with Alyssa—the bartender. I knew her a little bit. I was in there a lot."

"What'd you talk about?"

The girl frowned. "I don't really remember. Just small talk. We used to talk about movies, TV shows. Stuff like that."

"Okay. So you were waiting for this guy . . ."

"Yeah, so, he texted me to tell me he couldn't get away. It was already around eleven. I had one more drink, and then I left to go home." She laced her fingers together in her lap, a pale, tense knot. She was still as she spoke, but every muscle seemed rigid. "I remember going through the door to the stairwell—the door stuck a little bit, and I remember thinking, good thing there's not a fire. I got in and I started down the stairs. And then . . . things get all fucked up in my head." Grace paused for a moment, her lower lip trembling slightly, but when she spoke again her voice remained matter-of-fact. "I don't know where exactly my memory starts to gray out. It's like when you go to the dentist and they start to put you under and you don't even notice the moment you let go. You just come to later, and you can kind of remember the dentist moving around overhead, and the sound of the drill, and the vibration in your skull, but you can't put it together chronologically."

Veronica nodded. "Do you think you might have been drugged when you were at the bar, right before you headed downstairs?"

"No, I was sitting right in front of the bartender the whole time and wasn't talking to any guys. All I'm saying is, stepping through the stairwell door is the last distinct memory I have. And for a long time, *all* I could remember beyond that point was being attacked. I remembered something hitting me again and again. Here . . ." She touched her ribcage, below her breasts. "Here. And here." She ran her hand along the side of her face, her jaw, her collarbone. "I remembered hearing something snap and thinking: *Fuck! My fucking nose.* And I know it's probably going to sound frivolous to you, but I remembered thinking . . . *I have an audition next week. How am I going to be Hedda Gabler with a crooked nose?*"

Veronica knew from experience that it wasn't frivolous, that it was impossible to predict or police the thoughts that floated through your mind, even in a moment like that—but Grace kept talking.

"And then I felt something pressing down on my neck."

The girl's long, pale fingers curled instinctively around her throat, gentle and protective even as they demonstrated violence. "I couldn't breathe. I scratched at whatever it was and felt my fingernails bite in. That was when I realized he was choking me. He shook me. My head smashed up against something a few times."

She looked up. Her eyes were clear, her expression bland. It would have been easy to see it as affectless—Veronica assumed that was probably how the sheriff's deputies had read it—but Veronica saw something else. She saw the face of a girl who'd been taken apart with violence, and who'd then put herself back together with sheer willpower. She saw a girl who refused to let the story, told and retold, hurt her all over again.

"When I woke up I was in the hospital," Grace went on. "Everything was still fuzzy; they had me on a ton of painkillers. I had a concussion and a bunch of broken bones. And he'd damaged my throat so bad I couldn't talk. For some reason I got it in my head that I'd be mute for the rest of my life. I couldn't shake that fear even after the doctors kept telling me I'd be able to talk in a few days."

It all rang true: the horror, acute and paralyzing, of everything that'd been taken from her in one moment. Her body. Her sense of safety. Her voice.

"For a long time I couldn't remember the guy's face. It was just this horrible blurred image lingering in my brain. And I kept having these nightmares. I'd wake up screaming. My neighbors called the cops once, it was so bad—they thought I was being murdered in my bed." She gave a hollow laugh. "Anyway, a few weeks ago I just . . . I finally saw his face again, in my dream. And I woke up and I knew it was real—that I could ID him. My therapist says it's fairly common in cases with trauma. Sometimes it takes a while for the information to process. So I called the Sheriff's Department. I gave them the description. They had me come in and look at some photos, and . . . and there he was." She swallowed hard, her fingers clenching. "Right there in the book of photos. Miguel Ramirez. The guy who raped me."

"Did anything else come back to you then? Like how he got you out of the building?"

"No. I must've been unconscious for that part."

Veronica frowned. "Grace, you said you spent a lot of time around the Grand. Did you ever notice Ramirez before that night? Did he ever try to talk to you?"

She shook her head again. "No. I mean, I spent most of my time in the bar, or in a room. I don't think I would've bumped into a laundry guy in the hall."

"Oh? Did you stay overnight at the Grand often?" Veronica raised an eyebrow. "Pretty posh digs for a college student."

"Oh, is that not in my *file*?" Grace asked with a slight sneer. "I assumed you knew. I had a married boyfriend. That's where we used to meet. The cops drilled me on that so many times I assumed it'd be there in bold."

It had, in fact, but Veronica didn't rise to the bait.

"Can I ask why you took the stairs that night?" Veronica asked. "Fourteen stories in stilettos? There have to be easier workouts."

"I always took my shoes off. Otherwise I'd have broken an ankle." Grace shrugged. "My boyfriend was a little bit paranoid. Didn't want the elevator camera to track which floor I got off on because someone might trace it to him."

"But you said that night he canceled."

"Yeah. I don't really remember why I took them that night in particular, but it was kind of force of habit. I almost never took the elevator down." Grace picked at a cuticle.

Veronica jotted *Extreme secrecy re: "boyfriend"* in the notepad.

"Look, I understand why you didn't want to tell the cops who your boyfriend was. But if we're going to figure out what happened that night, I really need . . ."

"No." Grace's voice was sharp. Veronica glanced over and was unsurprised to see her eyes narrow, her chin jutting belligerently. "There's no reason to talk to him. He wasn't there that night—he wasn't *involved*."

"I believe you." Veronica looked directly at her, trying to show sincerity, though she wasn't sure *how* she really felt. "But it strengthens your case against the Grand if we can show *definitively* that he wasn't involved."

"Once they have his name, the case becomes an out-of-control media wankfest. He'll be a philandering pervert and I'll be a home-wrecking slut. They'll use it to totally discredit me."

"They're going to do that anyway," Veronica said.

"And these are the people you're working for. You feel good about that?"

Veronica had been waiting for that jab from the moment Grace sat down; it's what she would have said if the situation were reversed.

"When this goes to trial, Grace, the Grand's lawyers are going to get his name, one way or another," Veronica said. "And yes, they will do anything they can to discredit you, regardless of my feelings on the matter. You should be prepared for that."

Grace stared at her for a long moment. "It's not going to

trial, Veronica. You know as well as I do that they're going to settle. Look, they hired an undocumented immigrant who turned out to be a *rapist*. They're in the wrong—and they're not going to take their chances in court."

"Are you still seeing him? Your boyfriend, I mean."

Grace hesitated. "Our relationship was more or less physical. I mean, I really liked him. And he liked me. But it wasn't like he could take me out on dates or anything. After what happened, I was . . . not so interested in sex. So we broke it off."

Not exactly a fairy-tale romance, Veronica thought.

"It was mutual," Grace added a little defensively, seemingly reading Veronica's mind. "It wasn't like he decided I was damaged goods and threw me off. I just knew I needed a chance to get my shit together, and that wasn't the kind of relationship we had. But that doesn't mean I'm ready to throw him to the jackals. He's got kids, for Christ's sake. I don't want them hearing about any of this."

Grace looked down at her lap again. The scar across her cheek was barely visible. On stage, under makeup, no one would notice. But this close, it looked like a thin, pale question mark.

"I just want it to be over. Medical bills, therapy bills—they're all stacking up, and the work-study gig barely scratches the surface of what I owe. I have no idea how I'm going to pay for tuition next semester." She bit her lip. "Hearst is the first place I've ever felt like I belonged. I don't know what I'll do if I have to leave. If I can win this suit, I'll be able to . . . to really move on. The Neptune Grand took something from me. I just want it back."

Veronica faced the stage for a minute, leaning back in the

red velvet seat. From this angle, she could see the little Xs of glow-in-the-dark tape the actors used for blocking and the plain wooden blocks that stood in for furniture while the set was being constructed.

"I remember you, you know."

Her head snapped back to Grace. Her hands were clasped tightly on her lap.

Veronica nodded slowly. "I wasn't sure if you would."

"Yeah. You, and Duncan Kane." The girl's expression was unreadable. Her lips curved up slightly, but her eyes were flat and hidden. "The big, bad baby snatchers."

"I didn't have anything to with that," Veronica said, lying reflexively.

Grace's odd little smile didn't waver. "You know, for a while I used to think you were going to come back for me. I used to imagine it while I was falling asleep in the crawl space. I could see it so clearly. You'd open the closet, just like before; at first I wouldn't be able to make out your features because I'd been in the dark so long. You'd just be a dark silhouette. But then I'd see your hand, stretched out for mine. If I could just reach it—if I could just grab it—I'd be free. I'd be whisked off to wherever Faith and Duncan were shacked up." She shrugged. "I thought you were a big hero."

The words hit, a sucker punch that first inspired pain, then a powerful impulse to strike back. She'd never put much stock in heroes; it wasn't her job to save the day. And legally speaking, she'd done her due diligence for Grace: She'd told Dan Lamb what she'd seen in that house, assuming he'd turn the information over to Child Protective Services. Hoping someone would do something. She'd only helped Duncan take the baby because it was his, and because Meg had begged her from her deathbed to make sure her parents didn't get custody. But what more could she have done for Grace?

Really, Veronica? You couldn't think of a single thing to do for her? Not with all your supposed ingenuity, your willingness to see the rules as profoundly optional?

For a moment, she didn't trust herself to speak.

"I know you have no reason to trust me, Grace," she said finally. "I know I'm working for the other team. But I want to get the guy who did this to you."

"Bullshit. You want to prove I'm a liar and make this all go away for the Neptune Grand."

"Grace, I wish there was some way to say this where I don't look like an asshole . . . but I get paid either way," Veronica said, shrugging. "So can we please just let my mercenary motives go for a moment? Look, I've seen the photos of you after the attack. You should believe that I want to see the guy who did that to you suffer." She pulled a business card from her wallet and handed it to Grace. "Call me anytime, day or night, if there's anything else you want to tell me."

Grace looked down at the card, clearly skeptical, but she nodded and slid it into a pocket. Her voice was full and ringing when she spoke.

"'Oft have I heard that grief softens the mind, and makes it fearful and degenerate; think therefore on revenge and cease to weep.'"

Veronica wasn't sure which play the quote was from, but she knew exactly what it meant: You get tough. You get even.

You get tough. Had Mars Investigations been the sort of outfit that bothered to draft a list of its "Core Values," that would've been a top fiver.

CHAPTER TEN

"Ms. Landros will see you now."

Veronica stood up from the plush gray sofa and smiled at the woman behind the desk. It was about forty minutes after her meeting with Grace Manning. *And now for something completely different.*

"Fantastic," she said, attempting to bury the irony.

Her feet made no sound on the thick carpet. The reception area had the kind of muted quiet that only hovered around executive offices and university libraries, the air rarified and free of the clatter and clang of day-to-day life. She pushed one side of the heavy oak double doors open and entered the office of one of Neptune's most powerful people.

Veronica hadn't taken for granted that Petra Landros would agree to see her. The last time they'd worked together, Petra had made sure Veronica had everything she needed to get that case solved. But this time, it was Petra's business that stood accused of wrongdoing. And even though it was Petra's own insurance agents who had hired Veronica, she wasn't counting on the same red-carpet treatment.

It felt almost ridiculous to call the room she stepped into an "office." *Veronica* had an office; she had a desk, a chair, and a plant. This? This was a *study.* A *library.* A *throne room,* even. The floor was a gleaming mosaic of inlaid mahogany. Dark green drapes hung in the floor-to-ceiling windows, and Veronica had no way to be certain, but she would have bet money that the large painting of a lounging woman was, in fact, an original Matisse. A French cut-crystal chandelier hung from the molded ceiling, sending delicate rainbows across the floor.

Petra Landros sat behind an enormous wooden desk. Her dark hair was pinned up in a simple twist, and reading glasses perched on the end of her nose. Studious as she looked, there was no hiding the fact that Petra Landros was a bombshell. In her youth, she'd been a supermodel. Veronica distinctly remembered the *Sports Illustrated Swimsuit Issue* gatefold that occupied a place of honor in Logan's locker back in high school. Ten short years after wearing a silver mesh bikini on the shores of St. Lucia, Petra now owned the Neptune Grand, along with an ever-growing swath of restaurants and nightclubs. She was a dominant force on the Chamber of Commerce—and it was partly her influence that kept Dan Lamb in power, not because she liked or respected him, but because he was a useful tool. Skeptics dismissed her at their own peril.

She looked up as Veronica closed the door softly behind her.

"Ms. Mars. We meet again."

"Thanks for finding time for me, Ms. Landros."

"Of course. I'd like to get this cleared up as much as anybody." Petra gestured to a small bar against the wall. "Can I get you anything to drink?"

"Thanks, but no. I'm all right." Veronica sat, flipping open her notepad. "I just came from a meeting with Grace Manning."

Petra nodded slowly, taking off her glasses. "And did you learn anything that'll help with the case?"

"I don't know yet." She met the woman's eyes, frowning. "You seem awfully calm for a woman getting sued for three million dollars."

Petra waved her hand dismissively. "That's why I have insurance." She smiled wider at Veronica's expression. "Do you realize how many lawsuits come our way every year, Veronica? Every time someone slips on a rug or loses an earring. Every time someone sleeps through their wake-up call and misses a meeting or a flight. I have had more than one person threaten to sue us for destroying his or her marriage, after finding out the adultery took place here." She shook her head. "This is just another day at work for me."

Veronica's blood pressure blipped, but she maintained outward composure. "This was a rape. There's kind of a difference," she said, her voice level.

Petra's smile disappeared. For a moment, she looked somber. "It is terrible, what happened to that girl. I'm not denying that. As to the Grand's liability, that's for the lawyers and the insurance people to decide."

Veronica shook her head. "You don't think you'll take a PR hit if the media finds out someone was raped by one of your employees on hotel grounds?"

"If we settle, there'll be a no-publicity clause in the settlement. If we go to court, it'll be because we're sure we can win." Petra tapped a pen on her desk. "It's not that I'm cavalier about a crime happening in my hotel. But I trust that you understand: The business side of this will be handled as dispassionately as possible."

Veronica sat motionless, staring across the desk at the woman. This woman was best known for walking down a runway in a twelve-million-dollar sapphire-studded bra, and here she was giving Veronica a lesson in Machiavellian politics.

Petra seemed to guess what she was thinking. She put down her pen and laced her fingers together in front of her. "So how can I help you, Ms. Mars?"

"I'd like to get a list of everyone who was staying here that night, for starters."

Petra exhaled impatiently. "We had almost six hundred guests that night. I doubt you'll be able to narrow it down from that."

"No—but if we get a lead, I want access to that information so I can verify it myself."

Petra's eyes narrowed. "You're not going to harass my guests, are you?"

"I'm not about to cold-call six hundred people, if that's what you're asking." Veronica leaned back in her chair and folded her hands. "Look, I don't plan to talk to anyone if I can help it. I just want to be able to verify who was there that night."

"I suppose that's reasonable," Petra said. "All right. Talk to Gladys on your way out; she'll get you that list. Is there anything else?"

"What can you tell me about Miguel Ramirez?" Veronica asked.

Petra shrugged. "I never met the man. He was one of six people caught in the ICE bust—the others were all in housekeeping. I fired two people in HR for that mess. The Grand has always had a policy against hiring undocumented immigrants."

I'm sure you had a firm policy against getting caught, at very least, thought Veronica.

"Have any other complaints against him surfaced?"

"None that I've heard. Then again, the entire service staff has clammed up since the raid. No one's talking—the Sheriff's Department has already been sniffing around trying to get information from them."

"Nothing puts a disenfranchised group at ease quite like armed men in uniforms," Veronica said. "Mind if I try my luck?"

"Sure. Gladys can give you a pass card to get you down to the service corridor."

With that, their interview wound down to a close. Veronica shut her notebook and slid it into her purse. Then she paused, looking back at the woman on the other side of the oversized desk. A folded newspaper sat in front of her, Dan Lamb's picture leering up from the photo. Veronica's jaw tightened.

"Still voting for Sheriff Lamb in the election?"

Petra looked amused. "Who else is there?"

Outside the office, Veronica paused at the reception desk. The nameplate perched on the corner read Gladys Corrigan. The woman behind it was short and matronly, her red hair set in a stiff bob. She smiled up at Veronica over her monitor.

"Ms. Landros told me you'd like the guest roster from March sixth. Do you have a flash drive?"

Veronica didn't have time to wonder what arcane bureaucratic magic had delivered the message so fast. She rummaged in her purse, found the stray flash drive she always kept handy, and handed it across. Veronica watched the woman's fingers fly over the keyboard, entering her personal login information to access the database. A moment later the flash drive was back in Veronica's hand.

"Thanks." She slid the drive in her purse. "I was also wondering if you could look up who was working at the Eagle's Nest that same night?"

"Sure." Another flourish across the keyboard. She paused. "Looks like it was Alyssa Winchell that night."

So that part of Grace's story checks out, at least. "She doesn't happen to be working right now, does she?"

"No, ma'am, but I can give you her number."

Veronica wrote the digits down in her notebook, just in case. It would be better to come back and talk to her here, though, in the place where it happened. Memories were sometimes a little stronger at the scene of the crime.

"And you wanted to talk to the laundry employees as well?" Gladys cocked her head. "Is this about Miguel Ramirez?"

Veronica blinked. "Did you know him?"

Gladys gave a sad nod. "We both went to St. Mary's. Sweet, sweet young man. I just don't believe he could have done what . . . what they say he did."

"Did you ever see him at work?"

She looked mildly scandalized. "Of course not. The laundry workers are in the basement. I don't go down there." She handed Veronica a white plastic pass card. "This will get you onto the service elevator. The laundry is straight down the hall from where you get off."

If Miguel Ramirez were a rapist, he wouldn't be the first one called a "sweet, sweet young man" by an acquaintance who refused to believe it. Still, Veronica made a mental note while she waited for the elevator. If nothing else, now she knew something else about him: Monster or not, he charmed the church ladies.

Instead of going straight down to laundry, she rode the elevator from the third floor administrative offices all the way up to the Eagle's Nest. She paused to glance around the quiet bar—it was late afternoon, still too early for the happy hour customers—then went into the stairwell. She wanted to take the stairs from the roof to the basement, to retrace Grace's steps as closely as possible. She descended the concrete stairs slowly, examining the walls and floors as she did. She didn't expect to see any sign of a struggle—Bundrick and Foss had swept the stairs for blood evidence months ago to no avail—but it was worth keeping her eyes peeled, just in case.

The stairwell somehow felt both utilitarian and surreal—murky light, all the normal sounds of the hotel muted and far away while her own footsteps echoed up and down the deep vertical corridor. It was easy to imagine Grace Manning there with her, just a flight or two ahead, walking into unsuspected disaster. Veronica picked up her pace, anxious to reach the bottom.

She didn't meet a soul until the fourth floor, when she caught a whiff of tobacco smoke. She looked over the edge of the railing to see two women in maid's uniforms sharing a cigarette and speaking in Spanish a few flights below. Though they were talking in low voices, their speech reverberated strangely against the walls, creating an illusion that they were much closer. When they caught sight of her, they quickly stubbed out the smoke and went silent, though they didn't leave their perch. She had to squeeze between them to get past.

No cameras in the stairwell. And the employees seem to know it.

Finally, she got to the bottom of the stairs. She swiped the card Gladys had given her and went through the door marked EMPLOYEES ONLY.

The service corridor was long and windowless. Fluorescent track lighting ran along the ceiling. There was a large employee lounge through one door, with vending machines and threadbare furniture. When Veronica poked her head in, the only occupant was a woman in a maid's uniform, stretched out on a sofa with a newspaper over her face. A handful of workers, most of them Hispanic, passed her in the hallway, but none spared her more than a passing glance.

The laundry stood behind a pair of swinging double doors. As Veronica entered, a blast of hot air pushed against her. The machines' roaring and whooshing sounds filled the cavernous space. There were five employees, all in red polo shirts with the Neptune Grand crest on the breast pocket. One broad-chested woman shoved an armful of sheets into a washing machine. At a large table, a man and a woman worked together to fold clean linens. Two more women stood at a station surrounded by garment bags, ironing clothes. Shelves full of clean sheets and towels covered most of one wall.

As she moved deeper into the room, she spotted a row of wheeled, fabric-sided linen bins. She paused to look them over. *Definitely room for a body—especially one as small as Grace's. But I still can't see how he'd get her out of the building without the cameras picking it up.*

The woman who'd been loading the machine was the first to notice Veronica. She was no taller than Veronica, but she was stocky, her body compact and muscular. She approached with a wary expression, wiping beads of sweat from her forehead.

"*Hola,*" Veronica said. "*Mi nombre es Veronica Mars. ¿Hablas inglés?*"

"A little," said the woman. Her accent was heavy, but her words were carefully enunciated. She waited, her expression unreadable.

Quickly, Veronica considered her options. There weren't many. Anyone who actually knew Miguel Ramirez wouldn't want to discuss him with some perky blonde *gringa* they'd never seen before, particularly after an ICE raid. Deportations tended to get people scared, and scared people didn't talk. But she had to try.

"I'm working for the Grand's insurance company," she said, consciously avoiding the word "investigator." "I'm trying to find any information I can on a man named Miguel Ramirez. He worked here until a few months ago. Do you remember him?"

Something in the room changed at the mention of the name. The employees stopped what they were doing and looked up at her.

The woman shifted her weight. "I don't remember."

Veronica nodded. "Please, Señora, may I ask you how long you've worked for the Neptune Grand?"

"Six years," she said. "All legal."

"So you were here when Mr. Ramirez worked here?"

"I don't remember," she said again, her expression unchanging.

Veronica looked around the room helplessly. "I'm not trying to get anyone in trouble. I just need to know more about him. Can anyone here help me?"

For a moment, the woman stared at her, unblinking. "No one remembers him. He was not one of us."

Veronica nodded slowly. It was obvious that the interview was over. "I see. Thanks so much for your time." She turned and left, feeling their eyes on her. There was no point in continuing this line of questioning. If Ramirez's coworkers knew anything about the attack, they weren't about to share it with *her*. She'd have to find another way.

CHAPTER ELEVEN

When Keith pushed open the door to Mane Attraction on Monday afternoon, a single bell hanging on the handle clattered against the glass. The little salon occupied a storefront in a strip mall just a few blocks from the Camelot Motel. The name of the shop was stenciled in pink tempera paint across the windows.

Someone had once made an effort to give the space a little flair, but now the pink walls were smudged gray with a decade's worth of handprints. Faded photos of outdated hairstyles hung over the mirrors, along with dozens of glittery fake butterflies, their antennae bent and broken. There were three stations, but only one was currently in use. A middle-aged woman sat in the chair beneath a purple smock. Behind her stood a tall, wiry woman, her hair teased in an extravagant bouffant.

The hairdresser glanced up as she heard the door. "Be right with you, hon." Her voice was soft and a little gravelly.

"Sure. Take your time." Keith pretended to look at his phone while the woman in the chair resumed a story about her ex-husband's new girlfriend.

"He tried sushi with her. *Sushi.* When he was with me he wouldn't even try a new brand of *cereal.*"

The hairdresser made little *tsk* noises in response, shaking her head as she worked. Keith could see that she was younger than he'd first thought—maybe in her early thirties. Her face was caked with makeup, but it couldn't quite cover up the pitted scars across her cheeks. Her fingers, though, were slender and clean, her nails sculpted and painted pearly blue.

She's not using now, Keith thought. *If she were, those nails would be bitten to the quick.* But she still had the gaunt, hollowed-out look of a meth addict.

"All right, Carla, take a seat over here." She patted the arm of an ancient-looking dryer chair just across from her beauty station. The older woman sat down, and the hairdresser adjusted the bowl of the dryer over her head. "I'm gonna see to this gentlemen. It doesn't look like it'll take too long. Just a little off the top?" She winked at Keith.

He chuckled, hands in his pockets, waiting for her to get the woman set up with the dryer full blast in her ears.

"So what can I do for you?" The woman picked up a broom and started sweeping hair away from her chair.

"Are you Casey Roarke?"

She froze for a split second. "Yeah, that's me. And who's asking?"

He held up his hands in a placating gesture. Glancing at Carla to make sure she was safely involved in her *Cosmo*, the dryer blasting in her ears, he spoke in a low, calm voice.

"Ms. Roarke, I'm Keith Mars. I'm a private investigator. I'm sorry to bother you at work, but I was hoping I could ask you a few questions."

Her expression turned cagey. "What about?"

"I'm sure you've heard about the lawsuit against the Balboa County Sheriff's Department—the one that's accusing them of planting evidence to boost their arrest numbers."

She shook her head. "I don't know anything about any of that."

He looked down, shifting his weight slightly. He was a solidly built man, but over the years he'd learned to morph into a less imposing figure when he needed to put someone at ease. Shoulders and belly relaxed, thumbs hooked in front pockets, a hint of Andy Griffith in the voice, sans the overt rurality. "Well, if I'm not mistaken, in August 2012, you were pulled over for speeding. Deputy Douglas Harlon searched your vehicle and found three grams of crystal meth in your glove box. From what I heard, you denied it was yours for more than a week, before changing your story and pleading guilty to a misdemeanor drug charge."

Casey's face hardened. "Fine, I'm a tweaker. So what?"

"I don't think that meth was yours," he said evenly. "I think Deputy Harlon planted it in your car because you already had a record and because he needed an arrest that night."

Her fingers tightened around the broom handle. "You don't know what you're talking about."

"I know you put in a call to the ACLU on August twenty-first. You told the volunteer that you'd been clean for eight months when the cops found that eight ball."

She shrugged. "I was looking for a way out of jail." She leaned toward him. "Haven't you ever met an addict before? We're *liars*."

Keith didn't miss a beat. "Doug Harlon was the same deputy who arrived on the scene when my client was shot. He made sure there was a Glock in his hand when backup arrived. And you aren't the only two with stories like that."

"Yeah, but that's all you've got. A bunch of stories." She shook her head. "You know what I've got? Three kids I *just* got back from CPS. You have kids?"

"A daughter."

"Well, imagine if someone could take her from you." Her voice was like glass, sharp and clear. "Just for a second, imagine that you had a choice to make. That you could keep your mouth shut and maybe get your kids back, or that you could stir up shit and lose everything. Think about that before you come asking me about any more *stories* you've heard, all right?"

She knelt with a dustpan and deftly scooped up the scraps of hair. Then she stood and looked him in the eye.

"Now, if you'll excuse me, I got a lot of work to do."

Back in the car, Keith collected his thoughts before starting it. Leading up to Eli's criminal trial, he'd found dozens of people willing to testify about the planted evidence. But to strengthen the civil case, he wanted to make sure he could show that Deputy Harlon, the officer who'd signed off on Eli's arrest, was a part of this pattern. So far he'd struck out; Casey Roarke had been his third interview of the morning, and they'd all gone about as well. Lawrence "Duck" Gibbs, a former heroin dealer and small-time thug, had let his two pit bulls out in the yard when he'd seen Keith at the gate; he'd shouted over their frenzied barking that he "wasn't no kind of snitch." And Benji Saroyan, one of Neptune's itinerant homeless, had started to cry in the middle of Keith's pitch and refused to answer any questions—though he'd taken Keith's outstretched twenty eagerly enough.

It didn't matter; there were plenty of witnesses. And they were trying to show institutionalized corruption, anyway—

not just Deputy Harlon's itchy evidence-planting finger. He thought they'd have enough with or without Harlon's victims. But it troubled him to see how many people were still scared. It meant that even with all the press, the Sheriff's Department was still squeezing the underclasses as hard as they dared.

He glanced up and down the street. So far, no oncoming trucks. And he had three more people to try to talk to before he gave up for the day. He turned the key in the ignition and glided back out into traffic.

CHAPTER TWELVE

When Veronica's alarm went off at seven on Sunday morning Logan was up, his side of the bed already empty. She sat up in the rumpled sheets, looking around.

Back in high school, the only thing that'd gotten him out of bed early was the promise of good surf conditions. Since his return from the *Truman* he'd been up before her almost every morning, sometimes hitting the beach with Dick Casablancas, but often just fixing breakfast or going for a jog. *It's like he's a grown-up or something. Weird.*

For a moment she considered nestling into the sheets and going back to sleep. She hadn't slept well all that week, which was normal when she had a case with so many details and dead ends. Her brain just wouldn't shut down.

Which is why you can't go back to bed, remember? You've got work to do. And if you don't hurry up, you're going to be late for church.

Gladys Corrigan had said she and Miguel Ramirez went to St. Mary's. It was a long shot. She anticipated the same reaction she'd gotten in the laundry room. But if she were lucky, other parishioners might remember him. If she were very lucky, they would be willing to talk about him.

She showered, pinned her hair back, and donned a pink

flowered skirt and a white peplum blouse. Then she opened the bedroom door and emerged.

An accented female voice spoke from the living room. Veronica stopped in the doorway, frowning.

"*Motasharefon bema'refatek.*" The voice paused. "Nice to meet you, masculine. *Motasharefatun bema'refatek.*" Another pause. "Nice to meet you, feminine."

Veronica poked her head into the living room. Logan sat at the kitchen counter, a half-eaten bagel on a plate next to him. He was looking at his laptop. On the screen, a dark-haired woman spoke slowly and clearly as Arabic lettering appeared beneath her.

"*Sabah al khayr.* Good morning. *Masa'a al khayr.* Good evening."

"*Sabah al khayr,*" Veronica repeated.

"*Sabah an noor,*" Logan said, giving her a sheepish grin and shutting his computer. He was already dressed in jeans and a PROPERTY OF THE US NAVY T-shirt. "Aren't you whole-some this morning?"

"Gotta look good for Jesus," she said, leaning in to kiss his cheek. "It's not even eight. You've been up, out for bagels, and learning a foreign language with the sunrise? Who are you and where's my boyfriend?"

"I'm practicing for when you finally get your way about that puppy you keep going on about," he said. "We both know who's going to be rolling out of bed and taking it out to do its business." He went into the kitchen and grabbed a bag from the bread box. "I got blueberry, sesame, and plain. Pick your poison."

Veronica shifted into a spot-on Yiddish accent. "Three years I lived in New York—three! I *know* from bagels, *bubeleh*. And now you want I should eat this Trader Joe's *chazzerei*?"

"Sesame it is, extra schmear." He picked up a heavy bread knife and sliced the bagel before popping it into the toaster.

She climbed up onto the stool he'd just vacated, opening his computer. The lesson had automatically paused midsentence when he shut it. "What's with the Arabic? You didn't experience any reprogramming in the Middle East that you haven't shared with me? Any well-worn rugs I should avoid giving to Goodwill?"

Logan narrowed his eyes. "I harbor no feelings that should concern you or my native land, to which I remain fully loyal. But Allah willing, the Great Satan Hulu Plus will soon pay the price for blocking *Archer* Season 5 in Iraq."

Logan grinned and shrugged. "I'm just messing around with it. My CO said I should think about taking some classes. Might be useful, you know?"

She frowned as he slid a cup of coffee in front of her. "That's funny. I didn't think they spoke a lot of Arabic in San Diego."

"You don't order a lot of shawarma, do you? I need my pita crusty but still moist inside; meat shaved thin; no eggplant. Plenty of *skhug* and fresh-cut lemons on the side." He shrugged. "Tough to pantomime all that."

She didn't answer. Logan's shore duty was supposed to last another year, and she'd been hoping that his fleet would be rotated out of the Persian Gulf by the time that was over. If he was trying to learn Arabic that meant *he* was planning—or at least expecting—to stay in a war zone.

And more upsetting than the news itself was the element of surprise. The possibility that she might have misread his intentions. That they might always have had starkly different visions for the future.

She opened her mouth to argue, and then closed it. Did she really want to start a fight on a peaceful Sunday morning? Or did she want to nibble on the truthfully-just-as-good-as-New-York bagel her boyfriend handed her. To enjoy the sight of him, lean and muscular in the kitchen's sunlight?

"Thanks," she said, sipping the coffee.

He smiled. "*Al'afw.*"

St. Mary's was an imposing Romanesque cathedral in Neptune's Old Town, next to Founder's Park. Veronica arrived just as the nine o'clock bells rang out across the neighborhood. She joined the crowd making their way toward the double doors and did her best to blend.

Her eyes took a moment to adjust to the Catholic gloom. Patterns of red, blue, and green spilled over the cavernous nave from a massive rose window. Towering organ pipes jutted upward behind an altar draped with white cloth. She noticed most of the people in front of her dipping their fingertips into a shell-shaped font of holy water as they entered, but deemed it best to pass on that particular rite. *Bursting into flame would definitely blow my cover.*

She took a seat in one of the back pews and looked around at the milling parishioners. Young families herded children and soothed fussy babies. Three very old women, two with canes, walked tremulously to the front of the church, bowing to the altar before taking their seats. A man in an Argyle sweater laughed loudly, then was shushed by his wife.

She gave a little start as she caught sight of Liam Fitzpatrick, looking uncomfortable in a button-down shirt and tie. His face was pitted and scarred now—time, and the criminal life, had taken its toll. He was surrounded, as usual, by cousins and siblings. Veronica recognized Danny Boyd, Liam's loutish cousin, and Ciaran Fitzpatrick, who'd been a third-year senior when she was a freshman at Neptune High. The Fighting Fitzpatricks were Neptune's most notorious crime family, though their influence was fraying. They seemed almost quaint these days compared to the savagery just ninety miles south in Tijuana. According to Keith, Liam had managed to stay out of prison in the last decade only by throwing more and more of his underlings to the wolves. The PCHers weren't even afraid of them anymore.

Veronica was distracted by the sound of a familiar voice. She glanced to the other side of the aisle. Halfway back she saw short red hair that she recognized as Gladys Corrigan's. A younger woman with sandy-blonde curls sat close next to her—a daughter, maybe, or niece.

Without warning, the organ let out a few bombastic bars of music. The parishioners rose in one fluid motion, making it all but impossible for her to see anything. She stood too, a half second too late. Then they all started to sing.

"Immaculate Mary, your praises we sing. You reign now in splendor with Jesus our King. Ave, Ave, Ave Maria . . ."

Next to her, a tiny, wizened-looking woman in a pale pink suit leaned over, holding her hymnal so Veronica could see the words. Veronica gave her a grateful smile and joined in.

Father Patrick Fitzpatrick—yet another of Liam's brothers—made his way down the aisle in vestments of emerald green. Bull-necked and florid, he looked more like he belonged on a bar stool at the River Stix than in the sacristy. But as far as Veronica knew, he really was on the straight and narrow. She wondered just what Ma Fitzpatrick had done differently with him.

The crowd sat down as he took the podium.

"The Lord be with you." His voice boomed out over the nave.

"And also with you," chorused the congregation in a practiced, rote manner.

"I invite all who are gathered here in worship to take a moment to contemplate our need for salvation." Father Patrick's eyes moved along the pews. It might have been Veronica's imagination, but she thought his gaze lingered for an extra second or two on Liam and the other members of Clan Fitzpatrick. "Let us pray."

Mass went on, punctuated with hymns, prayers, and recitations. Father Patrick read several passages from Scripture, including good old Matthew 19:24, which to Veronica's mind bore witness that Neptune might actually be hell: "Again I say to you, it is easier for a camel to pass through the eye of a needle than for one who is rich to enter the kingdom of God." There was a short homily about greed, followed by Communion. The whole thing took about an hour.

Finally, Father Patrick gave the final benediction. "May almighty God bless you, the Father, and the Son, and the Holy Spirit."

"Amen," replied the crowd.

And then everyone was on their feet. Some people wandered to the statue of the Blessed Virgin standing over the bank of votive candles and lingered to pray; others gathered in the aisles, talking to friends. Veronica watched as Liam Fitzpatrick—followed by the bulk of his crew—made straight for the door. A few tweedy older women surrounded Father Patrick, fluttering their eyelashes and basking in his attention.

"Veronica?"

She jumped at the sound of her name. When she turned, it was to look into the face of Jade Navarro. She stood in front of Veronica with her little girl in her arms. Valentina had just turned four, and she peered at Veronica with enormous, shy eyes fringed with long lashes that were unmistakably her father's.

"Hey, Jade. Hi, Valentina." Veronica adjusted her purse over her shoulder and tried to look natural. *Just another sinner on Sunday—nothing suspicious here.*

The little girl hid her face against Jade's neck. Veronica gave Jade an apologetic smile. Jade didn't smile back.

"What are you doing here?" she asked. "I've never seen you at St. Mary's before."

"No, I . . . I haven't really been before." *Well, except for the one time I planted a hidden camera in the confessional. But that was a special case.* "How are you? Is Weevil . . . I mean, Eli, here with you?"

The woman's lips tightened, almost imperceptibly. "Eli doesn't come to Mass anymore."

Veronica wasn't sure what to say. Jade's expression was hard, accusatory.

"You know, Eli used to talk about you all the time. Hard-ass Veronica Mars who didn't take any crap and who helped him out of more jams than he could count. I wonder if you think you helped him by getting him back on that bike."

"I didn't get him back on that bike," Veronica said. "But let's not kid ourselves. Becoming 'old Weevil' probably kept him out of prison."

"For the moment." Jade shrugged. A splotch of red from the stained-glass window fell across her dark hair, giving it a bloody cast. "But that won't be much comfort if he gets busted for something he's actually done. He's back in the game now, Veronica. He thinks I don't know, but I'm not stupid."

A half-dozen rejoinders popped into Veronica's head. *What did you want, Jade? For him to sit back and let some lying opportunist deliver him to Lamb's doorstep like a pizza? Sure, you'd be able to visit your morally upright husband in prison on the weekends. That'd be a real consolation.*

Instead, she opted for diplomacy.

"Look, he's trying to make things right. Has he told you about the lawsuit? If he wins, it'll totally vindicate him. Lamb will look—"

"I don't give a *fuck* how Lamb looks. And neither does Eli. That's all you." Her voice dipped to a hiss when she swore. She quickly crossed herself, and for a moment she seemed to be fighting for control. Then, shaking her head, she simply turned away and hurried toward the door, Valentina's tiny face watching Veronica over her mother's shoulder.

Veronica watched Jade go, fighting the urge to chase after her, to keep arguing. She'd never tried to frame herself as some quixotic warrior. She'd never claimed to be able to save anyone.

But don't lie to yourself, Veronica—it really does please you to believe you wear the white hat here in Neptune. Just you and your dad. But it's hard squaring that noble idea with taking money from people whose hats are so unmistakably gray.

She took a deep breath. Then she saw Gladys Corrigan disappearing out of sight into one arm of the transept.

If she was going to act, she had to do it now.

CHAPTER THIRTEEN

A stairway in the transept led Veronica down to the cathedral's subterranean multipurpose room. It was a large space with linoleum floors and fluorescent lighting, more high school cafeteria than Gothic catacomb. A kitchen was visible through an open door at one end. Several people sat talking and laughing at the long folding tables. Children ran around the open space, playing a game with rules obvious only to themselves.

Gladys Corrigan came out of the kitchen balancing a silver tray heaped with Oreos. She placed it on a small table next to two large carafes of coffee, and was busily straightening the sugar packets when Veronica stepped up next to her.

"Hi, Ms. Corrigan. I don't know if you remember me, but my name's Veronica. I met you at the Neptune Grand a few days ago?"

The woman blinked rapidly, then took off her glasses and polished them on the edge of her blouse. "Veronica. Yes, I'm sorry, you startled me. Hello."

"It's okay. I'm sorry to sneak up on you like this." She smiled, doing her best impression of affable. "I was wondering if you could help me."

Gladys hesitated, her brow knit into a complex tangle of lines. She glanced around the room. "What is this about, dear? If it's something work related, I can't really . . ."

"I'm trying to find someone . . . anyone . . . who can talk to me about Miguel Ramirez. You mentioned that you knew him through church. How well did you know him?"

Gladys twisted her lips in a thoughtful pout. "Well, we talked after Mass sometimes. When my husband died a few years ago, he came by once in a while to help me mow my lawn. It was so sweet of him. I was too . . . you know, too heartbroken to see to it myself." She shook her head. "But I didn't know much about his personal life, if that's what you're asking."

"Is there anyone here who might know more?"

Gladys straightened herself up, one hand going to her hip. "Miss Mars, these people are here for *church*. You can't just ask—"

"You sounded very sure that Miguel was innocent," Veronica interrupted. "If that's true, don't you want his name cleared?"

Gladys fell silent for a moment. At the tables around them, people chattered on, oblivious to the tension at the snack table. A small child darted between them, grabbed an Oreo, and ran off to join his friends again.

She gave Veronica a strange, searching look. "He's already been deported. It doesn't matter."

Veronica took a deep breath, frustrated.

"It *does* matter. I'm trying to save the place you work millions of dollars. I could also restore the reputation of someone you believe is a sweet young guy who couldn't have done what he's been accused of."

The woman's eyes dropped down to the dirty linoleum floor. Veronica knew the details of the crime were probably common knowledge among the staff of the Neptune Grand.

"I don't want to bother anyone, or get anyone in trouble," Veronica continued. "But unless I can find some way to either rule him out or find him, this case is going to fall apart."

Gladys looked up, her lips pressed tightly together but shaking. She took a deep breath. Then she held up her hand, calling out to someone across the room. "Bianca, honey. Can you come here for a second?"

Veronica watched as a young woman in a yellow sundress turned toward them from the table where she sat. Her black hair was cut short, and she tucked the ends nervously behind her ears as she approached.

"What's up, Gladys?" She crossed her arms over her chest in a gesture that seemed more self-protective than hostile.

"Well . . . if you have a few minutes . . ." Gladys gave a sad little smile. "This young lady has some questions about your husband."

Veronica and Bianca sat together on an oak-shaded bench in Founder's Park, just across the street from the cathedral. Eucalyptus and palm trees dotted the expanse of the neatly manicured lawn. Paved trails wove through the greenery, joggers and speed-walkers hurrying past. Their bench faced a playground where Bianca and Miguel's four-year-old son, Gabe, shrieked with laughter as he chased another boy.

Bianca angrily wiped a tear from her eye. "I can't believe I didn't know."

The feeling is mutual, sister. Veronica had been prepared to question churchgoers about Miguel, but finding out that he had wife—a wife who had no idea that he was accused of any crime, much less a vicious rape and beating—had left her reeling.

"It's strange. If local law enforcement ran any kind of identity check on Miguel, you and Gabe would have come up," Veronica said, leaning forward, bracing her forearms against her knees.

Bianca sniffed. "Not necessarily. 'Miguel Ramirez' wasn't his real name. And we weren't . . . we weren't legally married." Her voice dropped, ashamed. "We always really wanted to be. But he didn't want me to get in trouble if he got caught. No one at church knows the truth—we told everyone we were married in San Diego."

Bianca pulled her phone from her purse and, after pulling up the photos, handed it to Veronica. The screen showed a smiling Miguel with Gabe on his shoulders, somewhere down by the Boardwalk. Carnival lights flashed in the background, and Gabe held a towering cotton candy high over his head. It was hard to reconcile this image with that of the sinister-looking alleged perp in his mug shot. But then, that was the nature of mug shots. They could make Bruno Mars indistinguishable from Rondo Hatton.

"He told me he was undocumented before we even had our first kiss," Bianca said softly. "He knew what it could mean for me. For us."

"Couldn't he apply for citizenship once you were married?" Veronica asked.

"It's not that simple. You have to go back to your home country to apply for a green card, but there's a law that anyone who entered the country illegally is banned from reentering for ten years. So we decided to risk it and stay here. I've been constantly afraid he would get pulled over for a bad taillight or something. That's all it takes for them to get you."

"Are you in touch with him now?"

"Of course I am." Bianca tucked her hair behind her ears again and frowned. "But if you're hoping I'll put you in touch with him—no way. Just no *way*. Miguel can't possibly have done this . . . thing you say he's accused of. Look, Ms. Mars, Miguel is the gentlest man I've ever met, okay? He never raised his voice with me or with Gabe. He never even slammed a door. I'm sure that's exactly what you'd expect me to say, but it's true."

"Maybe so. But with him out of reach, no one here has a good incentive to prove him innocent. Think about it—if you were, say, a lazy, corrupt deputy, would you put much effort into finding an accused criminal once he'd disappeared into Mexico? Or would you throw your hands up and assume he's guilty so you can move on with your day?"

She'd phrased it carefully. She wanted Bianca to hear the word *innocent* before she heard *guilty*. She wanted Bianca to trust that she would take either possibility very seriously.

"Mommy! Watch me!"

Gabe's high-pitched voice wafted back to them from the playground. He started to climb up the miniature rock wall—a three-foot ledge with hand- and footholds bolted to the side. Bianca's eyes followed him closely as he scaled the wall. When he'd gotten to the top, he waved. She waved back. When she spoke again, her voice was soft, broken.

"I grew up getting the shit beat out of me on a regular

basis. Grew up watching my mom get the shit beat out of her too. I used to watch her cover for my dad at the hospital. Bruises all over her body, broken wrist, broken nose, and she told the cops she walked into a door. I swore up and down I'd never let anyone treat *me* like that. Never."

Veronica fought the urge to reach out and touch the woman's hand. She knew it would not be welcome.

"Whoever said this about him is lying." Bianca tugged at a lock of her hair, looping it tightly around a finger. "You said there was DNA evidence?"

"Yes. If we could get a sample from him . . ."

The woman shook her head tightly. "He's in Michoacán, on his sister's farm. It'd take you weeks to find him and get him tested." Her eyes stared out over the playground. Gabe ran along the playscape to the fireman's pole, leapt onto it, and squealed as he slid to the ground. "There's another way, though, right?"

Veronica didn't answer. She'd been hoping Bianca would have the idea for herself—and she didn't want to say anything that might accidentally change her mind.

"Gabe, *mijo*, come here for a second, please." Bianca gestured for the boy to come over. The child ran over, tripping on his shoelaces once but getting right back up.

"You can take his, can't you?" The woman scooped the boy up and pulled him in her lap.

Veronica hesitated. "I could," she said. "Do you mind?"

Bianca's nostrils flared. "Do it."

The little boy stared up at her with wide, baffled eyes. Veronica used the tweezers she kept in her purse to pluck five glossy black hairs from his head and put them into a plastic bag. This sample, of course, wouldn't be admissible in court. It would be too easy for a lawyer to claim—for a while at least—that there was no proof Gabe was Miguel's son. However, it would determine her next step. If the samples matched, that would be enough to get the FBI interested in tracking down Miguel Ramirez, or whatever his name really was.

And if they didn't . . . Well, it wouldn't completely rule Ramirez out. But Veronica would start looking damn hard at other suspects, other possibilities. Because she sensed that, like all survivors, Bianca Ramirez was a kind of amateur detective herself. Anyone who'd spent a childhood waiting for the other foot—or the other fist—to fall knew how to sense danger. And she didn't get the feeling that this was a woman who'd tolerate a threat in her home for very long.

CHAPTER FOURTEEN

On Thursday, not quite a week after Veronica's visit to St. Mary's, she and Logan joined about thirty journalists, activists, civic voyeurs, and well-wishers in the cramped lobby of a midtown office building to bear witness to the official announcement of Weevil's lawsuit.

"Thank you so much for being here." The lawyer's name was Lisa Choi, a rising star who projected the riveting charisma and no-bullshit focus of Helen Mirren on *Prime Suspect*. Veronica had been shocked to learn that the nationally lauded prosecutor with the Hillary pantsuit and black-framed glasses was just thirty-two years old—three years her senior. "Today we have filed a lawsuit against the Balboa County Sheriff's Department. In January of this year, my client Eli Navarro was attempting to render aid to a citizen whose vehicle had broken down. He was shot at point-blank range for his trouble, and he still suffers chronic pain and disability from this unwarranted attack. Yes, Mr. Navarro is lucky to be alive. But luck certainly wasn't in his corner when the Balboa County Sheriff's Department arrived on the scene."

Weevil stood to Lisa's right, looking uncomfortable in the same slacks and button-down shirt he'd worn for his criminal trial. Keith and Cliff lingered on the sidelines, trying to draw as little attention as possible. Both men had long, contentious histories with Lamb, and Veronica knew that Lisa wanted the trial to be perceived as all about Weevil, not a political vendetta.

"The night my client was shot, deputies of the Balboa County Sheriff's Department planted evidence on him to falsely indicate that he'd been attempting to rob the woman he was trying to help. Mr. Navarro was later found innocent of all charges. For all of us who believe in equal justice under the law, that's a start. It's a good start." She paused for effect and turned to Weevil, whose stoic face was flushed from the effort of suppressing his emotions. "However," Lisa continued, "this still fails to undo much of the damage that's been inflicted upon his career, his health, and his mental well-being. It fails to undo the injustice perpetrated on my client and on the *community of Neptune at large.*" She looked around the room at that, as if challenging someone to disagree. "When we lose faith in our officers of the law, it harms all of us. It cripples our criminal justice system. It threatens the most vulnerable parts of our community. It allows money and power to subvert justice."

"I miss money and power," Logan whispered in Veronica's ear.

Veronica pressed her lips together to suppress a laugh, then turned her attention back to Lisa. *What she's doing— that could have been my life, if I'd wanted it.*

Veronica had gone to law school in part to get away from the PI life, convincing herself she wanted to be comfortable and detached and . . . and what? Normal? Whatever that was supposed to look like. In the end she hadn't been able to stay away.

Did she have regrets? Maybe. But she'd had half a year to accept the choices she'd made—to stay in Neptune, to work in her father's profession, to give up law. Now it all felt inevitable. But there was no denying a twinge of envy as she watched Lisa command the room.

"We will show that the officers who planted that gun on my client are not, as the department has claimed, outliers, but that they are part of a pattern of corruption infecting the department at large—a pattern reaching all the way up the chain of command." She hadn't named Lamb outright, but Veronica knew the journalists in the room would immediately zero in on the sheriff. "The Sheriff's Department has been manufacturing its own twisted version of justice for years now. My client was only the most recent victim of this pattern. Our aim is to expose as much of this endemic, unchecked corruption as possible so Neptune can once again have a *justice* system worthy of the name."

Glad she's on our side, but I hope she's got a bodyguard. Veronica glanced over at her dad, who stood next to a potted ficus on the other side of the room. Someone had tried to kill him for daring to ask too many questions. Now Lisa Choi was asking those same questions, with a bullhorn.

"I'm ready to take any questions you might have," Lisa concluded.

The room exploded in a chaos of TV, radio, and print reporters' urgent voices.

"What kind of damages are you seeking?"

"Are you suggesting that Sheriff Lamb knew about the planted evidence?"

"Are you planning to name Mrs. Kane in the suit as well?"

Veronica had heard enough. She gave Logan a little nod, and together they pushed out the glass doors, onto the covered sidewalk. It was almost three p.m. and visible waves of heat rolled up from the concrete. She was temporarily blinded by the sun's glare reflecting off windshields in the parking lot.

"Well, that was romantic," Logan said as she rummaged for her sunglasses in her bag.

"Why, darling, what could be more romantic than uncovering systemic corruption through a grueling process of investigations, subpoenas, and litigation?" She tilted her head and grinned. "But I guess, if you want, we could do something more, you know, light and fun?"

He did a mock double take, wiggling his index finger in his ear as if clearing it out. "I don't understand. What's this 'fun,' and how do you do it?"

"I've heard some people do it two days a week," she said. "Maybe we could take a drive up the coast? Have dinner later tonight?"

"Dinner, like, at the same place, at the same time?" He raised an eyebrow. "Now that sounds suspiciously date-like."

"Yeah?" She leaned up to kiss him. "Play your cards right, maybe I'll take you home after."

Before he could say anything else, her phone trilled from the depths of her bag. She dug it out and checked the screen.

It was Preuss Insurance.

"Let me take this real quick, okay?" She held up one finger toward Logan, then answered the phone.

"Hi, Veronica, this is Joe Hickman. I'm calling to let you know that the hair you sent in—Ramirez's kid? The DNA doesn't match."

Her heart picked up speed. She moved the phone to her other ear and took a few steps away from Logan.

"I knew it. Have you talked to the victim's lawyers yet?" She hadn't talked to Grace since she found out Ramirez had a family; she'd wanted verification first.

"Not yet. Now that we know he's in Michoacán we've sent someone down there to take a sample from Ramirez himself."

"Great, so now I'll focus on finding Grace's boy—"

"I'm sorry, Ms. Mars. I don't think you understand," Hickman interrupted. "We hired you to determine if Ramirez was guilty. Based on what you've found, we're reasonably satisfied that he's not."

She paused, her shoulders going rigid. "So you're saying I'm off the case."

"No, I'm saying the case is *closed*." His tone was firm. "We do get several cases a year that require the assistance of a private investigator, and we'll certainly call you the next time that happens. It's been a pleasure working with you."

She kept her voice measured. "Of course. Let me know if there's anything else you need."

As she hung up, she caught sight of Lisa Choi, still declaiming from the podium. She thought about her dad, nearly dying to get at the truth about the Sheriff's Department; about Cliff, who defended people the rest of Neptune wanted to throw away.

Grace's words floated back to her. *I thought you were a big hero.* She had an image of Grace as a child, waiting for Veronica to come back. Waiting for her to open that closet one more time, and tell her it'd be okay.

Veronica's decision came clearly in that moment, as

unavoidable as it was surprising. Concepts like heroism and moral certainty were so far from her normal worldview, naive at best, delusional at worst. Yet here she was, determined to keep working the case. She shoved her phone in her bag, and turned to Logan, a hundred apologies on her lips. But then she saw he was looking at her with a knowing smile.

"Our plans just got canceled, didn't they?"

"Logan, I'm so sorry. I've got to—"

"I know." He leaned in to kiss her cheek. "I'll see if Dick's around tonight. Maybe *he's* up for a romantic drive."

She gave a wan smile. "You get going. I'll grab a cab home later."

He gave her a final lingering look, then nodded, heading across the parking lot to where he'd parked the convertible. As soon as he was out of sight, she pulled out her phone again, and dialed Grace's number.

The phone rang three times before the girl picked up.

"Hello?"

"Hi, Grace. This is Veronica Mars. Can you talk?"

There was a short pause.

"Okay."

"I just have some follow-up questions for you about the night of the attack."

"I already told you everything I remember."

"I know. The thing is, Grace, we've managed to get DNA evidence that proves it wasn't Miguel Ramirez who raped you. I know you were really certain it was him, but . . ."

Grace exhaled sharply. "DNA evidence? How? I thought he was in Mexico."

"He is, but his son's here in the US and we were able to get a sample. They're working on getting Ramirez's DNA just to be sure—it might take a few weeks, but they're pretty sure it'll clear him." Veronica chose her next words carefully. "No one's accusing you of lying, Grace. You went through a lot. It's possible your brain injuries scrambled some of the details. I mean, maybe you'd seen Ramirez around the Grand before, and so he popped up in your memory when you were trying to reconstruct the attack. Or maybe it was someone who looked a little like him, or . . ."

"Don't act like you're trying to help me." Veronica could just make out the tremble in the girl's voice. "All this time you've been trying to prove I'm lying. Don't ever think I've forgotten: You're working for *them*, not me."

"No, I'm not working for them. Not anymore. As far as they're concerned I've done my job and I'm off the case. Which means right now they're probably on the phone with your lawyer, telling him your suit is falling apart. But I still want to figure this out, Grace. And if I'm going to help you, I need to know the truth."

The girl was silent for a long moment. When she spoke again her voice was steady.

"So what does that mean?"

"That means I need the name of the guy you were there to meet that night." The deputies who questioned her were assholes, but they weren't wrong. In 99 percent of cases, the assailants were boyfriends or husbands. Without ruling Grace's out, the case couldn't move forward.

"You're just like those cops, you know that?" Grace said. "They kept asking and kept asking, trying to catch me in a lie. They came to my hospital bed and talked to me while I was high on morphine before the nurses finally chased them off. And here you are, playing good cop, acting like you're my friend. Good cop, bad cop. It doesn't make any difference—none of you give a shit about me." She took a ragged breath. "Forget it, Veronica. I've already told you what happened. If you don't believe me, you can just join the fucking club."

With that, Grace Manning hung up the phone.

CHAPTER FIFTEEN

The Eagle's Nest was even more dazzling in person than on video. Fragrant herbs and flowers overflowed from recessed planters. At the central bar, backlit rows of top-grade liquor lined a crescent-shaped wall. The ocean was visible beyond the other buildings downtown.

It was still early, and the bar was almost empty. Two men in suits, their ties loosened, sat talking quietly in chairs that looked out over the vista. A young woman with hair knotted in a tortured-looking bun read a paperback at the bar. Other than that, the only person was the bartender—the exact person Veronica was looking for.

Alyssa Winchell was in her late twenties, with dark hair cut in a bob around her cheekbones and a silver hoop in her left nostril. She stood behind the bar, yawning as she dried a glass. Veronica sat on one of the high wooden stools, a few seats down from the girl with her book.

"Hey, hon, what can I get for you?" The bartender put down the glass and braced her weight against the counter.

Veronica handed her a card. "I'm looking into the assault that happened here back in March. I was wondering if you had a moment to answer a few questions."

Alyssa's eyes widened. She stared at the card for a

moment, then looked up. "Shit. You're that private eye who busted the girl who faked her kidnapping, right?"

My dear stepsister, Veronica thought drily. Aurora Scott— her mom's new husband's daughter—had used Hayley Dewalt's disappearance to stage her own, hoping to reap the reward money.

"That's me," Veronica said. "Do you have a minute?"

"Sure." The woman leaned in toward Veronica. "I don't know how useful I'll be—I already told those cops everything I know. Total dicks, if you ask me," she said. "They treated me like I was some kind of criminal because I couldn't tell her ID was fake. It's not worth my job to serve eighteen-year-old kids. If I'd known, I wouldn't have. But—I mean, the license looked fine. And you've seen her, right? She looks like she's older. What nineteen-year-old carries a fucking Fendi handbag?"

Chatty, defensive, observant. My new favorite witness.

Veronica smiled sympathetically. "Yeah, well, they were probably just trying to cover their own asses. That whole investigation's been a royal clusterfuck from the get-go."

Alyssa smirked. "Typical douche-nozzle cops."

"Hear, hear!" Veronica drummed her knuckles on the wooden bar top. "So, did the victim come in pretty often?"

"Oh, yeah, she was in here a lot. Three, four times a month."

"Did you ever see her meeting anyone in the bar?" Veronica asked. "Did she talk to anyone?"

A sly smile crossed Alyssa's face. She glanced up the bar at the reader, still immersed in her novel. Then she looked back at Veronica.

"Nope. Never saw her talking to anyone here, except the

staff. I mean, plenty of guys *tried* to talk to her, but she made it pretty clear she wasn't interested. She'd just come in, have a few drinks, pay her tab in cash, and leave. She was a good tipper."

"That's so *strange*," Veronica said, injecting a note of earnest confusion into her voice. "Why would she come in here all the time if she wasn't meeting anyone?"

"Yeah, well, I've got a theory about that." Alyssa leaned in a little. Veronica hid a smile. Chatty, defensive, observant, *and* a gossip. *Jackpot.* "I mean, I'm guessing you've seen the surveillance tape. You saw what she was wearing, right?"

Veronica nodded.

"The girl was flashing some serious labels. And that was totally normal for her. She'd come in here on a weeknight, dolled up like she was going to a movie premiere." Alyssa looked at her significantly. "You've heard about her boyfriend?"

"I heard she had one," Veronica said carefully.

"Yeah, well, my impression: older dude, married. Kind of guy that loves to throw his cash around," she said. "Eventually he gets a little soft around the gut—maybe in the sack too—but as long as he can buy his girl some diamonds, he feels powerful."

Veronica frowned. "Did Grace ever talk to you about him?"

Alyssa shook her head. "Nope. She was pretty discreet about personal stuff. Sweet girl, though. If she was in on a slow night we'd talk sometimes. She's smarter than she looks."

"What makes you say that?" asked Veronica.

"I've met more than my fair share of dumb, mercenary bitches working here." Alyssa tucked a lock of hair behind her ear. "But Grace uses words like *pivotal* and *Brechtian* when she talks about TV shows. She can't dumb herself down even when she's trying."

The reader at the end of the bar waved her hand, trying to get the bartender's attention. Alyssa held up one finger toward Veronica, a *just-a-minute* gesture, and went to see what she wanted. For a moment, Veronica just sat and watched as Alyssa pulled out half a dozen liqueurs, chatting easily with the customer while she mixed, shook, and poured the complex drink. Then she came back, smiling apologetically. "Sorry about that. What was I saying?"

"Do you remember any other particular nights she was in here? Did anything ever stand out to you?"

Alyssa thought for a moment. "I don't remember specific dates, if that's what you're asking . . ." She bit the corner of her lip. "Actually, she was in here the night of the fight."

"Fight?"

"Oh, man, it was epic." Her eyes flashed. "Somehow both Jimmy Ray Baker—a stubble-faced slab of man meat—and Oneiroi were in town the same night, and guess where they both were staying?"

Veronica gratified her with an open-mouthed gape, only half feigned; it *was* kind of funny. Former rodeo champion, super patriot, and noted NRA-apologist Jimmy Lee Baker was one of the top-charting country singers in the US. His latest No. 1, "Welcome Home, Sergeant Jake," was an over-the-top weeper in which a high school football coach reconnects with his legless former star tailback at a Veteran's Day parade. Oneiroi, on the other hand, consisted of three emaciated junkies in corpse paint who shrieked black metal suites about insect-headed succubi.

Alyssa grinned at Veronica's expression. "I know, right? I don't know what started it, but Baker's bass player lost his shit and took a swing at one of the Oneiroi fans. Everyone was wasted, so of course it instantly turned into a full-on brawl. Grace left just before it happened. I remember telling her afterward that she'd missed the best show of the night."

"What night was that?"

Alyssa frowned. "It was back in December, I think. . . . I can't remember the specific date."

"Thanks so much. You've been really helpful." Veronica dropped a twenty in the tip jar—an investment in future goodwill—and eased herself off the stool.

She had one more stop to make. Her dad still had some old friends from his days as sheriff, including a retired deputy who just happened to be a security guard at the Grand. It looked as though she needed to cash in a favor.

CHAPTER SIXTEEN

In the cab on the way back to the office, she called Mac. "What are you doing tonight?"

"I have a feeling the answer might be 'working late.' What's going on?"

"I'll tell you as soon as I get there."

When she arrived at the office twenty minutes later, the neon Mars Investigations sign was off but Mac was, as always, at her computer.

"Thanks for staying," Veronica said without preamble. "I'll add you to the list of people I owe big. My boyfriend's on top but you're bum-to-belt-buckle with him."

"Yeah, I'm not sure how I feel about that image," Mac said.

Veronica caught Mac up on the phone call and all it meant for the case. "Okay, so we're not working for Preuss anymore," she said. "But that doesn't mean we have to stop working."

Mac looked at her for a long moment. Then she gave a quick nod. "You'd better see what I've been doing, then."

Her monitors were filled by all the different angles of the Neptune Grand's security cameras, playing at double speed. Grace entered the front door and crossed the lobby. She got in the elevator, then, a few beats later, she got out again at the Eagle's Nest.

"I've been watching all the footage between ten p.m. and seven a.m.," Mac said. "As far as I can see, exactly forty-two people leave in that time span. I've got screenshots of all of them, and I've been logging all their movements." She showed Veronica her tablet, where she'd scrawled a complicated timeline with her stylus.

11:01—PSU BASKETBALLERS SNEAK IN POOL.
11:07—BALLERS CHASED OUT OF POOL.
11:13—RED-HEADED MAN GOES TO BATHROOM IN BAR;
       MANNING ORDERS 2ND DRINK; SANTIAGO (GUARD)
       TALKS TO COHEN (CLERK) AT FRONT DESK.
11:16—RED-HEADED MAN RETURNS TO BAR STOOL.
11:20—RAMIREZ PUSHES CART UP THE SERVICE HALLWAY.

The words were color-coded, indicating if the subjects were staff or guests, and in places the text was cramped, the increments of time becoming ever smaller as Mac filled in every minuscule movement she could track.

"Wow," Veronica said. "I don't know whether to be impressed or set up an intervention. This looks like Russell Crowe's wall in *A Beautiful Mind*."

"I've been trying to figure out if any of them could be the victim in disguise," Mac said. "Wearing a wig, or . . . whatever. But it's impossible." She sped up the footage by another click. Veronica watched as Grace disappeared into the stairwell. After that there was little movement other than employees gossiping in the lobby or moving around the lower floors. "Sixteen hotel employees leave at midnight, through the service entrance. None of them are hauling anything big enough to hide a body. Then there are four people who leave the bar when it closes at two, but they're on camera the whole time—none of them are ever unaccounted for. Then there are the ball players at five a.m."

"Unless she's on stilts, Grace Manning isn't with them." Veronica's eyes narrowed. The players all had identical black rolling duffels. It was hard to tell how big they were—the players were so tall they dwarfed everything. "Do you think she could fit into one of those bags?"

Mac leaned over, frowning. "Well, the wainscoting here is about three feet tall," she said, pointing to the wooden paneling on the wall of the lobby behind one of the players. "So I'd say the bag is two feet long—two and a half, tops. I don't know, that seems tight."

"She's pretty tiny, though." Grace Manning was barely taller than Veronica and weighed maybe one-ten. Any of the towering men on that team could have picked her up—but she wasn't sure if that translated to wheeling her out the door in a bag. Veronica watched as one by one, the players boarded the bus. The bus door faced away from the camera, toward the street beyond, so there was no way to track the bags past that point. She imagined they were filling up the hold beneath the bus.

"All those bags end up on a bus full of people, though. How would the attacker get her off the bus and into that field without everyone seeing?"

It was a good point. Veronica thought about the cover-ups she'd heard about in the past several years, stories of corruption in college athletics, where players' crimes were an open secret protected by their teammates and even their coaches.

Drugs, beatings, rape, even murder had been hushed up by group assent. But it was hard to imagine an entire busload of college kids—including managers and coaches and a chartered bus driver—agreeing to dump a wounded girl on the side of the road without a single leak in the months since.

Veronica squinted at the screen, then shook her head. She grabbed her bag and rummaged for a moment until she found an unlabeled disc. "Mind popping this in?"

Mac took the disc and put it into the drive. A moment later, they were looking at a new set of surveillance images.

"What's this?"

"Security footage for December fifteenth from the Neptune Grand." She leaned down over Mac's shoulder and watched. "They usually record over the footage after a month, unless there's an incident. Lucky for us, there was."

The angles were exactly the same as those the night of Grace's rape, but now Christmas decorations hung all over the lobby and the bar. A fifteen-foot tree stood just catty-corner from the front desk, gold and silver orbs glittering from every branch. On the roof, garlands looped along the bar, and both the bartenders wore Santa hats. Veronica noticed Alyssa at once, though her hair was a different color, dark red, and a bit longer than it was now.

The time stamp read 9:30. Just as Alyssa had said, the bar was packed to bursting with an eclectic crowd. Men in cowboy hats and embroidered Western shirts sat around the fire pit, talking to girls in Daisy Dukes. Gathered around the railings was a crowd sporting black vinyl bondage gear and zombie-eye contact lenses. Every now and then someone in one group would gesture at the other, or cast a furtive look their way.

"There she is." At 9:32, Grace Manning entered the lobby. This time her hair was loose, curled into Veronica Lake waves that framed her face. She wore a gray trench that hit mid-thigh, her long legs bare beneath it. She headed to the elevator. Inside, the close-up of her face showed her carefully made-up face. She stood facing the doors and smoothed her hair.

Up at the bar, Alyssa was mobbed with people clamoring for drinks, but as soon as she saw Grace, she nodded at her and leaned in close. After a moment, Alyssa moved away to mix a drink. Grace took off her coat to reveal a low-backed black dress.

In the far corner, a stubble-faced Jimmy Ray Baker— wearing his denim shirt unbuttoned halfway down an admit- tedly impressive set of pecs—pulled out a guitar and started noodling. A girl with big Texas hair and pink cowboy boots climbed up onto one of the benches and began to dance, while another did an impromptu lap dance, grinding against one of the entourage.

Alyssa slid a martini glass across the bar to Grace, and Grace walked with it to the railing, looking out over the city. For a while all they could see was the girl's bare back. At one point, a cowboy walked up to her and appeared to talk to her. A few minutes later, he slunk away, leaving Grace alone again.

"Shot down," Mac said, impressed.

At 9:57, Grace set her empty glass on the bar and headed toward the stairwell, giving both Goths and goat-ropers a wide berth. She disappeared into the dark portal without a backward glance.

A minute later, a fight broke out. Mac paused the video, just as Jimmy Ray Baker drove his fist into a wraithlike metalhead's face.

"So . . . why are we watching this?" she said.

"If Grace was there that night, then so was her boyfriend, assuming he didn't cancel on her again." Veronica nodded at the screen. "Fast forward. See what time she goes back downstairs."

Mac clicked a key, and the images rushed forward. In the Eagle's Nest, the skinny kid was getting mobbed by men in cowboy hats. Alyssa and the handful of other guests dove behind the bar to get out of the way.

"I feel like 'Yakety Sax' should be playing in the background," Mac said.

"Or the score to *West Side Story*," Veronica said.

In the lobby, there was no sign of Grace Manning. They watched as security ran across the lobby toward the elevator doors, hotel guests watching with startled eyes. Upstairs on the roof, an Oneiroi fan was waving a broken beer bottle. The security guards barged into the scene, deputies a moment later. Some of the warring factions were led away in cuffs, while others melted into the night. The bar cleared out. Back downstairs, a manager in an ill-fitting suit stood talking with desk staff, probably debriefing about the fight. A news crew showed up and was rebuffed.

At 1:14 a.m., the door to the stairwell in the ground-floor lobby swung open. Grace Manning stepped out, as cool and put together as she'd been when she'd first arrived. She had the trench coat wrapped tightly around her again. On her way out of the rotating glass door, she waved familiarly at the valet. He waved back with a grin.

"A little over three hours," Veronica said. "So the boyfriend was definitely there. If we can find out who was staying there that night, we can narrow down who he might be."

Mac stared at Veronica. "Petra doesn't strike me as naive.

I'm guessing she'll have pretty good network security. It might take me a couple days to hack my way into her reservations database."

"Then it's a good thing I have a password," Veronica said. She grabbed a pen and a Post-it note from the desk. She jotted down two lines.

```
Login: corrigans
Password: pumpkin _ and _ princess
```

Mac raised her eyebrows. Veronica shrugged. "I watched Petra's assistant log in."

Mac's fingers flew over the keyboard as she made her way into the Neptune Grand's system. After signing in as Gladys, she clicked several times until she found the correct date. "There were five-hundred thirteen people staying at the Grand on the night of the fifteenth," Mac said. "But only twenty-one with local zip codes attached to their billing addresses."

Veronica leaned in closer. "How many are men?"

A tiny crease formed between Mac's eyes. She stared at the screen for a moment, then highlighted a few more names. "Fourteen men, one 'Avery,' who could be either, I guess."

Veronica narrowed her eyes. "Any way to find out how many have stayed there in the past, say, year?"

"Yeah, just a second." Mac ran the names through the system one by one. The silence stretched out, Mac's face pale in the light of the monitor. Veronica waited, watching names and dates flit across the screen.

Then Mac's shoulders went rigid.

"What?" Veronica asked. When Mac didn't answer, she frowned. "Did you find him?"

"Yeah. I found him." Her voice was strange, low and flat.

Veronica looked at her curiously. "Well?"

Mac finally tore her eyes away from the screen and looked straight at Veronica. "It's Charles Sinclair."

The name fell between them with a dull thud.

Charles Sinclair. Madison Sinclair's dad—and Mac's biological father.

CHAPTER SEVENTEEN

Mac shoved abruptly back from the desk, running her fingers through her hair. For a moment Veronica thought she was about to cry. Then she realized her friend's grimace was one of bitter triumph, almost of satisfaction.

She's not surprised. The thought hit her with the certainty of an irrefutable fact. Mac may not have expected to see Sinclair's name on that list—but she wasn't shocked either.

Which meant Mac had been keeping tabs on her birth family.

Veronica didn't know why she was surprised by that. It was no less than she would have done herself. But they'd never talked about it—not since high school. Not since Veronica discovered that Mac had been switched at birth with their classmate Madison Sinclair, the poster child for spoiled '09ers. The mistake hadn't been discovered until both girls were four—at which point both families decided to keep the children they'd raised as their own. A hefty hospital settlement had allowed the Sinclairs to get richer; it gave the Mackenzies seed money to start a Jet Ski business that failed in less than three years.

"Well, it's not exactly news that Charles Sinclair is a dog," Mac said. She stood from her desk and went to the kitchenette. Instead of opening the fridge as Veronica expected, she pulled the bottle of whiskey down from the cabinet overhead. She sloshed some into the bottom of a coffee mug, took a sip, then poured a little more.

"What are you telling me?" Veronica asked cautiously.

"Just that I, um, may have looked in on the Sinclairs a few times over the years." Mac looked studiously through the dark window, avoiding Veronica's eyes.

Meaning, Veronica knew, that Mac had hacked into their personal information—their e-mail, their bank accounts, their medical histories.

"Charles and Ellen were in marriage counseling for a while. I didn't, like, try to get access to the notes. But, you know, you kind of assume."

"Mac . . ."

"I know. I'm pathetic." She ran the fingers of her free hand through her hair again. When they came away, locks of her short hair stood on end, giving her a slightly mad look. "I've never . . . bothered them or anything. I just wanted to know what their lives looked like." She gave a jagged laugh. "I mean, I only know the big stuff. Like, they went to Argentina last year on vacation. They took Lauren, my . . . Madison's sister. She was home on break from Sarah Lawrence. Um, and Ellen, she had a breast cancer scare a few years ago. But it turned out to be benign, so she's okay."

She took another slug from the mug. "As for Charles—I mean, I assumed he was screwing around. Ellen's away from home a lot. She does this charity thing, working with low-income women who have ideas for small businesses. It's pretty cool, actually. She's done a TED Talk and everything." She shook her head as if trying to clear it. "Like I said, I assumed he was a cheater. But nothing would have led me to believe he was a . . ." She trailed off, unable to say the word. When she spoke again, her voice was steady and sober, cracking only near the end.

"You know, my dad's been in a dead-end job for twenty-plus years, and he'd wallpaper the house with pictures of Dale Earnhardt if my mom would let him. But he treats my mom like a goddess. He'd never cheat on her. And he'd never, *never* hurt a woman. I know that. So fuck Charles Sinclair."

Veronica stood up and walked over to Mac. She wasn't sure if she should take the whiskey away from her or pour her another cup. In the end, she just leaned against the counter next to her.

"Look, we don't know anything for sure yet," she said. "Charles might not have anything to do with it. I mean . . . did he check into the Grand the night of the attack? Does he show up anywhere on camera? Does he have any kind of motive for this? We need to dig a little deeper before we jump to conclusions."

Mac tossed back the rest of the whiskey. Then she put the cup in the sink and brought the bottle back to the desk, where she sat it next to her computer and resettled into her chair, her eyes alight with new determination.

"So let's dig," she said.

Charles Sinclair had stayed at the Neptune Grand seven times in the past six months, each time for a single night. Each time, he racked up quite a room service tab, order-ing bottles of Krug, plates of chocolate-covered strawberries, oysters on the half shell, caviar. Mac was able to match each visit with a trip Ellen Sinclair had taken out of town. But he hadn't stayed at the hotel the night of the attack. His name wasn't on the guest list, and none of his credit cards had been used. And there was no sign of him on any of the security footage.

"Maybe he has a secret way in—the same way Grace was taken out." Veronica leaned back in the office chair she'd pulled up beside Mac's, staring at the ceiling. "Or maybe Grace wasn't attacked at the Neptune Grand at all. Maybe she got out of the hotel somehow and met him off-site."

Mac rubbed her face, exhausted. "But then, why suddenly attack her after all those months of feeding her caviar? It doesn't make sense."

Veronica hesitated. It was possible Sinclair had been abusing Grace all along, that the attack was the final escalation. Or maybe he'd decided the girl was a liability—if she'd threatened to go public, for instance. Which would also explain her steadfast refusal to name him. If his goal had been to silence her, he'd succeeded.

Not that she wanted to say any of that out loud. "First things first. We can answer at least some of those questions if we get a DNA sample."

"Easy enough," Mac said quietly. "We just swab me, right? That was enough with Ramirez's son."

Mac's jaw was tight, her eyes narrow. *She's taking this personally,* Veronica thought uneasily.

"It might come to that," Veronica said. "But I think I have a better idea."

CHAPTER EIGHTEEN

Sinclair & Ives was the premier graphic design firm in Southern California. Their clients included Nike, Calvin Klein, Disney, Pepsi. If a company had a commercial written up in *Artforum*, a logo recognized worldwide, a font that inspired hosts of knockoffs, chances were good that Sinclair & Ives had a hand in it—and that the original creative spark came from Charles Sinclair, the agency's superstar art director.

The firm's offices occupied a full floor in a chic office building downtown, decorated with color-blocked walls and sleek modern furniture. On Monday morning Veronica sat on a backless red sofa, clutching a portfolio and jiggling one leg up and down in a good imitation of nerves. She wore combat boots and a slouchy boy's blazer; her hair was looped through a rubber band into a sloppy bun. A pair of nonprescription glasses with heavy black plastic frames finished the look: casual, Bohemian, this side of edgy. A sandwich board over her shoulders, block-lettered ART STUDENT, couldn't have been more overt. Which was the idea, because Veronica had a job interview with Charles Sinclair. And she needed to pass as a viable candidate for the few short minutes it'd take to accomplish two specific tasks: determine whether he knew Grace, and find an object with his DNA on it.

Veronica hadn't wanted to involve Mac further, but a quick background check revealed that Sinclair had graduated from the California College of the Arts. It also provided his private line. Veronica, doing her best college counselor impression, placed a quick call that morning, informing him that she had a talented photography grad student looking for work, and would he mind meeting with her? His voice on the phone had been warm. Sure—he had twenty minutes just before lunch.

So now Veronica sat in the waiting room, holding a portfolio of her own hastily curated photos. The receptionist—a young man with carrot-red hair gelled in a high arc above his forehead—kept glancing at her with surly amusement over the top of his monitor.

"Gretchen Spengler?"

Veronica gave a little start. She'd expected the receptionist to make her wait as long as possible before showing her back to Sinclair's office, but here was the designer himself, watching her from the doorway with an indulgent smile.

Charles Sinclair was tall and lean, with dark hair receding from a craggily handsome face. He wore a suit jacket and a button-down shirt, no tie, and he leaned against the doorway with confident ease. *The very picture of middle-aged richfuck entitlement,* Veronica thought. *He doesn't seem like a guy who'd hesitate to take what he wanted. But—rapey or merely insufferable?*

"Mr. Sinclair!" She shot to her feet, walking toward him with her hand outstretched. "Thanks so much for meeting with me. I can't tell you how grateful I am."

"It's always great to meet a fellow CCA alum." They shook hands.

She followed him through a large, open workspace. One full wall was made of blackboard material and covered with doodles. Four people were crouched over drafting tables or computer stations, surrounded by empty coffee cups or soda cans. It looked as if everyone else was gone for lunch.

Sinclair's office was large, but cluttered. A corkboard lined three-quarters of the wall, covered with clippings of everything from athletes in motion to woolly-faced sloths clinging to branches in the jungle. Two twenty-seven-inch monitors sat side by side over his computer, and an angled drafting table sat next to the window. A coiled yoga mat was propped against the wall by the door, a grubby-looking hand towel jutting from the center.

Her eyes darted around the room, taking in the details. If he had as many empty cans at his station as everyone else in the office did, then this would be easy. But there was nothing.

Okay, so I'll just have to get creative.

Charles pulled an Aeron chair out from under his computer desk and motioned for Veronica to take a seat. He settled into a molded, green plastic chair just a few feet away from her. It felt strange, not having a desk between them—a bit more exposed than she'd have liked.

"Thanks so much for making the time to see me, Mr. Sinclair. I'm such a fan of your work." Veronica pushed her glasses up her nose. "The spread you did for Rolex a few years ago is, like, half the reason I went to design school."

His smile widened a little. "That's one of my favorite campaigns. And not just because I got to meet Marion Cotillard." He crossed his legs, resting his fingers on his knee and regarding her with interest. Veronica realized with a shiver that his eyes were the same light blue as Mac's. "So you're a photographer?"

She nodded, then unzipped the portfolio in her lap and started sifting through the pictures. "I interned with TBWA in Los Angeles last summer and did a lot of product test shots for them. But my thesis work was all on portrait." She handed a book of photos to him and he started to leaf through.

Veronica had spent hours going through her own prints the day before. She'd been taking pictures since she was a kid, and her best work was pretty good—certainly passable as a talented student's portfolio. She'd included an array of images—shots of historic buildings and ocean vistas, pictures of birds and flowers, a few photos of cheese platters and cupcakes—but more than anything else, she included portraits. Most were of friends back in New York, from her days at Columbia; she didn't want to run the risk of showing him anyone he might recognize.

With one important exception.

She watched his face closely as he looked through the prints. He lingered on a few—one she'd taken at Coney Island's Mermaid Parade two years ago, showing three young women in shell bikinis and green wigs; another of a broken window in an abandoned elementary school. Then he turned another page, and froze.

Grace Manning's posed portrait didn't entirely fit in with the rest of the images. Veronica's pictures were generally more photojournalistic in tone. Grace's professional head-shot was meant to show her at her most generic, a blank slate for directors' imaginations. Her expression was serious—lips closed, eyes ingénue-wide, hair loose around her face. The picture was from before the attack, and Veronica thought she could detect a subtle difference in the girl's features. Or maybe it was just her expression that had altered—some lightness in her eyes, some of the casual ease in her muscles, was gone.

Charles's eyes locked onto the portrait, his mouth opening and closing a few times in a frantic bid for composure. First he went pale—then he flushed, his cheeks and neck darkening to red. Veronica hid a smile.

Gotcha.

Veronica leaned over as if checking to see what he was looking at. "Oh, you like that one? God, I lucked out with her. She's an actress who hired me to do her headshot. Kind of an innocent, girl-next-door vibe, right? But vulnerable too—kind of breakable."

She saw his fingers tremble, then curl around the edge of the book. But before he could say anything, another voice broke in. A petulant, horribly familiar voice. A voice that still affected Veronica like a battery acid IV.

"Daddy, you've *got* to fire that guy at the front desk. He always acts like I'm some kind of *nuisance.*"

Madison Sinclair stood in the doorway, wearing a canary-yellow sheath dress and a pale pink cardigan. Her brows were arched in characteristic disdain. She stopped in her tracks when she saw Veronica.

Veronica was momentarily flummoxed, unable to think or process. Madison Sinclair had insulted, bullied, and belittled her every day in high school—as well as at their ten-year reunion a few months earlier. The only upside had been that Veronica had gotten to do what she'd dreamed of for years: punch Madison square in the face.

"What are *you* doing here?" Madison said, her voice dripping with loathing.

Charles looked up from the prints spread across his lap. He fumbled the book shut and handed it back to Veronica. "Oh, do you know each other?"

"Oh my gosh, you're Charles's daughter?" Veronica plastered a winning smile onto her lips, standing up from her chair. "I knew your last name was Sinclair but I don't think I ever put those two things together. It's so nice to see you again."

Madison blinked. This was clearly not what she'd expected.

Lucky for Veronica, Charles seemed almost as eager to cut the interview short as she now was. "I'm so sorry, Ms. Spengler—I forgot that I had a lunch date with my daughter. We'll have to cut this short. But your photography is . . . really interesting, and if you'll leave me a copy of your CV . . ."

"*Spengler?*" spat Madison. "What the—"

"Thank you so much for making the time to meet me, Mr. Sinclair." Veronica stuck out her hand, and after hesitating a moment, he shook it. "It's been a real honor." She turned toward the door, beaming at Madison. "Have a great lunch, Madison."

In the three seconds it took her to get to the door, Veronica's eyes flickered frantically back and forth, combing the room. She'd gotten the reaction she'd wanted from the picture—but she hadn't gotten what she really needed. No soda cans, no half-eaten food, no strands of hair just sitting conveniently out for her to grab. Once she left, there was no way she could come back. Madison would tell him that she was a private eye, and it would be over.

And then she saw it. The crumpled white hand towel on the yoga mat, propped by the door. She had a sudden image of Charles Sinclair in a humid, sweltering yoga studio, covered with sweat. Coming out of Warrior pose to mop his face. Then rolling it up in the mat, keeping it there for next time.

As she sailed past Madison, she plucked it lightly from where it stuck out. Veronica hurried through the workroom, Madison's voice ringing behind her.

"Why did you call her Spengler? Her name is Veronica Mars, Daddy, and she's total trash."

She didn't stop to hear his response. Instead, she sped up, breezing past the receptionist and wondering if she had proof of the attacker's identity clutched in her hand.

CHAPTER NINETEEN

Friday morning, Logan was leaning against the kitchen counter watching Veronica stir pancake batter when he said unexpectedly, "Let's do it."

She glanced up at him, amused. "Again? It's been ten minutes. I need some breakfast if you expect another performance like that."

It was just after ten a.m. Veronica had decided to take the day off—there wasn't anything she could do at work until Sinclair's labs came back, and she hadn't picked up a new job in weeks. Keith had seized upon this lull to wheedle Veronica into helping resolve a feud between two rival pawnshop owners, one of whom was seeking proof that the other was hiring gang members to vandalize and pilfer from her store. A quick background check on the client had cast doubt on her story: a total of nine false accusations, nuisance lawsuits, and interactions with the state mental health system. Even so, proof of effort was needed to collect the base fee and send the addlepated old dame on her way.

Today, though, Veronica was taking a quick break from that mutt of a case to spend a little time with Logan. She was still in her bathrobe, a half-finished cup of coffee next to her on the counter. Sunlight filtered through the curtains, and for the first time since the Manning case had landed on her desk, she felt almost peaceful.

"Not that. Though now that you mention it, check back in with me on that front in just a moment." Logan picked up a piece of bacon and crunched down on it. "No, let's get a puppy."

She turned to stare at him, her mouth hanging open in mute disbelief.

He grinned. "Huh. Veronica Mars, speechless. I'll have to write this one in my feelings journal."

"Are you serious? You're . . . I mean, it's a huge commitment, and . . ."

"So what? So's everything worth doing." His expression was half playful, half urgent. "Come on. You can keep doodling dog faces on every blank pad in this apartment, or we can just take the leap. Why not?"

Maybe it was something about the way he looked at her when he said it, but for once, she couldn't answer that question. At that moment, all she could do was put her arms around him and kiss him, her mind deliciously blank.

The pancake batter lay forgotten on the counter as they made their way back to the bedroom. . . .

Two hours later they were making their way along the fenced enclosures at the animal shelter when Veronica stopped short. From the other side, a tiny black puppy stared up at them, her head cocked inquisitively to one side.

"This one. This is the one."

Logan knelt down in front of the little dog and looked at

the puppy with a serious, measuring expression. She put a paw up against the chain link and wagged.

"This is seriously threatening my hardboiled persona," Veronica said, "because I have never wanted to squee so badly in my life."

"It says here she's going to be between ninety and a hundred pounds," said Logan, looking at the flyer on the outside of her enclosure. "Where are we going to put her?"

"I lived in a two-bedroom with a territorial pit bull. I'm pretty sure we can make it work." She knelt down and slid her fingertips through the fence. The puppy followed her with her honey-brown eyes. It was impossible to say what mix she was—her nose was long, her ears floppy, and her paws were three times too big for her body.

The little dog licked her finger.

"This one," she repeated softly.

An hour and a half later, after they'd gone into the small enclosure to meet the puppy up close and thrown a balding tennis ball for her to chase, they sat across from an adoption counselor to fill out paperwork. Then they walked the puppy out to the car and got back on the highway. Veronica noticed that Logan hung back from the dog, kneeling down to let her sniff his hand, as if afraid he might scare it. As she drove, she glanced at Logan from the corner of her eye. His light brown eyes tracked the puppy in the rearview, almost wary.

Is he as into this as I am? Or is he just trying to keep me happy?

The day was heating up, the sun glaring out from a thin web of clouds. They flew up the PCH, the ocean sparkling blue to their left. The puppy stuck her nose out of the sliver of space Veronica had left in the window, sniffing the salt air.

"What should we name her?" Veronica asked, glancing at Logan as she drove. "Athena? Joan of Arc? Christiane Amanpour?"

"Those seem a little . . . aspirational," Logan said. He looked back at the puppy, who was now on her back, gnawing the squeaky toy they'd gotten at the shelter, her paws flopping in the air. Regardless of what she'd grow into, the puppy had a body type that could only be described as *roly-poly*. "I'm thinking something more like Doodlebug."

"No way! The other dogs will tease her!" Veronica exclaimed. "How about Havoc? Or Mayhem?"

"Is she a puppy or a supervillain?" Logan raised his eyebrow. "Sugar Cookie. That's my final offer."

They headed back into town, laughing as they volleyed names like Nitro, Snuggums, Cerberus, and Peaches. In the backseat, the puppy wriggled and played.

"Mind if we swing by the office?" she asked as she exited the highway toward town. "I want to check in, make sure they don't need me for anything.

"I thought this was going to be a day off," Logan teased. "Or do you just want to show off the new baby?"

"Hey, I believe we have a duty to help the puppy-impaired."

The response in the office was predictable, though it wasn't Mac who cooed the loudest; it was her dad.

"Who's a big fierce monster dog? Who's a bloodthirsty hound from Hell? It's you. Yes it is." Keith knelt to the floor and tickled the puppy's pudgy stomach. Veronica and Logan watched, amused.

"I didn't know he was *this* anxious for grandchildren," Veronica said.

"Just for the kind that can't talk," Keith said. The puppy struggled to her feet and started bounding in circles around him. Her dad brushed the dog hair off his leg as he stood up. "Do you remember when we first got Backup? He was so tiny he fit in your mom's purse."

"Yeah, before he chewed it to pieces, along with half the house. I seem to remember losing three pairs of shoes, the baseboard in my bedroom, and the better part of my Ninja Turtles collection, all in the first week."

"He was just getting settled," Keith protested. "You know, you're in a new house, you have to fluff the pillows a little."

"Or rip them apart, as the case may be."

The puppy capered over to Logan suddenly, setting one paw against his shin and gazing up at him. Veronica fought the urge to coo. *Channel Philip Marlowe*, she told herself sternly. *Come on, Veronica, Sam Spade doesn't coo.*

"She seems to like Logan," Keith said.

Logan gave a nervous laugh; he was always strangely formal around her dad. He leaned over and stroked the little dog, his movements tentative and very gentle.

"Did you ever have a dog when you were a kid?" Mac asked him.

Logan shook his head. "Nah. Mom was allergic, and . . . Aaron worked a lot." The puppy leaned against his leg, and a faint smile spread across his lips. "We didn't really do pets."

"Well, prepare to be owned," Keith said. "Looks like this one's already figuring out how she's going to work you over."

They were still playing with the dog a few minutes later when the door opened and Cliff McCormack entered, carrying a bankers box of paper, followed by Lisa Choi and Weevil. Cliff raised one dark eyebrow, looking around. Mac was on one side of the room, the squeaky T-bone in one hand, and Veronica was on the other side, poised to catch it in a game of keep-away. The newcomers distracted the puppy entirely from its game; she ran to Cliff, her tail whipping back and forth, and jumped up against his legs.

"Did I get the time wrong, or did you start a doggie day care while I was out of the room?" Cliff asked.

Mac quickly hid the squeaky toy. Veronica hurried over to scoop up the puppy. It wriggled in her arms, licking her cheeks and chin in raptures of affection. Her dad stood up from the sofa. "Sorry, Cliff. I lost track of the time."

Lisa Choi was as efficient-looking as ever in a dark red pantsuit, a black briefcase at her side. Veronica was suddenly painfully aware of her rumpled T-shirt, now speckled with dog hair, and the suddenly adolescent-seeming Vans she'd donned that morning. Lisa gave Veronica a blink-and-you-missed-it smile as their eyes met.

"You're Keith's daughter, right? It's nice to meet you."

"Daughter and partner." Veronica wasn't sure why she said that, but it was out before she could stop it. "I'm a PI too." She gave what she hoped was an authoritative nod. The puppy picked that moment to start licking her ear.

"These files aren't exactly light. Where are we working?" Cliff broke in, shrugging to get a better grip on the box.

"Sorry, yeah. My office." Keith gestured toward his open door. Cliff went through, followed by Lisa and Keith. Weevil hung back for a moment.

"Lisa's a ballbuster," he muttered. "She already told me I gotta get rid of the bike. Says I gotta clean up my appearance if I'm gonna win this thing."

"Yeah?" Veronica shrugged. "Well, I'd listen to her if I

were you. The county's not going to roll over and let you take their money. If they can make you out to be a petty thug, they will."

He exhaled loudly. "Yeah, I know. They been doing that my entire life."

"Well, get ready for more because discrediting you is their plan A, B, and C," she said. Weevil shook his head morosely.

Logan, who'd watched this exchange with a deepening frown, interjected: "But you've got their plan D, right?" He looked at Weevil, let one hand slide toward his belt buckle and discreetly whirled the other in the *c'mon, c'mon* sign.

Eli looked puzzled for a moment, then sighed. With a wan half smile, he cupped his crotch with one hand and muttered, "Dese nuts."

"Better!" Logan exclaimed, stepping up to Weevil and enfolding him in an overlong bear hug. "You can't let the *cuicos* bust you down, *carnál*. Stay strong."

Over Logan's shoulder, Weevil raised his brows at Veronica.

"Eli? We want to get started." Keith waved from the doorway of Veronica's office. "We're running kind of late and have a lot to cover."

"Yeah, Mr. Mars, I'm coming." Weevil gave Veronica and Logan a cool nod and disappeared into the office.

"Wow, heartbreaking," Logan murmured. "I know this is wrong, but I want to put a big greasy bike chain in his hand, slap him on the butt, and tell him to start trashing the place. Just to get some of the old thug brio back. I mean, Weevil and I were never tight, but I always respected the fight in the guy."

Veronica stared at the closed door. "Yeah, I know what you mean."

But then, he's never had so much to lose. She thought about Jade and Valentina, sleeping on a pull-out sofa in Jade's mother's little house. She thought about the plywood-covered windows in the garage Weevil had closed four months back.

"Well, hopefully two million dollars can get some spring back into his step," Mac said. She sat the squeaky toy on the edge of the desk. "I've never totally bought that 'can't buy happiness' thing."

The office phone's ringtone cut through the room. Mac snapped it up. "Mars Investigations."

Veronica knew who it was from the way Mac's eyes widened. Veronica handed the puppy, who'd conked out in her arms, to Logan. The dog made a small grunt of complaint, then burrowed into the crook of his elbow. Logan looked startled to be holding her. He stood still, staring warily at the little animal.

"Okay. Yes. Yes, I understand. Thanks so much." Mac slowly put the receiver back in the cradle, her lips a wide, thin line. She looked up at Veronica.

"That was the lab," she said, her voice a forced calm.

"And?"

Mac slowly shook her head. "It's not a match. The DNA from the night of the attack doesn't belong to Charles Sinclair."

CHAPTER TWENTY

It was just over a week later that Keith first realized he was being watched.

The car was parked up the street from his house, a silver Ford Fusion with tinted windows. He could just make out the silhouette of a broad-shouldered man in shades behind the steering wheel. Keith checked out the kitchen window five or six times before he was sure. The car and its driver were there for hours, watching his front door.

Either this is amateur hour, Keith thought, *or Lamb wants me to see him and be intimidated.*

He'd expected something like this since the lawsuit was announced. Lamb and his deputies would be watching his every move now. They'd drop in on the witnesses they'd intimidated to begin with. No doubt someone would be keeping an eye on Eli too.

It was a clumsy, desperate move, and he knew it wouldn't be the last. Lamb would lash out any way he could.

Keith's knee twinged as he stepped out onto his front porch and locked the door behind him. He couldn't remember the accident, but he still felt its effect in his bones and joints, and in the lingering aches and pains throughout his body. He avoided glancing left or right as he made his way down the steps and straight to his car.

As he'd expected, the Fusion tailed him ineptly. He watched it in his rearview, a few cars behind him. It would have been easy to lose him, but Keith had nothing to hide. Not today, anyway; he was just going to the office. He amused himself by slowing down and speeding up, forcing the driver to pace himself accordingly.

At the office, the puppy—which Veronica had started calling "Pony" as a joke that ended up sticking—scampered toward Keith, wagging and capering around his shins. He knelt down and scooped her up in his arms, and she licked his chin. Then he looked up and realized Veronica was there in front of him, looking almost as eager as the puppy.

"You're not going believe this," she said.

Behind her, at reception, Mac gave a smug smile. Keith looked back and forth between them.

"Hmm. The atmosphere's a half shade less doleful than usual. What's with this relatively unfettered joy?"

Veronica grabbed his sleeve and dragged him toward Mac's desk. "Just wait. Mac, you have it up?"

"I sure do."

Mac had the *Neptune Register*'s website opened on her largest monitor. Keith stood behind her chair to watch as she clicked on a link. Then his jaw dropped.

"Sheriff's Race Heats Up as New Candidate Enters the Stage?" he read out loud.

Veronica clapped her hands a few times, schoolgirl style, but he barely noticed. He'd just seen the subtitle beneath the headline.

> Retired Army Brigadier General Marcia Langdon announced her campaign this

```
morning, stating that the time has come for
change in Neptune.
```

Marcia Langdon. It couldn't possibly be the same Marcia Langdon.

But the accompanying photo was unmistakable. She was thirty-plus years older, in military uniform, but he recognized her raptor nose, her heavy jaw. More than anything he recognized her eyes—sharp and hard as a flint spearhead.

```
Citing departmental corruption and
system-wide incompetence, Marcia Langdon
announced Thursday afternoon that she would
run against incumbent Dan Lamb in the
sheriff's race this November. Langdon, who
retired from active service in 2013, moved
back to her hometown of Neptune last year
after ending a thirty-year career in the US
Army.
```

He skimmed ahead. She'd been awarded the Legion of Merit, the Meritorious Service Medal, the Defense Distinguished Service Medal, the Defense Superior Service Medal, and the Bronze Star Medal. She'd climbed the ranks in CID, holding command for the last seven years of her military tenure.

The article included a quote from Langdon herself near the bottom of the page. "I grew up here. This is my home. And as much as I was looking forward to retirement, I can't in good conscience stand by and watch the Sheriff's Department run roughshod over the basic tenets of justice."

"Did you notice how she used the words 'conscience' and 'Sheriff's Department' in the same sentence?" Veronica looked up, eyes dancing.

Keith smiled slightly. "Yes. Yes I did."

Veronica stared at him incredulously. "I thought you'd be thrilled, but you look like you've seen a ghost."

A ghost? Maybe. He could still see Bobby "Tauntaun" Langdon, his face paper white as Deputy O'Hare shoved him in the backseat of the cruiser. Could still picture Langdon's mother, a messy, weak-chinned woman in a denim house-coat, crying on the street as they drove away. And Marcia. Seventeen years old, her slacks pressed with precise creases and her face an impenetrable mask, watching from the porch.

"No, it's nothing," he said. "It's just . . . I haven't seen her in a long time. It's just kind of surprising."

"You know her?" Veronica suddenly looked interested. He smiled a little.

"I used to. Like I said, it's been a long time. And she's been busy."

"What was she like?"

He looked at the picture again, not sure how to answer. After a long moment, he said, "Honest. And . . . determined. Very determined."

They were the kindest words he could think to use. Veronica seemed not to notice his hesitation.

"I'll take it," she said.

Mac leaned back in her chair and looked up at them. "Think she's got a chance? It's so late in the game, and Lamb's been fund-raising for months now."

"I don't know, but they mention the lawsuit," Veronica said. "Quote: 'The department has been rocked by a series of scandals in the past year. A pending lawsuit, Navarro vs. Balboa County, alleges that deputies planted evidence on thirty-year-old Eli Navarro during an armed robbery investigation. Mr. Navarro was acquitted of all criminal charges, but in October his lawyers will try to prove that the county unconstitutionally targeted him and falsified their findings to gain a conviction.'"

"'Sheriff Dan Lamb could not be reached for comment at press time.'" Mac read.

Veronica smirked. "God, I wish I could be a fly on the wall in the Sheriff's Department right now."

"Yeah, well, I'm glad you're not," Keith said. He frowned. "Stay clear of Lamb for the next few months, all right? Between the trial and the election, he's going to be on the warpath."

Pony wriggled against his chest, and he knelt down to put her on the ground, ignoring the achy pull in his back. Marcia Langdon for sheriff. It made a sick kind of sense. *No, that's not fair,* he thought. *You don't know what really happened. You don't really know what went down in the Langdon house that afternoon in 1982, in the hours before we busted down their door. You just know the rumors.* He suddenly realized he was one of the last people around who'd even remember that much. Most of the other kids from the block had moved away, died, or burned out.

Thirty-three years was a long time; a lot could have changed. But looking at the photo, he couldn't help but see the shadow of the teenage girl who'd turned in her own brother.

CHAPTER TWENTY-ONE

Two weeks later, Veronica had given up on the Manning case entirely. The last credible lead had evaporated like steam from a teacup. In the meantime she had been trying to refocus on the low-rent (and yet rent-paying) gigs she'd been ignoring.

On Wednesday afternoon she stood next to a concession stand at the Santa Anita racetrack, peeling the foil top off a single-serving of down-market white wine. She'd retreated to the shaded mezzanine walkway to escape the unseasonably hot sun. Down below, oblivious to the heat, were five hundred or so hardcore gambling addicts taking in some claiming races. Happily, the man she was tailing sat just ten rows down, enabling her to spy on him in relative comfort.

Parking her plastic wineglass on a condiment table, Veronica got out her mini camera and clicked several shots of her person of interest, a doughy, unwell-looking gent in a threadbare MIDNIGHT OIL 1988 WORLD TOUR tee. The final two snaps were keepers. One showed him on his feet, rooting his horse to the finish line. The other was taken right after the finish. It caught the guy with his head flung back in despair, clutching double fistfuls of his lank, greasy hair.

These, along with a previous shot of him at the betting

window, would be plenty to satisfy Veronica's client, the man's sister—who also was executor of their late mother's estate. The will specified that he had to quit gambling to earn his share of the inheritance. Thanks to Mars Investigation's tireless quest for truth, the sister would now be able to claim her sibling's share of the boodle—if any still remained.

Veronica knocked back the remainder of the wine in one gulp. She glanced heavenward. *Yeah, yeah, I know: I am your daughter, in whom you are well pleased. No need to make a fuss over me, though. Just pay it forward by letting St. Vincent have a platinum album or something.*

As she was heading for the exit, her phone rang and Mac's face appeared on caller ID.

"Mac Attack. What's up?" Veronica said, cupping the phone to drown out a sudden, blaring eruption of between-races music. She ducked into an empty women's restroom to escape the noise.

"I need you to take a look at something," Mac said, sounding psyched, perplexed, and exhausted all at once. "Can you get down here right now?"

"Is something wrong?" Veronica asked.

In the moment of silence that followed, she guessed the reason for Mac's agitated state: She'd once again ignored explicit warnings to stay away from the Grace Manning case.

Veronica groaned. "Didn't you have a teeth-cleaning appointment this afternoon? Because something tells me you blew it off to binge-watch the same fifteen hours of hotel security video you've already seen, like, three hundred times."

"Sorry, sorry, sorry," Mac said. The words came in a rapid-fire tumble, half apologetic, half desperate. "There's just this *thing* I've got here and I need you to tell me if I'm crazy to . . ."

"Yes. You are. Now please, as a friend and as a fellow high-risk relapse candidate, just turn that computer off right now."

"Veronica, I've found something we missed before," Mac blurted, her voice suddenly firm and resolved. "I'm not saying it's a huge breakthrough. But I have feeling it might be. And I really need you to see it for yourself."

"Okay—wow," Veronica said, trying not to sound as intrigued as she was. "Look, thanks for calling me, Mac. Forget the dentist; I'll be there in twenty minutes."

Fourteen minutes later—after shaving six off by driving illegally around a highway construction barrier—Veronica sat next to Mac back at the office, watching sped-up images zigzag across her thirty-inch monitor.

"This looks better than before," Veronica said. "Did you enhance it somehow?"

"Just a little exposure gain in the shadows. It helps a lot for what I'm about to show you." Mac slowed the video to normal speed and Veronica saw a numbingly familiar scene: Pacific Southwest University basketball players emerging from the Neptune Grand lobby with rolling gym bags, heading for their team bus. This camera, mounted just above the hotel's main front entry doors, afforded a wide-angle view of a semicircular drive used mainly by guests who were checking in or out. Currently, the entire middle foreground was filled by the PSU Kestrels' bus.

Mac, who'd looked alarmingly wrung-out when Veronica had first come through the door, now seemed to crackle with static energy. Impatient with the parade of drowsy, crotch-scratching hoopsters, she hit Fast Forward and turned to Veronica.

"Well, I guess we've seen this enough times already," she said.

"Yep." Veronica sighed. "Whoa! Heads up, Ice Cube!" Two seconds later, they watched for the umpteenth time as a burly player in retro Jheri curls walked face-first into a potted palm's low-hanging frond, then angrily swatted it as his teammates cracked up.

"Don't worry, we're getting to the interesting part," Mac said. As she spoke, the last few players, coaches, and trainers approached the bus for boarding. Each, in turn, passed around the back of the vehicle and out of sight—presumably to stuff their rolling duffels into the driver-side storage bin. When the final straggler, a diminutive trainer, trotted out the front door and behind the vehicle, Mac paused the video.

"Okay, boss, watch closely now. Here we go." She hit Play again and, less than a minute later, the bus started to move, slowly gliding out of view on the screen's right side. Veronica now saw another familiar scene: the crescent drive occupied by only a lone bellman sneaking a few hits from an e-cigarette. Veronica cocked her head and watched the static scene for a few more seconds, then turned to Mac.

"Well, I saw all the *Paranormal Activity* movies and clocked every spooky drifting balloon and ripple in the dog's water bowl. But you've got me. What did I miss?"

Mac pointed to the top of the screen, a shadowy area beyond the entry drive. "The background—*all* the way back. The part we haven't seen until now because it's been blocked off by the bus. What can you make out?"

"A parking lot," Veronica said, leaning into the screen

and squinting at the dim, poorly resolved area on the outer limits of the camera's range. She knew the area well; it was the hotel's short-term parking lot, thirty or forty spaces used primarily by guests loading or unloading heavy bags. There were a couple of shuttle vans, a motorcycle, and six—no, seven—cars visible. Suddenly, she understood. "We've never watched the video this far, have we?"

"No. At least not with any real attention to this parking lot after the bus leaves. So okay, do we want nineteen more minutes of foreplay or . . . ?"

Veronica lunged for the remote and Mac smacked her hand away. "Straight to the money shot it is!" she said, pressing Fast Forward. The image flickered under extreme acceleration, but no physical motion was visible until, as the eighteenth minute raced to its end, the headlights on one of the cars in the parking lot came on. Veronica and Mac watched, now at regular speed, as a small white compact car backed out of its space. It could be seen in full profile, but a parking lot light's glare on the side window obscured the driver from view. The car unhurriedly crept toward the street exit, turned right onto Neptune's wide central boulevard, and passed out of sight.

"To answer your obvious question," Mac said, "those vehicles you can see after the bus pulls out are the same ones that were there before it arrived and blocked our view."

"And later on?" Veronica murmured in amazement, suddenly realizing she'd watched the final few seconds with hands pressed to her face a la Munch's *The Scream.*

"The parking lot view is clear all night. And from the time that one car pulls out, right up to when Grace is found, only two other people leave: A desk clerk who's empty-handed and a teenage girl with a purse in one hand and a bouquet of flowers in the other. So I think it'd be very interesting if we could find out who's driving that car, don't you?

Veronica turned to Mac and slipped her a congratulatory low five. "You rule, girl," she said. "How many times did you have to watch this, at what ungodly hours? Don't answer that. All I've got to say is, if anyone wants to throw shade on the OCD community, they best not do it around me, because I will mess them up good."

Mac grinned. "But I feel obligated to step on our buzz a little. We may have just watched an incredibly stealthy rapist leaving a crime scene. But it just as easily could've been some guy out having brews with his bros. And afterward they dropped him off at his car while the bus was blocking our view."

Veronica closed her eyes and drummed her hands furiously on the counter.

"Right," she said. "All this tells us is that someone, somehow, managed to leave the hotel without getting ID'd on video. That doesn't prove they're the perp. And whoever the perp is, we still have no clue how he got Grace out of there." She mulled this over as she scooted into the kitchen to grab a bag of salted caramel pretzels and a carafe of iced coffee, and hustled back to Mac's desk.

They both munched for a long while in thoughtful silence, then Veronica picked up the video remote and backed the video up to the point where the first of the PSU players started ambling through the lobby and out the front door.

"Can I safely assume you have godlike total recall of everything that happens from here until, say, seven in the morning?" Veronica asked, not even looking up to register Mac's *Bitch, please!* look.

"Speak to me of luggage, Mackenzie," she said as she pointed to one of the players' gym bags. "Other than these ballers and the mega-duffels they're carrying, I don't remember anyone else who checks out after this *and* who has anything bigger than a backpack. Am I right?"

Mac nodded absently. Then, as the weight of Veronica's question sunk in, her hands fell to her side in disbelief. "No way, Veronica," she said. "Those bags aren't remotely big enough. I mean, look at 'em. You could stand one on end and it'd barely even reach above these dudes' kneecaps."

Veronica didn't answer. She grabbed the mouse and dragged the video back to the scene where the basketball players trooped steadily out the door. The bags were Nike, soft black duffels on wheels with retractable handles. She opened an Internet browser on Mac's smallest screen, and typed in *Nike roller duffel black.* Immediately, several models popped up. She started scrolling through, trying to find the right one.

"Are you hearing me, Mars?" Mac said. "I'll grant you these guys are amply proportioned. But there's no way their jockstraps and shorts and whatnot take up as much space as a grown woman's body would. Even your midget ass couldn't fit in there."

"But what if it could?" Veronica said.

"It doesn't fucking matter!" Mac groaned, her face pink with exasperation. "The rapist has a bleeding, semiconscious woman in his bag. So when they get to the outskirts of town is he like, 'Hey driver, you mind pulling over next to that big, muck-filled pit and popping the luggage bin? I've, um, got something I need to drop off. No peeking, guys!'"

"I didn't say he got on the bus. We never see any of these PSU guys actually boarding because the door's on the far side, out of view. We've just assumed they all did because they're *a team*, and once the bus drives away, they're all gone. But what if one of 'em, while everyone else is getting into the bus, rolls his team bag—with Grace Manning in it—straight out to his little white hatchback?"

"Coach Fennel!" Mac chirped when her old classmate picked up the phone. "I hope you're enjoying these last heady days of summer vacation."

Wallace's voice was instantly wary. "Funny. This sounds like Mac, but that's the patented Veronica Mars I-need-a-favor tone. Let me guess. You two belles are looking for a strapping black man to do something boring, strenuous, or illegal for you?"

"Look, Wallace," Veronica chimed in, "all we really have is a sports gear–related question. I just texted you a photo and I need you to tell me how we can get one of these things very quickly."

Seconds later, Wallace replied, "Well, it looks like you got this picture off of Amazon. Have you considered a Prime membership?"

"No, it kind of has to be today. And we're more interested in just, you know, seeing it and poking around inside it than actually buying," Mac said.

"Good luck, ladies. This is the biggest selling bag on the market right now, so those store managers may be a little on the unhelpful side."

"Wallace, I'm going to cut to the chase here," Veronica

said. "We need to know if this is a gym bag that's big enough to stuff an unconscious woman into."

There was a long silence before Wallace spoke. "You know, Veronica, we go way back. And I've done all kinds of dubious favors for you without pushing for any explanations. But I kind of think I'm owed one here."

"Oh, come *on*, Wallace! Why get all 'morally culpable adult' on me now, after all these years?"

Wallace sighed explosively. "Fine. I have a bag exactly like the one you're talking about. You and Mac can come check it out if you like."

"That is so awesome! But, um, is there any way you could maybe bring it over for us right now? I'll owe you a nice warm batch of chocolate chip cookies . . ."

"What the hell. I can bring it over for you. *Had* thought about spending this afternoon bodysurfing with a special lady friend—but whatever. Driving used athletic gear across town works too. Oh, and one other thing: No chocolate chip. Snickerdoodles. Nonnegotiable."

CHAPTER TWENTY-TWO

Veronica paced up and down the office as they waited for Wallace, her limbs electric. Just a short while ago she'd felt utterly defeated. Now she couldn't sit still. She tried not to get ahead of herself, though. Mac wasn't wrong to be skeptical; those bags did look awfully small.

Back at her desk, Mac's fingers flew over her keyboard. The Neptune Grand's internal database appeared on the screen, and she entered a query for every car parked at the hotel on March sixth, the night of the attack.

"Okay, we're in," Mac said, rattling the pretzel bag to dump the last few fragments into her palm. "I'm sure there'll be dozens of white compacts, but if we can figure out the exact make and model of the one in the front parking lot . . ."

It was at that moment they heard footsteps on the stairs. A minute later, Wallace came through the frosted-glass door. He wheeled a black duffel behind him, his expression coolly sardonic.

"Gym bag delivery for Ms. V. Mars," he said, plunking the bag at Veronica's feet.

"Wallace, you're the best." Veronica knelt next to the bag and unzipped it. It was empty, but a ripe, sour smell wafted out. She pinched her nose, and gave Wallace an appalled look.

"What do you *keep* in this thing?" she asked.

He crossed his arms over his chest. "What do you think I keep in there? It's a gym bag! I sweat, woman! You were expecting what? Lily of the Valley?"

Veronica stepped into the duffel, lowered her body, and curled tightly into a ball in the bottom. Wallace stared down at her.

"Am I allowed to ask what this is all about?" he asked.

"Trust me. The less you know, the happier you'll be." She tried a few positions, hunching her shoulders, tucking her head. After a moment, she looked up. "Okay, zip me!"

Mac leaned over and fiddled with the pull. A moment later, there was a loud zipping sound, and Veronica's world disappeared into darkness.

"Unbelievable!" she heard Mac say.

Veronica's breath started coming in gasps, and this time it wasn't just the smell of Gold Bond Powder and male body funk. Now it was all too easy to imagine Grace in a bag just like this one. Confused, gagged, dimly aware of voices outside. Or had she been too traumatized to feel anything but pain?

"Let me out," Veronica said. Then, because it seemed to be taking forever: "Let me out of here, Wallace!"

"Okay, okay, hang on." Wallace yanked the zipper open and helped Veronica up. She wobbled on her feet, hungrily drawing in the cool, clean air. When she felt her heart stop racing a bit, she turned to Mac, who was shaking her head in disbelief.

"So—I guess these things just look tiny when they're next to a guy you could hitch a U-Haul to, huh?"

"Trust me, they're not exactly roomy," Veronica said, staring down at the cramped space she'd just occupied.

"Well," Wallace said, grabbing the bag, "I'd love to stay, but I must be on my way. If I hurry, I still might be able to get in a little bodysurfing."

Veronica nodded at him. "Thanks, Wallace. Fresh-baked cookies are coming your way this weekend."

On his way to the door, he bent over to give Mac a hug, but pulled up short when he saw what was on her screen: Pacific Southwest players scuffling across the hotel lobby, duffels in tow. "Huh. The PSU Kestrels," he said. "And those same lady-sized bags. Part of me wants to know what's up here, but another part is terrified to ask."

Despite her long, no-secrets relationship with Wallace, Veronica played this one close to the vest. "It's no big deal," she said. "They just happened to be at the Grand the night of a case we've been working. And like you said, those bags are everywhere now."

"This was back in March, right? Yeah, that's it. I saw 'em play Hearst. We got smoked." He shook his head disgustedly at the memory and again turned toward the door.

"Hey, quick question before you go," Mac said. She went behind her desk and leaned over the keyboard. "Can we avail ourselves of your manly automotive knowledge? We're trying to visually ID the model of a car from a low-res TV image."

Wallace shrugged. "I can try. But you'd do better just sticking your head out the window and hollering at the first fat white dude you see with a shaved head and foot-long beard. I'm not really into cars unless they're cheap, basic, and the kind of thing they can fix at Sears." He and Veronica followed Mac behind the desk to look over her shoulder. Mac still had dozens of windows open, showing different angles of the security footage.

"Well, then, I expect this will be right in your wheel-house." Mac said, advancing the video to the parking lot scene at the moment the white hatchback backed out of its parking space and showed itself in profile. "Look familiar?"

Wallace chuckled. "Believe it or not, it does. That's a 2013 Mazda 3."

Veronica and Mac exchanged triumphant glances. "You sure?"

"One hundred percent," he replied. "It's pretty much the official car of the Neptune High School faculty these days. We're into those budget-friendly rides, you know. I even test drove one myself before I decided to give our local repair-men some love and buy American."

Veronica looked at Mac. "Anything matching that description on the parking roster from that night?"

Mac opened another window and started scrolling through a list. After a moment, she let out a soft, sharp laugh. "Got him." She highlighted a line item on the screen. Veronica leaned in to read over her shoulder. "There were three white 2013 Mazdas at the Neptune Grand that night, but just one hatchback. A rental from Lariat driven by a hotel guest named Mitchell Walter Bellamy."

Wallace's eyes narrowed. "Mitchell Bellamy?"

Veronica's head snapped up. "Uh-huh. Why? You know him or something?"

"Oh yeah, from way back," Wallace said, walking up to the screen and peering for a moment before pointing to a tall, blonde, middle-aged man in a Kestrels polo shirt. "That's him right there. Mitch Bellamy. He's one of the PSU assistants. He was a badass college baller in his day. Sweet-est three-point stroke I ever saw. We used to call him 'Drain

Man.' Not that long ago he came out to Neptune and looked at a couple of our players."

Veronica grabbed Wallace's arm hard enough to draw an indignant yelp. "Do you remember the date he came to the school?" she asked fiercely.

"Yeah, the day after they played Hearst, right before spring break in March."

"The Kestrels had another game that weekend," Veronica said, recalling their itinerary. "They drove straight to Stanford and arrived at three that afternoon. Mac, I need to know when Bellamy checked his car back in with Lariat." She then turned back to Wallace. "Do coaches have to ride the bus with the players?"

Wallace rubbed his arm where she'd grabbed him. "Mostly. But assistants do have their own cars sometimes. Especially if they've got recruiting stops along the way."

Mac, who'd long had access codes for every car rental company in Neptune, was already logging in to Lariat Rent-a-Car.

"Here you go, Chief," she said two minutes later. "Bellamy returned that car on March tenth. *Three days* after the team bus left Neptune. So on the morning the team checks out of the Neptune Grand, Mitch rolls his bag with his victim inside right through the lobby and disappears behind the bus. We assume he gets in with the team. Instead, he gets into his rental car, unseen by the surveillance cameras, and nineteen minutes later leaves to find an empty field where he can dump her body."

Wallace stared at her in disbelief. "Say what?"

Veronica didn't answer him. She stared down at the information on Mac's screen, her eyes hard. All the math worked—the timeline, the dimensions of the bag, the shape of a girl's broken body curved to its boundaries. Yes, they'd put together a picture of Bellamy the rapist. But it wouldn't do them any good. Not yet.

"We've got to figure out a way to get to Mitch Bellamy," Veronica said to Wallace. "I need you to help me right now."

CHAPTER TWENTY-THREE

It took Veronica less than an hour to come up with a plan, but there was a lot she had to do before putting it into action. Two days later, on Friday morning, she dialed the number for the Pacific Southwest Athletics Office. She sat with her feet on the coffee table in the Mars Investigations waiting room, Wallace on the sofa across from her, Mac at her desk, and waited while the switchboard patched her through to a recruiter in the basketball program.

"This is Dwayne Williams. How can I help you?"

"Hi, Dwayne!" She pitched her voice to sound earnest and sweet natured. Wallace, who'd heard Veronica work endless variations of this con over the years, just shook his head. "My name's Heidi Jensen, and I'm calling on behalf of my little brother Otis. He plays ball for Neptune High?"

The quick intake of breath on the other end of the line told her he recognized the name. She gave her friends a thumbs-up and plowed ahead.

"Anyway, Otis is going to be a senior this year, and we want him to have a chance to look at all his options before the pressure to sign really starts. I think he met one of your coaches in the spring—Coach Bellamy? Otis really seemed to like him. We were hoping we could come down and talk with him a little more."

"We'd love to show your brother around, Ms. Jensen," Dwayne said eagerly. "I've had the privilege of seeing him play a few times. But I'd heard Texas was ready to sign him."

"Well, Otis thinks he might be happier sticking closer to home. He's definitely interested in seeing what Pacific Southwest might have to offer."

Across the table from her, Wallace had looked up from where he was looking at the university's website, and mouthed *Nothing* very clearly. She shrugged. On the phone, Dwayne's voice had picked up speed. "That's fantastic! Let's get something on the books in maybe late September. He can sit in on a practice, stay the weekend . . ."

"I was really hoping we could come down next week, actually. We'd really like to get a head start on things. You know how crazy the recruitment season is—we really think it'd be best if Otis had a chance to see the real PSU, without all the up-selling."

There was a long pause on the other end of the line. Evidently that was not how Williams had imagined the meeting. Veronica held her breath, aware that both Mac and Wallace were watching her closely for a sign of what was happening.

"Well, the thing is, the summers aren't exactly the best time for a visit. It's pretty bare bones—the guys are mostly just in the weight room or doing laps. The NCAA restricts our practice time quite a bit."

"Oh, that's all right," Veronica said. "I'm sure we'll find out what we need to."

After a little more wrangling back and forth they settled it. Otis would come down on Saturday and stay the night.

He was eager to see the whole campus . . . but he was particularly eager to meet Assistant Coach Bellamy.

When she hung up the phone, Wallace flopped backward, hiding his face in his hands. "You know, one of these days, you're gonna get me fired," he said, his voice muffled.

She'd had to tell Wallace who she was investigating—and why—to get him to go along with her plan. It hadn't been hard. Wallace had been friendly with Meg Manning and, as it turned out, Neptune's best basketball player in two decades owed Wallace. Wallace had caught Otis buying beer at the local Sac N Pac earlier that summer and hadn't turned him in to the varsity coach. Instead, Wallace had met him early in the gym for two weeks of extra sets of suicides, a punishment Otis welcomed over expulsion from the team. Wallace had forged a relationship with Otis from his days coaching him on the freshman squad. And since Otis was already eighteen, he didn't need a parent to accompany him on a recruiting trip.

Now Veronica gave Wallace a mock-incredulous look. "Fired? For giving Dwayne Williams the best news he's gotten all week? For telling him a six-nine kid who's being wooed by Stanford and Texas wants to give little old Pac-SW a look-see?"

"So it's all set up?" Mac asked. "You think you'll be able to get a DNA sample?"

Veronica held up one of the DNA swabs she'd taken to keeping in her purse. "Don't you know they call me Veronica, Reaper of Cells? Or they might, by the end of this case. Anyhow, we've got an in. I'll have a better chance of getting a sample from there than I will sitting here and waiting for DNA evidence to rain from the sky."

Mac wrinkled her nose. "There is no good way to visualize that one."

Pacific Southwest University, home of the Kestrels, was a private research university occupying just over two hundred acres of green lawns and orderly avenues in northern San Diego. At the center of the campus was the Eddie Castillo Stadium and Sports Complex, the home to Pac-SW's Division I basketball team—and home to Mitch Bellamy's offices.

That was where Veronica, Wallace, and Neptune High's star varsity forward, Otis Jensen, headed on Friday afternoon, led by Dwayne Williams. Dwayne turned out to be a young African American man with a dimple in one cheek and an easy, energetic manner. He was almost as tall as Otis, whose head had skimmed the roof of Veronica's RAV4 on the drive down.

"Big O! It's great to meet you," Dwayne had said when he'd met them in front of the main building, clipboard in hand. He shook Otis's hand vigorously. "We're really excited you're checking us out."

"Hi," said Otis. Otis looked like a combination of farm boy and draft horse, with shaggy blonde hair, pale freckled skin, and legs like a Clydesdale's. In spite of his size, he had stereotype-busting speed.

Dwayne turned to Wallace and Veronica next. "Now I know Coach Fennel by reputation—I started as a freshman the year after you graduated. Saw you take Hearst all the way to the conference finals that year, man—that was something else."

Wallace grinned. Any lingering complaints he had about the plan were obliterated by the ego stroke.

Dwayne turned to Veronica and looked her up and down—more as if trying to figure out just who she was than to check her out. "And you must be . . ."

"Oh, that's my mom," Otis blurted.

Dwayne blinked a few times, clearly doing some quick math. Veronica laughed lightly.

"Stepmom. Dee-Anne," she drawled in an accent cloned from half-remembered CMA Awards acceptance speeches on *Entertainment Tonight*. "I mean, it was borderline *criminal* when I married his dad—I was practically a child bride!"

She'd dressed for the part of wholesome older sister— pink cardigan, white button-down blouse, a mid-length skirt. It didn't work nearly as well for the former jailbait "spring" in a May-December marriage, but it would have to do.

She shook hands with Dwayne, hoping he didn't remember her voice well enough from the phone to realize that Dwayne's sister sounded exactly like his stepmother. "But I don't want to get in the way. I'm just along for the ride, here to make sure Otis gets the most out of the visit."

"Well, nice to meet you, Mrs. Jensen. Let's head up to Castillo, shall we?"

"We shall!" she cooed. Wallace's eyebrows shot up, a look that clearly said *overselling just a bit*. She ignored him and fell into step behind Dwayne as they headed up a narrow campus road.

As they walked, Dwayne kept up a running patter of information about the program. "We've got a brand-new practice space with top-of-the-line equipment, steam room, sauna, Jacuzzi—anything you need. Every player on the team gets one-on-one attention from the coaches. And besides that we've got massage therapists, personal trainers, and a team nutritionist who fixes lunch for us every day. Between you and me . . ." He leaned conspiratorially toward Otis. "Oksana's meals are a definite step up from the dining hall."

The campus was as abandoned as Hearst had been a few weeks earlier. The few people around appeared to be administrators on coffee break or summer students on their way to class. The group approached an enormous modern sports complex surrounded by a graceful Xeriscape of flowering desert trees, river stones, and yucca.

Well, I've got my ticket in, she thought. *Now all I have to do is find what I came for. Preferably without being arrested or getting Wallace fired.*

Instead of going in the main entrance, they followed Dwayne around to the side. He pulled a magnetic card from the key pocket of his casual slacks and swiped it through a reader by the glass door.

"Will Otis need one of those to look around?" she asked, touching Dwayne's arm and noting that the top of the card protruded slightly from the pocket where it had been retucked. Dwayne smiled at her. He had the perfect face for a recruiting agent. His playful, innocently flirty grin was probably great at deflecting fussy moms. And he was unflappable enough to pretend not to notice when Otis had to sound out the sign over the door reading AQUATHERAPY.

"He'll be with me or with one of the guys, so he shouldn't need one for now. Don't worry, we're not going to lock him out!" With that, he turned and opened the door.

The halls had a sheen and smell unique to brand-new institutional buildings. Enlarged action shots of past and present Kestrels stars lined the walls. Trophy cases were packed with awards and plaques under dramatically angled spotlights. They passed the weight room and the locker rooms on the way to the gym. From the far end of the hall, Veronica could hear the echoes of bouncing basketballs and squeaking sneakers.

"We'll come back, don't worry," said Dwayne. "I'll show you all around. But first, I want to introduce you to the guys."

In the gym, nine players were practicing free throws. For every miss they ran a lap. Their deep voices echoed off the walls as they talked smack aimed at rattling shooters.

Two steps through the door, Veronica came up short. Otis knocked into her from behind.

"Sorry, Mom," he mumbled. But she didn't answer.

Sitting in the bleachers with a clipboard on his knee, watching every movement on the court, was none other than Mitch Bellamy.

She'd seen his picture online, of course. For the past week she'd been finding out everything she could about Mitchell Walter Bellamy, the Drain Man. He was forty-one, divorced and single, with two teenaged kids who lived with their mother. His college career had been, as Wallace said, legendary. It had looked like a sure bet he'd move on to the NBA. Clippers coach Larry Brown openly gushed over the idea of Bellamy as part of a three-guard rotation with Ron Harper and Mark Jackson.

Then, late in Bellamy's junior year, he shredded his MCL and ACL. Multiple surgeries restored guy-on-the-street mobility but not the joint strength to handle an eighty-two-game pro season. His playing career at anything above a YMCA level was over. Coaching offers flooded in, though.

And for two decades that had been his career—including the past twelve seasons with PSU.

Bellamy had thinning, sandy-brown hair and the look of a muscular man gone slightly to fat. In pictures she'd seen of him on the court, he usually wore a suit and tie, but for today's practice he had on a pair of cargo shorts and a T-shirt. He watched his players intently, making marks on his clipboard every now and then, his watery blue eyes focused on the court.

Dwayne walked over and leaned in to say something in Bellamy's ear. The assistant coach glanced over at Otis, Wallace, and Veronica in the doorway, and nodded. A moment later, he blew his whistle.

"Hey, guys, looking way better today. Spencer, you're leaning in too far. Do that in the opener and Braxton's gonna cross you over all night. Abioto—like your off-the-ball D. You've got your head in it today. Okay, fellas, let's take a break. I want you to meet someone."

The players all turned to look at the newcomers. Veronica recognized a few from the surveillance video—kids who'd been there the night of the attack—along with some new faces. Bellamy walked toward them, hand outstretched.

"Otis, it's great to see you again, son." He shook hands with Otis, and then he turned to Veronica. He was about six-foot-six, more than a foot and a half taller than she was, and it was disconcerting to stand in his shadow. His expression, now that he'd stopped watching the players with a critical eye, was mild and almost paternal.

"Mrs. Jensen, is that right?" He held out his hand.

Is this the hand that left those bruises on Grace Manning's neck? It was enormous, meaty, but surprisingly cool and dry as they shook. She ignored the shudder it sent up her arm and tried to seem breezy. "So nice to meet you, Coach Bellamy."

"Can we get you anything? Water? Coffee?"

"I'll take a Gatorade," Otis said. Dwayne disappeared immediately.

"I'm good, thanks." Veronica smiled. "Coach Fennel?"

"Uh, yeah, I'm good too." He glanced at Veronica, and she gave an infinitesimal nod. "Nice to meet you, sir. Saw you guys play Hearst in the spring—first week of March?"

Bellamy's grinned and thumped Wallace on the shoulder, all ball-busting camaraderie. "Oh yeah! I remember that game. Man, that was gruesome." He whistled softly and shook his head. "After a while, I just had to turn my head. Did Hearst ever bother showing up?"

So no sign that he remembers that date as anything but a basketball win. Not that that means anything.

"It must be *exhausting* being on the road for games all the time," Veronica broke in. "I hope they at least put you boys up at the Grand. There ain't nowhere else worth staying in Neptune."

"You know, in fact, that's just where we stayed," Bellamy said with a nod. "No complaints. I slept like a baby."

For a moment, their eyes met. She stared hard at him for as long as she dared, trying to somehow see inside his head, trying to read him. Was it her imagination, or was there a hint of a smirk around his mouth? She honestly couldn't tell.

At that moment, Dwayne returned from the hallway, Gatorade in hand. "Here ya go, Big O!"

Veronica grabbed him by the arm and squeezed. "Look at this guy. He's already been so great to us. What a cutie pie he is too!"

She'd seen enough women bring Wallace plates of cookies and brush invisible lint off his coat to know that flirty moms were a definite type. And she was pretty sure that Dwayne Williams—cute, charismatic, and expressly charged with keeping recruits and their families entertained—had met more than his share. She hoped his comfort level with grabby moms would keep him from minding that she'd slipped her arm around his waist. Or noticing as her thumb and forefinger snagged the jutting tip of his key card.

His eyes widened as he felt her hand against his hip. He edged slightly away from her, but the finger he waved at her was more playful than admonishing. "You're going to make me blush, Mrs. Jensen," he said, his eyes sparkling.

Playing it off as a game, keeping everyone's feelings from getting hurt. The guy was a pro. Luckily, so was Veronica.

She palmed the card, and slid it into her pocket without anyone noticing.

CHAPTER TWENTY-FOUR

That night, Dwayne took the Neptune visitors, along with three players they'd met earlier, for steak and seafood at a waterfront restaurant. The decor was mahogany and green carpet. A jazz quartet played in the bar. Lights from passing yachts twinkled in the bay. Otis sat between Josh Randall, a forward from some hog-farming burg in Missouri, and Isaiah Dempsey, a fast-talking guard from L.A. Across the table sat Art Templeton, a center from Juneau who looked like a six-ten Kurt Cobain. Between mouthfuls of rib eye and prawns, they engaged in a scholarly project of rating Nicki Minaj, Miley Cyrus, and Azealia Banks on a Mostly Hot to Mostly Crazy continuum. Veronica picked at her green beans and sipped Nebbiolo. During a lull in the conversation, she broke in.

"So, do you guys like Coach Bellamy?"

Art's eyes lit up. He swallowed the mashed potatoes he'd just shoveled into his mouth. "Oh, man, Coach is great. I mean, all the coaches are—Coach Zabka is one of the smartest guys I know. He pushes us really hard, doesn't let us slack. But Coach Bellamy's more about encouraging us. Building us up."

Veronica had met Coach Zabka that afternoon, a wiry

man in his mid-sixties who wore a trim-cut suit. He'd greeted Otis without fawning—he was businesslike and polite, asking questions about Otis's game and his goals, all of which were answered in mono- and duo-syllables.

"So Coach Bellamy's the good cop?" Veronica asked.

"Yeah, I guess." Art shrugged. "I mean, I want to get better, you know? You gotta have the bad cop around too. But we hear about every little thing we do wrong, so you learn to appreciate someone like Coach B."

"He ain't always good cop," Josh said, eyebrows raised significantly. "Remember Tucson?"

"What happened in Tucson?" Veronica asked, putting her fork down.

The boys exchanged glances. It was Josh who spoke.

"Two years back, we went to a Thanksgiving tournament in Tucson and played Northern Arizona in the championship game. Well, when we all went back to the hotel, Coach B was just fine—but the next morning, he came down to the bus beat *all* to hell. Black eye, broken nose, the works. We were all ready to go find who'd jumped him but he told us he'd been out getting a beer the night before, and on his way home he saw a guy beating up his girl in an alley. He said he just kind of . . . snapped. Went berserk on the dude. He kept saying, 'Guys, it wasn't heroic, it was stupid, I should have just called the cops,' but we were like, Coach B's the *man*, you know?"

Veronica mentally filed *Northern Arizona game; 2013; Thanksgiving tournament final*. She took a sip of water, struggling to keep a neutral expression. It could be nothing, of course—a drunken brawl with a stranger, just like Bellamy said. But she pulled out her phone and texted Mac.

Maybe she can check the game date on the 2013 schedule, pull up the Tucson hospital admits and police statements from that night, see if there's another side to the story.

The waiter drifted up with the water pitcher, refilling all around the table. Otis put down his fork, his plate scraped clean, and stared longingly at a passing dessert cart.

Veronica's phone buzzed. It was a text from Mac.

> Nothing from a cursory search, but I'll dig.

Veronica took a deep breath and settled in for another course.

Campus was dark when Veronica pulled into the arena's parking lot. It was almost eleven, and she'd just dropped Wallace and Otis off at the San Diego Hilton. Wallace had given her a resigned wave as she pulled away from the curb. By now they'd be in their room, watching *SportsCenter* and getting ready for bed.

It was time for Veronica to clock in.

The Castillo Center loomed as she approached. Through the windows she could see the pale security lights that lit the halls. She stepped lightly up the walk to the plain glass door where Dwayne had swiped them in earlier. Some key cards were attached to timers and wouldn't work past certain hours. She held her breath, hoping this wasn't one of them.

The red light on the reader turned green as she touched the card to it. She heard the lock click softly.

Veronica's footsteps echoed with unnerving loudness as she

made her way up the hall. She'd been half afraid she'd run into janitorial or security, but so far there was no sign of anyone.

Thanks to the tour Dwayne had given them that afternoon, Veronica knew the coaching offices were in a large suite on the third floor. If she could get into Bellamy's office, she should be able to find a stray hair on his chair, a used tissue. *Something.* She started up the stairs, not wanting the ding of the elevator to alert anyone to her presence.

A few steps from the top, she froze. Somewhere, muffled and distant, she could hear voices. She clutched the railing with one hand, listening hard. The sound wasn't getting closer or farther away. Someone was stationary, maybe behind closed doors, in conversation. She crept up the last few stairs, listened for a second at the stairwell door, and slipped into the third-floor hallway.

The sound was louder here, though still muffled. She hugged the wall as she stepped toward the open reception area. A lamp on the secretary's desk was lit, its downturned shade diffusing mottled green light through the room. She paused at the corner and once again tried to gauge where the voices were coming from. The doors, labeled with names etched in brass, were all closed.

The team had two assistant coaches besides Bellamy, along with a "Professional Development Coordinator." Coach Zabka's office was in the back of the suite, a personal assistant's desk sitting in front of it. From where Veronica stood, she could see light under his door.

She took a deep breath, then edged her way along the line of doors until she was at Bellamy's.

She pulled a hairpin from her wallet and snapped it in half. It was a simple lock, pin-and-tumbler. All you had to do was line up the pick just so; a few minutes of fiddling usually did the trick. She wiggled the hairpin back and forth, probing for the pins.

From down the hall, she heard furniture dragging across a floor and the click of a door latch opening.

The reception desk was right behind her. She dove underneath it, pulling the chair in front of her to block her from view. The light from the desk lamp above her swayed a little. She caught her breath in her throat as Zabka's door opened.

Footsteps came toward her, down the hall. A pair of brown leather loafers shuffled into view. She couldn't tell who they belonged to, but she could hear a low murmur down the hall—there were more than two people in Zabka's office. The loafers stopped right in front of her, so close she could see their fraying tassels. The man seemed to be looking through a stack of paperwork on the desk over her head.

Veronica pressed her knuckles to her lips, breathing as shallowly as she could. Above, she could hear things being moved around on the desk. She waited.

Finally, the man heaved a sigh, turned, and walked back down the hall. A moment later, the door opened again. This time she could make out the sounds of dribbling and courtside noise. *They're watching game tape,* she realized. A moment later, the door shut, and the sound was muffled.

Veronica sat very still for several long moments, listening. Then slowly, carefully, she crawled out from under the desk and went back to Bellamy's door. After a few more quick twists of the hairpin, the door swung inward with a soft groan. She stepped through and closed the door behind her.

She snapped on her penlight and swept it over the dark room. The office was immaculate. She could make out a leather loveseat against one wall, a green plaid throw folded over one arm. The desk was almost Spartan, with nothing but a computer and a container of pens. A framed photo of two teenagers, a boy and a girl, sat on a bookshelf. The walls were covered in roster photos, all of them signed by former players.

THANKS FOR EVERYTHING COACH!

YOU'RE THE BEST, COACH B!

YOU'RE THE MAN.

She started to open drawers, moving quickly but carefully. In one there was nothing but a pair of scissors and a roll of tape. In another, a small assortment of screws and nails rolled on their sides. There were almost no personal effects—no sweater draped over the back of the chair, no hat hanging by the door. The wastebasket was completely empty.

Of course he has to be a neat freak. Of course.

She ran her hands over everything, looking for something she could use. Her frustration mounted. And then she saw it. A small smile spread across her face.

There, tucked behind the photo of his children, was a blue toothbrush case and a small tube of Crest.

Looks like Bellamy likes to stay minty-fresh throughout the day. Here's hoping he really works that gum line hard.

She picked it up and slid it into her purse. That was when the door swung open again, and light flooded the room.

It was Mitch Bellamy, plainly as stunned to see her as she was to see him.

CHAPTER TWENTY-FIVE

Rage blew across Bellamy's features like a storm cloud moving in. When he stepped toward Veronica it was fast—faster than she'd have thought a man his size could move. She'd just gotten her fingers around the Taser in her bag, when another voice came from down the hall.

"Hey, Mitch, I was thinking we should look at the Oregon State tapes too . . ." Coach Zabka appeared in the doorway behind Bellamy. He came up short as he saw them. "What the hell is going on here?"

Bellamy didn't seem able to speak, the veins in his neck swollen in sharp relief. He didn't look away from Veronica, and it was clear he was fighting for control, breathing fast, clenching his fists at his sides. Zabka looked from him to Veronica once or twice.

It was hard for Veronica to tear her eyes away from Bellamy, but instinct told her Zabka's presence was keeping her safe. She forced herself to look at the head coach and held up the toothbrush.

"Coach Zabka, I have to apologize—I haven't been entirely honest with you. My name is Veronica Mars. I'm a private investigator. I have reason to believe that Coach Bellamy was involved in a sexual assault in Neptune on the night of March sixth. I broke in here trying to find some DNA to prove it."

Bellamy made a sputtering sound. Veronica glanced at him from the corner of her eye. He was fighting to master his anger and look of outrage. "This is crazy. Tommy, you can't—"

"A nineteen-year-old girl was attacked in the Neptune Grand." Veronica spoke over him. It was a desperate move, blurting out the truth, but she didn't have many options. Zabka could call security any second and have her hauled off campus, maybe even report her to the police. She had to give him a reason not to. "She was raped, beaten, and left in the rain to die. Luckily, she didn't."

Zabka looked at Bellamy, then back to Veronica. "And she's accused Mitch?"

"If she had, you'd be talking to the cops instead of me."

Zabka stiffened. Veronica registered the fact with satisfaction; he obviously didn't want the police anywhere near his department. In this situation, she was the preferred option.

She continued. "She doesn't remember who attacked her. There was some brain trauma, and her memories are compromised. But I was hoping to get some DNA evidence and *quietly* find out if Coach Bellamy is a match." Her inflection on the word *quiet* was featherlight but obvious. Quiet, without press, without scandal. Without Zabka's name becoming synonymous with *Paterno*. "If he's not, that's great. I get to cross a name off my list, no fuss."

"I'm calling security." Bellamy moved toward the phone, but Zabka grabbed him by the arm.

"Hold on just a minute, Mitch. I want to get to the bottom of this myself." He peered at Veronica through his wire-frame glasses. "Are you testing everyone who was at the hotel that night, or just Mitch?"

She hesitated. "Only a few for the time being. We know Coach Bellamy wasn't on the bus with everyone else. He was in a car, by himself. Which gave him an opportunity to dump the girl on the edge of town."

Bellamy's face was deep purple. "I was *scouting*, you fucking . . ." He checked himself, taking a deep breath and turning to Zabka. "That was the day I went to Neptune High to check out Jensen and Rodriguez. I was in a separate car. Damn it, Tommy, this is absurd. This . . . *woman* broke into my office and went through my things. She needs to be arrested—tonight."

Zabka looked at Bellamy for a long moment, his face unreadable. Veronica waited. Her lungs felt tight.

"Do you have a swab?" Zabka said, turning to look at her. His mouth was a tight line, but he seemed more focused on developing his own plan of action than yielding to Bellamy's angry demands.

Veronica nodded. Zabka turned to Bellamy. "Give her a sample."

Bellamy looked as if he'd been socked in the stomach. "What?"

"Come on, Mitch, give her a sample. She'll see it wasn't you and we can all move on from this." He looked evenly over at Veronica. "I just want to make clear, I have perfect faith in my colleague. I'm letting you do this so we can clear his name. Once that's happens, I'll expect an apology. Then we'll put all of this behind us."

"Can't get any fairer than that," Veronica said. She pulled

a sterile-wrapped swab from her purse and ripped off the end of the wrapping. "Please open wide, Coach Bellamy."

At first she thought he'd refuse. His lips were closed tight together. But after a moment, he grabbed the swab from her and ran it inside his cheek. She held out the little plastic tube. He didn't break eye contact as he dropped it in.

"You'll let us know when you get the results?" asked Zabka.

"Provided it's negative?" She turned back to him, dropping the tube into a plastic bag and placing it in her purse. "You'll be the first person I call."

CHAPTER TWENTY-SIX

"So then we were out past the floats and the lifeguard made us get out for the rest of the day. It wasn't *fair* because the big kids can go all the way out to the other side of the cove and I can swim better than most of them." The little boy on Veronica's computer screen gave an indignant frown. "Some of them can only doggy paddle. I can do the crawl!"

Veronica sat on the sofa in her apartment, laptop propped on the coffee table. She'd taken the afternoon off to Skype with Hunter, her half brother.

"But other than that, camp was fun?" she asked.

"I guess so." Even at seven, Hunter had a somber, studied nonchalance. Veronica guessed it was a side effect of growing up in a house with so many secrets. She knew from experience that a quiet kid who could eavesdrop and stay mum about what he'd overheard could find out way more than a noisy one. "I didn't like canoeing. But I was the best scout for Capture the Flag. *And* I learned how to play the guitar."

"Oh yeah? Are you going to play me something?"

"I don't have a guitar yet. Mom said maybe for Christmas. They're expensive."

Lianne and Hunter had gone back to Tucson that April,

after the legal fallout from Tanner and Aurora's con had dissipated. Tanner was currently serving out a two-year stint in Ironwood State Prison for extortion and obstructing justice. Aurora, meanwhile, had gotten parole with mandatory therapy. Lianne had won custody, though Veronica wasn't sure why she'd want it. At the tender age of sixteen, Aurora had not only agreed to fake her own kidnapping for a cut of the ransom money but had double-crossed her dad in order to make off with the cash and stick him with the blame. Lianne had put her in a residential treatment facility for teens with "antisocial behavior," which sounded about right to Veronica; the kid had shocked Veronica with her own Taser before debating the merits of killing her and dumping her body in the desert.

Since they'd left, Veronica had only been able to visit Tucson once, but she tried to Skype with Hunter at least once every couple of weeks. Then in July he'd gone to sleepaway camp for a fortnight, an experience she'd quietly helped pay for. Lianne was barely making ends meet. And between the debt caused by Tanner and Aurora's legal fees and the cost of Aurora's treatment, there wasn't a lot left over for Hunter.

Veronica made a mental note to discuss guitars with her mother. She might be able to find a used one and send it to them, maybe prepay a teacher for lessons. Even after all this time, Veronica wasn't about to cut a check to Lianne.

"Well, you want to know what *I've* been doing the last few weeks?" she asked.

"What?"

She scooped up Pony from where she was snoozing in her dog bed and held her up to the camera. The puppy blinked sleepily. "Trying to convince my new roommate to stop pooping on the rug!"

Hunter's eyes got very round. "You got a dog?"

"We got a dog," Veronica confirmed.

He turned to look off camera. "Mom! Mom, come here, they got a *dog*!"

Even now, Veronica instinctively tensed up when Lianne appeared on the screen. *Old habits die hard.* But the Lianne who'd haunted her adolescence was gone. The woman who'd drained Veronica's college fund eleven years ago was different now. She smiled almost shyly at Veronica.

"Hi, hon—Veronica." Lianne interrupted herself. "Oh my goodness, who's this?"

"This," Veronica said, "is my Pony. And I was thinking . . . maybe when this case I'm working is over I'll take a few days, drive out for a visit. I can bring the puppy. Maybe Logan can get leave and come too. I'd like you to meet him, Hunter. I think you'd like him."

Hunter looked up at his mother. "Can they, Mom?"

"Of course, honey. Any time," Lianne said softly.

It was strange to see Lianne and Hunter, side by side. They favored each other, in the same way Veronica favored her mother. They all had the same light hair, the same delicate features. She'd always been closer to her father, even as a little girl, but Hunter's existence somehow brought home that she was Lianne's daughter as much as Keith's, no matter how strained things were between them.

Her phone suddenly trilled from where it sat on the sofa next to her. She leaned over to see who it was.

NEPTUNE LAB CENTER.

She lowered Pony back to the floor. "Mom, Hunter, I'm sorry to cut this short, but I've got to get this call. It's work."

"That's no problem," Lianne said. "Maybe we can talk next weekend."

"Bring the dog to see me!" Hunter yelled, waving.

"Bye!" She smiled into the camera until she was sure the call was disconnected. Then she grabbed her phone.

"Hi, Ms. Mars. This is Phil Curtis with Neptune Labs. We just got the results for the swabs you sent us this week."

"And?"

There was the briefest of pauses. Then:

"It's a match."

Veronica blasted down I-5 to San Diego, her windows down and the radio turned off so she could think. Her fingers tightened around the steering wheel. They *had* him. None of the intangible, circumstantial evidence—the bag, the bus, the car—mattered. DNA evidence didn't lie.

It was almost three when she arrived at the San Diego Police Department headquarters. Detective Leo D'Amato stood waiting for her just outside the main entrance. He was holding two cups of coffee.

She took the outstretched cup. "You brought him in?"

"Yeah, he's in interrogation room three. He's talking to his lawyer right now."

She'd known Leo since she was in high school. Back then, he'd been the cute new deputy in the Balboa County Sheriff's Department, with a smile that was part impish, part bashful, and one-hundred percent charming. They'd flirted shamelessly and even dated briefly. But Veronica's life had been too complicated for a nice guy like Leo. Not least of her problems had been a sudden and growing attraction to her dead best friend's boyfriend—one Logan Echolls.

Still, they'd stayed friendly. She'd called him as soon as

she'd gotten the lab results. Even though Bellamy's crimes were in Neptune's jurisdiction, she didn't trust Lamb's department to follow through.

Leo held the door open for her and led her through a bustling lobby to a bank of elevators. "I had a chance to look over the file. Is there anything else I should know before we go in to talk to him?"

Veronica briefed him as the elevator crept up, telling him her suspicions about the bag. "But the victim had severe head trauma that left her with short-term memory loss. She's probably not going to be able to give a positive ID."

"Yeah, not surprising." He grimaced. "I saw the pictures."

The elevator opened onto a bustling open room, subdivided into cubicles. Plainclothes detectives worked at computers and talked on phones. Corkboards and whiteboards lined the walls, scrawled with web charts and lists of names. A short, stocky woman spotted Leo and approached them.

"They're ready for you in there, D'Amato." She handed him a manila file folder. He opened it and glanced inside. Then he snapped it shut.

"All right, Mars. Let's do this," he said, opening the door.

It looked as though they'd picked Bellamy up straight from practice. He wore a Nike T-shirt and his whistle still hung around his neck. His face was flushed dark red, but otherwise he looked surprisingly composed. Next to him sat his attorney, Marty Campbell—an effete-looking little man in a fashionable, obviously bespoke suit. Every part of him that was capable of being manicured had been, from his sculpted beard to his scrubbed and trimmed fingernails. Both men looked up when Leo and Veronica entered the interrogation room.

"Coach Bellamy . . . Mr. Campbell." Leo shut the door. "I'm Detective Leo D'Amato. This is Veronica Mars, who's been consulting with us on this case."

Bellamy's eyes met hers, his jaw tightening almost imperceptibly. She didn't look away as she sat across from him at the rectangular table.

"We've met," she said, folding her hands on the table in front of her.

Campbell's lips curled tightly into a disparaging smile. "Detective D'Amato, this is ridiculous. You've hauled my client in on the flimsiest possible evidence. Let's end this before it becomes a major embarrassment for your department."

Leo's heavy eyebrows arched up. He opened the manila folder and removed a photo of Grace Manning's body, sliding it across on the table. Her face had been blurred out—even with the DNA evidence, they liked to be cautious with survivors' identities—but the severity of her injuries was unmistakable and shocking. Veronica watched Bellamy's face closely. His expression didn't change, but his pupils dilated.

"A nineteen-year-old woman was assaulted in Neptune the morning of March seventh," Leo said. "We have DNA evidence—which your client willingly provided—linking him to the attack. Lawyers usually don't find that kind of evidence *flimsy*."

"First of all, I'd hardly call the means by which your . . . uh . . . *associate* obtained the DNA swabs to be evidence of 'willingness,'" Campbell said smoothly. "She broke into his office and, when caught, accused him of sexual assault in front of his supervisor. He was pressured to provide that sample. Second, there's a rational explanation for the presence of his DNA at that crime scene."

"I'm all ears," Leo said.

It was Bellamy who spoke next. His eyes were still glued to that picture, his face and neck flushed. But his voice was quiet and deliberate, his words almost over-enunciated.

"I did have sex with that girl," he said. "But I didn't rape her."

Veronica couldn't contain her derision. "So breaking half a girl's ribs and choking her until she passes out is foreplay? Come on, Coach, even if rough sex is your thing no one's going to believe an innocent man dumps a girl's body ten miles from where they were last seen together."

"But I didn't." His pale blue eyes finally flitted up from the picture. "When she left my room she was fine. I don't know who did this to her, but it happened after we went our separate ways."

"Why didn't you mention this allegedly consensual sex when I swabbed you?" Veronica asked. "You knew what I was looking for. Why didn't you clear it all up when you had a chance, a week ago?"

Patches of purple sprang up across his face, a color that perversely resembled the mottled bruises in the picture in front of him. "Well, Ms. Mars, the fact is, I was embarrassed."

Veronica leaned forward. "Of what? Having sex?"

Bellamy crossed his arms. "No. Of having sex with a prostitute."

CHAPTER TWENTY-SEVEN

Veronica felt frozen to the spot. Her legs were heavy against the chair, her hands clenched against her thighs. She stared across the table, her mind a blank, all of her theories and assumptions floundering with one sudden electric jolt.

Next to her, Leo sputtered in shock. Bellamy leaned forward, elbows on the table, while his lawyer smirked beside him. For a moment the air felt scarce, the room too small and close.

It was Leo who recovered first. Swiping his hand over his face, he fought to regain composure. "So you're saying you *hired* this girl?" He looked down at the photos of Grace Manning's battered body, unable to keep a note of skepticism out of his voice.

But even in her numb state, Veronica had to admit it sounded plausible. She mentally replayed every conversation she'd had with Grace, every seemingly unanswerable question about the case. Bellamy's assertion credibly answered them all. It explained why Grace wouldn't tell them the name of her boyfriend. It explained why she used the stairs instead of the elevator, in an effort to stay off the surveillance cameras. It explained why Charles Sinclair hadn't been a DNA match even though he'd obviously recognized the photo. He wasn't *the* boyfriend. He was *a* boyfriend. Why had she not even considered that possibility before?

"My client has a very prominent position in the community as a representative of Pacific Southwest's basketball program," Campbell put in. "It's no surprise he'd want to avoid a scandal."

"Okay," Leo said, regaining his composure. "Okay. Let's start at the beginning. I need you to tell me everything you remember about that night, Mr. Bellamy. From the beginning."

Bellamy pressed his hands together, looking down at his fingertips. "We played Hearst that weekend. Our boys won and after the game we all went back to the hotel." He hunched his shoulders slightly, as if embarrassed. "I was lonely. I haven't had any time to date since my divorce a few years ago. Been too busy with work, you know? It takes over. Anyway, I was looking at some sites online, and I saw her ad. I'd never hired a call girl before. It'd never even occurred to me. But then, you know, kind of on a whim, I called her up. She sounded sweet—soft-spoken, easy to talk to. So I set up an appointment."

The footage Veronica had watched over and over spun through her mind. She saw Grace in her designer dress, her high heels, the makeup, all of it designed to make her look *expensive*.

"What time did you call her?" Leo asked, scribbling notes on a legal pad.

"I guess it would've been about nine, nine thirty." Bellamy cleared his throat. "She said she'd come to my room at eleven."

"All right. What did you do then?"

Bellamy glanced at his lawyer. "I killed some time in my room. Watched TV, checked e-mail. I ordered room service champagne for when she got there."

"Did she arrive on time?"

Bellamy nodded. "Yeah, she showed up just before eleven."

Veronica noticed that the man's eyes kept flitting to the photo of Grace's injuries on the table, lingering there as he talked.

"And then what happened?"

Bellamy actually blushed. "Well, you know, we talked for a few minutes. Had a glass of champagne. And then we . . . we had sex."

His forehead crinkled anxiously, and his face was droopy and hangdog. He seemed incapable of meeting anyone's eyes. Veronica had, over time, become well attuned to near-ineffable signs that could give away a liar. She had to admit she wasn't picking up any of those tells right now. Bellamy just looked like a scared, chastened, middle-age guy staring into the face of public shame and potential unemployment.

"After that, she went into the bathroom and tidied herself up," he continued. "I paid her, and she left. Like I said, she was fine when she left my room."

"Did you see how she left your floor of the hotel?" Veronica asked.

Bellamy gave her a blank look.

"Stairs or elevator?" she said impatiently. He shrugged.

"I don't know. I locked the door behind her and went to sleep."

"Around what time was that?" Leo asked, giving Veronica a quelling glance; she wasn't supposed to be asking any questions. She pressed her lips together.

"Around midnight. I paid her for an hour." He looked at the picture again. This time he stared openly. "Maybe she had another client after me. Someone who did this to her."

Veronica managed to keep her mouth shut, but her eyes narrowed at Bellamy. For a moment, he met her gaze, his watery blue eyes mild and almost apologetic. She thought of how cool he'd looked as he checked out of the hotel, how he'd known exactly how to act then too.

"Now, if that's all, we'll see ourselves out." The lawyer said. Leo nodded, and the lawyer and Bellamy stood. Veronica watched as Bellamy exited the interrogation room and headed toward the elevators behind his lawyer, free to go.

"It's a good-sounding story, and he sold it like Olivier, but he's lying," she said under her breath as soon as the door closed. Leo didn't answer. "I mean, come on. The last time we see the victim on camera, she's going straight to his room. And his was the only semen the medical examiner found."

Leo didn't respond. He just closed his notebook and pushed back from the table. "Come on, Veronica. I'll walk you out to your car."

She exhaled loudly, and nodded.

As soon as they were on the elevator, he turned to face her. "Straight up, Veronica—do you buy his story that's she's a prostitute? Or have you maybe known that she was one all along and kept it under your hat for some reason?"

He didn't sound angry so much as confused.

She shook her head exasperatedly. "If I'd thought so for even one second I'd have told you."

He rubbed the back of his neck and sighed. "But it's not like you to miss something like that."

"I didn't *miss* it. She hid it. *Well.* And we still don't know it for a fact. I'll be damned if I'm going to blow up this whole investigation just because Rape Suspect Number Ten Billion plays the 'it was consensual' card." Veronica paused as the elevator doors opened. She and Leo stepped off and walked through the lobby in silence, before pushing through the glass double doors onto a sunlit plaza beyond.

Veronica stopped to pull a pair of sunshades out of her handbag, then stared into the distance for a long moment. "Leo," she finally said, "We're not half as smart as people give us credit for."

"You're describing a problem with which I'm totally unfamiliar," Leo said, bewildered.

"Detectives in general, I mean. Conan Doyle deluded a century of readers into thinking we're all deductive geniuses."

Leo laughed. "You mean like: 'It's elementary, my dear Watson. The bird poop on this hat came from a species of lark that only exists in one village in Romania, so that's where our killer is from.'"

"Yeah. But that's not how it usually works, right?" said Veronica. "Often as not, it's some feeling or intuition we start with. And we'll charge straight ahead with that belief, even when the evidence for it seems . . . less than crystal clear. Look, we need to check out Bellamy's call girl story because it changes a lot of things. But true or not, a bottle of the finest Chianti says he's guilty."

"I believe you." He rubbed the back of his neck and sighed. "But this case is pretty much over now. You know that, right?"

She stopped in her tracks. "What do you mean, over?"

"Veronica, there's no prosecutor in the country who'd take this to trial. And if they did, the defense would just turn the whole thing into a bad joke."

"I'm not laughing," she snapped.

"Neither am I, okay?" For the first time a defensive note crept into his voice. "But I can't bring him in if the Neptune DA doesn't want to prosecute. You understand what I'm saying?"

Chastened, she looked away. "I'm sorry, Leo." The sun was starting to sink below the tree line. A cool breeze moved in off the ocean, but the day's heat still radiated from the ground. They started walking again, across the parking lot toward her car. "But I'm not giving up. There's got to be some way to get this guy."

"Yeah. Well, my CO's gonna have me on a short leash for a little while because of this, so I'm not going to be much help." He watched her for a moment, his face serious. "But Veronica, if there's something I can do, you let me know. Promise?"

She hugged him, a quick impulsive squeeze, and moved away by the time he realized what was happening.

"You're a prince," she said. She rummaged for her car keys in her purse, and then, finding them, opened her door. Before climbing in, she paused. "I'll call you soon, okay? I owe you big."

He lifted his hand in farewell as she backed out of the parking spot. As soon as she pulled out onto the road, she hit the gas pedal, hard.

It was forty minutes to Neptune, and she had a lot of questions that needed answering.

CHAPTER TWENTY-EIGHT

Grace Manning lived in a small apartment complex on a street lined with pawn shops, grimy convenience stores, and check-cashing operations. There was no landscaping to speak of, just cracked pavement littered with cigarette butts and broken glass. The cars in the parking lot were all at least ten years old, some on blocks. An overflowing Dumpster at one end of the property hummed with flies.

Veronica climbed the steps and knocked sharply at the door of unit 205. She stared baldly at the peephole and waited. Something moved behind the door. Then there was a silence that seemed to stretch on for minutes at a time. Finally, the door opened.

Grace Manning stood in the doorway in slouchy jeans and an OREGON SHAKESPEARE FESTIVAL T-shirt. Her hair was tied back with a red bandanna. She looked like a normal college girl.

"We need to talk," Veronica said.

The girl's expression was hard to read. She opened the door a little wider and gestured wordlessly for Veronica to enter.

It was like an oven in the little apartment, the air hot and motionless. The walls were paste-gray and cracked. A single north-facing window looked out on the parking lot, so dirty almost no light came through it. A twin-sized mattress lay directly on the floor. Next to that was a wooden cable spool with a laptop resting on top, Haim playing softly from the speakers. Clothes hung along a plain metal pipe on the ceiling, probably two dozen outfits total. No evening gowns, no silk, no sequins. Just the cotton and denim of an undergrad's wardrobe. A stained mini fridge and an ancient stove stood in the kitchenette.

Grace had obviously made an effort to give the place a Bohemian, theater-dressing-room feel. A pink jacquard bedspread was draped over the mattress. Playbills, signed by fellow cast members, lined the walls: *The Cherry Orchard*, *The Birthday Party*, *Endgame*, *Les Liaisons Dangereuses*. A bouquet of dried roses sat in a wine bottle on the windowsill. But the flourishes of color were swallowed by the shadows, and the whole effect was somehow sadder than if she hadn't tried at all.

Veronica wasn't sure what she'd been expecting, but this dismal efficiency didn't look like the kind of place a high-end escort would live in. The squalor somehow made what she was about to say seem like a slap in the face.

"There's not really anywhere to sit," Grace said. "Sorry."

"That's all right. We can stand." Veronica crossed her arms over her chest. "We found a DNA match for your attacker."

Grace's face drained of color, her eyes wide with naked panic.

Suddenly, Veronica had a visceral, gut-deep sense of déjà vu. It was like she was there again: That night, a little over ten years ago, when she and Duncan Kane had broken into the Manning house. That moment when she opened the hidden panel in the closet and saw the scared child, huddled in the cobwebs. *I don't wanna be tested*, she'd said. *Daddy said I'm not ready.*

The look on Grace's face now called up that little girl so vividly Veronica felt unsteady. In Neptune, the past was always grabbing at your ankles, trying to pull you back.

"Who?" The word was a hoarse whisper, barely audible.

"A guy named Mitch Bellamy, from San Diego." Veronica squared her shoulders. "But he had a really strange story, Grace."

The girl turned away abruptly.

"He said you were a call girl. That he'd hired you. But, if that were true, that'd be a pretty significant omission from *your* story."

Grace snapped back to face Veronica. "So because I'm a whore that means I can't be raped?" She spat the words, her panic breaking suddenly into fury.

Veronica, startled by the suddenness of Grace's admission, held up both her hands.

"That's not what I'm saying. Look, let's sit down, okay?" She knelt on the dust-colored carpet.

Grace stood still, her breath shuddering, her fingers clenched in her hair. Then, after a moment, she sank down onto the mattress, covering her face with her hands.

"I'm sure you must be shocked," she mumbled, her voice muffled. "Everyone expected this from Lizzie. From me, not so much."

Lizzie Manning had been two years behind Veronica in high school, peroxide blonde and notorious. Lizzie hadn't exactly passed the Purity Test. But Veronica hadn't known her well enough to judge.

Grace pulled her hands away from her face, staring down at her knees.

"All I wanted was to earn my tuition." Her voice was almost a whisper, directed at the carpet. "I've wanted to go to Hearst since I was fourteen years old. I saw their production of *Saint Joan* with my English class, and . . . I'd never seen anything like it before. I'd done a few children's theater plays, but this was real. It was *art*, not just a chance for some coddled little divas to get in the spotlight and help Mommy and Daddy impress the local culturati. So when I got older and started looking around at schools, I was determined to go to Hearst. Not that it mattered which program I preferred. I couldn't have afforded any of the ones I was looking at."

Veronica nodded. "And I guess it's not surprising your parents didn't step up. Beckett probably didn't strike them as a very effective witness for Christ."

Grace laughed bitterly. "You saw what they were like when I was eight. After Meg died they got worse. Before that Mom had held out against some of the crazier shit Dad wanted to do. I mean, at least she wouldn't let him withhold food or beat us bloody. But after, she was worse than Dad was in some ways. I guess she figured if they'd had more control over us she never would have lost Meg and Faith.

"I left the day I turned eighteen. I wasn't even done with my senior year, but I moved out and slept in my best friend's guest room for a few months. By that time I don't think they'd have paid for college anyway. They were going on and on about how it was my duty to marry a good and godly man and start churning out a Quiverfull."

"A Quiverfull?"

She rolled her eyes. "It's a thing in ultra-Christian circles. You know: *'Lo, children are an heritage of the Lord, and the fruit of the womb is his reward. As arrows are in the hand of a mighty man; so are children of the youth. Happy is the man that hath his quiver full of them.'"* She hugged her knees to her chest. "The point is, a woman's job is not just to have kids but to bust 'em out like a popcorn machine. And you don't need a degree for that.

"Anyway, I . . . I went ahead and applied to Hearst, even though I knew by then I couldn't afford to go. I thought if I got in, I could figure out the money part later. Well, I got in. But I couldn't get any financial aid, because they took one look at how much money my dad makes and determined I was ineligible. I wrote a bunch of letters trying to explain that I didn't have a relationship with my parents anymore, but it didn't do any good."

"Okay," Veronica said, her voice as neutral as she could keep it. "But, Grace. I don't want to sound judgmental . . ."

"Why didn't I take out loans, or get a job in the library?" Grace finished the obvious thought. "I want to be an actress, Veronica. A *stage* actress. A *classical* stage actress. When do you think I'll be making enough to pay those loans back?" She shook her head. "I knew what I wanted, and I decided to do what I had to do in order to get it."

Veronica nodded. That, at least, was something she understood.

"So, yeah. I started working. I did some research first—there are actually a ton of blogs out there written by call girls. I e-mailed a few for advice and spent the last of my money on a designer dress. I set up a website, and the responses started pouring in." She grabbed a pillow from her mattress, fidgeting with the tassel. "It was easy as that. I earned enough for a whole semester in a month and a half. And the truth is, until that night, it wasn't even that bad." She shrugged lopsidedly. "Most of my clients were actually . . . not awful. I'm not trying to candy-coat it or anything, but it was so much better than living with my parents. It was better than marrying some Bible-pounding asshole and letting him run his hands all over me just because it was God's will. I specialized in role-play, did a lot of 'Girlfriend Experience.' Which meant that a big part of my job was eating oysters and drinking wine."

Veronica didn't say anything. She just watched Grace, and waited.

"I'm telling you this so you'll understand that there's a big fucking difference between my job, and what happened to me that night." Grace's eyes flashed. "Because I didn't ask for that to happen to me."

"I never said you did," Veronica said. "I didn't come here to throw anything in your face. I came to get some answers. But you knew all along Miguel Ramirez didn't rape you. So why did you accuse him?"

A pale pink flush rose across Grace's nose. She took a deep breath.

"I was telling the truth when I told the cops I didn't remember the attack. I didn't. I still don't. I remember walking into the stairwell, and then—nothing. I saw the laundry guy's picture on the front page of that mug shot tabloid they leave at all the convenience stores. It said he'd been deported, that he'd been working at the Neptune Grand. So I thought: Well, this could be my chance to get enough money to finish school. They're not going to send Navy SEALs into Mexico to bring him back. And once he's been tipped off that he's a felony suspect, he's not coming back on his own."

Grace, suddenly looking disconsolate, gestured around

her barren little room. "God, you must think I'm total scum. But look, what you see here is all I've got left. I can't work anymore. I mean, I can't even go on a real date without having a panic attack. I sold my dresses, all the designer crap, all the jewelry. It's mostly gone to medical bills. And tuition is due in three weeks."

"So you accused an innocent man of rape?" Veronica tried to keep the edge out of her tone, but it was difficult.

"Like I said, he was already in Mexico. But if they did somehow manage to track him down for a swab he'd be exonerated by the DNA evidence. I could just say I'd been wrong, that I was confused." Her voice had a pleading note to it. "All I wanted was the money. I didn't want anyone to get in trouble."

Veronica felt her temper rising again. She bit it back, fighting for control. "You obstructed the investigation. You sent the cops—and me—off on a wild-goose chase."

A tear dropped loose from Grace's eye, but she smeared it away, almost angrily. "So my attacker would be in jail now if I'd just told the truth? Yeah, right. You know what the cops do if you report a rape when you've been working? They lock you up for solicitation. They have a big laugh about it. Then they fine you and they send you home. I know other girls who've been through it, Veronica, and not a single one of them has gotten a conviction. There's even an online forum where girls post about bad johns, to warn each other. Because they all know the cops won't protect them." She gave Veronica a hard look. "Tell me the truth: Did the cops seem ready to charge the guy you found with rape?"

Veronica didn't answer right away. She thought about

what Leo had told her—that the district attorney wouldn't touch it, that his captain would rein him in. All because the victim was a prostitute. Would it have been different if Grace had told the truth from the start? Instinct—and the memory of Don Lamb laughing Veronica out of his office twelve years earlier—told her no.

"I don't blame you for not trusting the cops. Especially not in Neptune. And I know you don't exactly have good reason to trust me. But I *really* want to get this guy," Veronica said. "And to do that, I need your help. I need to know details about your work, and what you remember from that night. But more than anything else, I need to know that what you're telling me is true."

Grace finally looked up. Her lip trembled, but when she spoke her voice was steady.

"Yeah. Okay. I'll help."

Grace went into the bathroom to wash her face. Then she poured two glasses of water from a Brita—Veronica noted that it was the only thing in the fridge besides three single-serve tubs of yogurt. She handed a glass to Veronica and sat back down on the edge of the mattress.

"I don't remember what time I got the call. It was kind of last-minute, I know that—sometime early Thursday night. We talked for about twenty minutes. He said his name was Dan."

Veronica nodded. That matched Bellamy's story. "What'd you talk about?"

"My rates, his preferences."

"Preferences?"

"I did a lot of role-play," Grace explained. "Sometimes it was just sort of banal. Naughty nurse, naughty schoolteacher, naughty maid. But some guys are really specific. You know, like, he's the president and I'm a Russian spy trying to get the nuclear codes out of him. Or I've got hypothermia in the mountains of Nepal and he's the strapping mountain guide who'll do whatever it takes to warm me up and save me. I had a Princess Leia wig I used for two different clients. One wanted to be Han Solo. The other wanted to be Jabba the Hutt."

Veronica closed her eyes for a moment. "Well, that's an image I'll never be free of."

Grace shrugged. "You wanted details. Anyway, I always did a pre-appointment screening on the phone so I knew explicitly what the client was asking for beforehand. That way I could turn down anyone asking for something I didn't do, without making it awkward for them or scary for me. This guy, Dan—or Mitch, I guess—he didn't want anything that crazy. He just wanted me to be submissive. Didn't want me to meet his eyes or talk above a whisper. But I've had a few guys ask for that, and none of them gave me any problems, so it didn't set off an alarm bell."

"Was rough sex ever part of the package?" Veronica asked.

Grace shook her head. "I had one regular customer who I let spank me. We had enough of a relationship that I knew I could trust him. But that was it. I didn't do any BDSM stuff. If that's what they asked for I'd refer them to a specialist."

"So Bellamy didn't ask for anything violent? No hitting, slapping, anything like that?"

"Not on the phone. He said he just wanted me to play meek and mild."

Veronica shifted her weight on the carpet. "Okay. What

do you remember about the session itself? Could you identify Bellamy if you saw him?"

Grace exhaled loudly. "I really don't remember anything after the bar. I wasn't lying about that. I remember going into the stairwell and starting down the stairs. And somewhere in there my memory just kind of . . . fades out. I must have at least gotten to the guy's room, but I don't remember it. I remember this, like, bodily sensation of being knocked down. And I remember something clenching around my throat. But they're really disjointed memories—I don't remember it as part of a chain of events." She took a sip of water. Veronica could tell how hard she was fighting to remain steady and matter-of-fact. "Then there's nothing else until I woke up in the hospital, three days later."

Veronica nodded. It had been the same for Keith after his accident. He remembered talking to Jerry Sacks in the car outside his house, but he'd never been able to recall the crash itself, or the first days afterward. *Brain trauma's a bitch.*

Grace continued. "I just kind of panicked when I woke up and realized the cops were asking questions." She looked down. "If I hadn't been injured so badly, I might not have even reported it. But I didn't really get a choice in the matter; my body was a crime scene. The docs had the police in there before I even woke up. I knew they'd be looking at the surveillance footage, talking to the staff, and they'd know I was around the Grand all the time. All I could think to do was make out like I had some high-powered sugar daddy I wouldn't name. I figured that'd sound better than telling them I was an escort." She sighed and looked toward the single window. The yellow light in the parking lot flooded through the pane. "I'm sorry. For all of it. For lying. For not being able to remember more. I mean, I know it sounds strange. Who'd want to remember something like this? But I really, really wish I could. Because not knowing what happened is so much worse."

Veronica hesitated for a moment. "I know. Trust me, I know."

Grace's pale blue eyes widened. For a moment neither of them spoke. Then Grace leaned forward and, surprisingly, grabbed Veronica's hand.

"That's the whole truth. I promise. And I'll do anything I can to help you."

CHAPTER TWENTY-NINE

Veronica went straight from Grace's apartment to Mac's building and pulled out her phone before starting up the stairs. It was almost eight. Logan would be home, maybe fixing dinner, or walking Pony. She jotted him a quick text.

> Working late tonight—don't wait up.
> xoxo

Then she took the stairs two at a time up to Mac's apartment. Mac opened the door before she even had a chance to knock.

"What happened?" Mac asked. "Did he confess?"

Veronica had called her on the way, saying only that she needed her help. Now she stepped into the apartment without preamble and asked, "How hard is it to retrieve a website once its admin has taken it down?"

Mac shut the door. "Well, most stuff on the Internet gets cached. It's pretty easy to find. If you really want to make a website go away there are ways to do that, but most people don't bother. It's kind of a headache."

Veronica threw her jacket on one end of the oversized sofa. The rugs and curtains had bright, geometric prints, and the air smelled like chai from the teashop downstairs.

"I need to find a webpage for someone named Chloé Huston." She pulled her laptop from her bag and handed it to Mac. "It would have been taken down in late March or early April."

"Sure," Mac said, her brow furrowed. "What's this all about?"

"Best to just show you, I think. And uh, be warned— there's probably going to be some adult content on there."

Mac blinked, but didn't comment. She sat down on the sofa, opened the laptop, and started to type.

Working late with Mac always felt vaguely collegiate. They ordered pizza—half olive oil and eggplant for Mac, half cheese and pepperoni for Veronica. She hadn't eaten since before San Diego, and was surprised at the surge of energy she got from righting her blood sugar. Before long she was pacing the living room, trying to determine what their next step should be, while Mac worked steadily at her computer.

It was an hour and a half before she found anything.

"Respect to the girl. She covered her tracks pretty well," Mac said, exhaling loudly. "But I've got the site up if you want to take a look."

Veronica sat next to her. On the screen, a black-and-white photo depicted a young woman sitting demurely on an outdoor terrace in a lace dress with a plunging neckline. Her face was turned away from the camera to gaze off over the city, but Veronica recognized Grace easily enough. There was a studied elegance in her posture.

Cursive script across the top of the page read *Chloé Huston*. Beneath that, in smaller font: *Your fantasy come true*.

"'Welcome to my world, gentlemen. I'm ready to share it with you,'" Mac read out loud. "'Refined, sophisticated . . . looking to share romance and adventure with generous, discerning men . . . enjoys intelligent conversation about art, music, philosophy, and *spirituality*'?" She looked up at Veronica. "What are we looking at?"

"Grace Manning's alter-ego," she said. "Or, rather, her former alter-ego."

"She's a hooker?" Mac gasped.

Veronica took the laptop from Mac and kept reading.

```
I'm a cosmopolitan but approachable
paramour who can provide a natural,
satisfying girlfriend experience, whether
we choose to go out or stay in. I also
specialize in different kinds of role-
play. I can make your dreams come to life.
Contact me for details.
```

"Nope," Veronica said. "She was a high-end escort. Trust me. There's a difference."

A gallery section had a collection of photos showing Grace, always looking away from the camera or with her honey-blonde hair obscuring her face, in a variety of provocative positions. Standing in front of a window in a corset and knee-high stockings; lounging chest-down on the deck of a sailboat wearing nothing but a bikini bottom. One showed her from the chin down, sprawled in a tangle of sheets.

The pictures were more pin-up than porn, and shot beautifully. But looking at them turned the pizza in her stomach into a leaden lump. *Because you've seen the "after" pictures. Because you've seen her when someone took away all this care and control and turned her into a victim.*

Veronica clicked on the section of the website marked "Donation" and scrolled through the pricing list. "Chloé

Huston" charged $500 for an hour-long "interlude." A two-hour "cocktail date" was $800; a four-hour dinner was $1,500. *Other fees may apply.* Mac's eyes went suddenly wide. "So all that time we spent trying to find her 'boyfriend' . . ."

Veronica put a hand on Mac's arm. "I'm sorry, Mac. I guess Charles was one of her regulars."

"Jesus," Mac said. She took the laptop back from her and stared at the website. A mix of shock and disgust registered on her face as she scrolled through the information. "Oh, great. She likes fine dining and walks on the beach. I'm sure they have that in common."

Veronica cleared her throat. "Mac, I hate to intrude on this reverie, but have you perchance checked out a vibrant little online salon called The Erotic Critique?

"The Erotic . . . ?"

"Critique," Veronica said, stressing the *eek* to help Mac with the spelling. "It's like Yelp—but for lonely, horny fellas."

When Mac gave her an incredulous stare, she shrugged. "Hey, hardboiled, remember? I'm on personal terms with the seedy underbelly."

Mac typed *The Erotic Critique* into her search bar. The site launched, and a helpful intro explained the service. Customers could type in their parameters to find the perfect girl, or could simply browse through names, clicking on profiles to see descriptions and reviews. Veronica had once used it to try to help a client track down a prostitute who'd sold the GFE role a little too well.

A list of names filled the screen. Savannah Duvall. Miko Minami. Taylor Moran. Bella Diaz. Chloé Huston. "Seriously, how did anyone pay for casual sex before the Internet?" Mac murmured.

Veronica pointed at the screen. "There—could you click on Chloé Huston's profile?"

Mac did. Instantly Grace's vital stats popped up: eye color, hair color, height, and weight, along with measurements (34-24-34), tattoos (none), piercings (navel), and "breast description" (natural B cup). Below that was a comprehensive list of sex acts with bright green check marks indicating which ones were offered.

And below that were the reviews. Chloé Huston had forty-three reviews, all from guys with names like lovebandit and continental_gentleman.

```
Full, firm tits, fit bod, made me feel
comfortable and at ease right away.

Has that something special u cant put ur
fingers on (but I did!!!)

I have always had a teacher/schoolgirl
fantasy and Chloé was awesome about making
it "cum" true.
```

"These sounds like dirty Yelp reviews," Mac said.

"Yeah. Raunchy lies and half-truths, a soupçon of single-entrendre humor, and a ton of dick-shaking—literally and figuratively. Ladies and gents, your American sex industry." Veronica stood up and started pacing again. "So, did anyone give her a bad review? Anything two stars or lower?"

"A few." Mac looked down at the screen. "One guy said she was 'cold and aloof.' He gave her two stars. One said some things I don't plan to read out loud, but the gist is 'unrefined technique.' One said she didn't follow instructions. The rest are just toxic gibberish."

Veronica stopped in front of a framed movie poster for *Nights of Cabiria* that showed a doe-eyed Giulietta Masina smoking a cigarette. Something in Masina's brittle, hopeful face made her think of Grace.

"This wasn't his first time."

Mac looked up. "What?"

Veronica turned away from the poster. The thought had been nagging at her since the beginning. "If I'm right, and Bellamy was the attacker, this wasn't his first time. Think about how calm he looks in the surveillance footage—he's standing right in front of a hotel clerk with a girl in his bag, getting the team checked out. A security guard is right there. A million ways he could get caught and he's risking all of them. He's forty-one years old. I seriously doubt that he just woke up one day after a life of respectful behavior and decided to start raping and brutalizing women. He's been escalating to this. And so far he's getting away with it."

Mac looked queasy.

"If we could find other victims we could prove a pattern. We could show that he's a repeat offender. It'd be harder for a jury to dismiss Grace Manning's injuries. But the thing is: How do we do that if no one's reporting?" Veronica said, now making her way toward the kitchen.

"The, uh, gentle hippie folk in the tea shop downstairs always know when you've come over to talk about a case," Mac said, lowering her voice and gesturing at the floorboards beneath them. Veronica smiled and stopped pacing. She walked back to the sofa and sat down next to Mac. The Erotic Critique was still up on the screen.

"Anyway, they list the reviews chronologically, right?" Veronica peered over Mac's shoulder at the computer. "Can you scroll down to the last few? Query the last date anyone reviewed her?"

Mac clicked a button labeled Search by Date and a dialogue immediately popped up: WELCOME BACK, VERONICA! WE SEE IT'S BEEN 9 YEARS, 8 MONTHS SINCE YOU ACCESSED THIS PREMIUM FEATURE. FOR DEEPER, MORE INTENSE SATISFACTION, CLICK HERE TO UPDATE YOUR PAYMENT AND ADDRESS INFORMATION.

Veronica groaned and Mac exploded in peals of laughter. Rolling her eyes, Veronica handed over her Visa card. A couple of minutes later, Mac was in the date-specific review, angling the screen toward her so she could see more clearly. "Looks like the last one is dated March twenty-eighth."

Veronica stared at the screen. There were five reviews posted after the night of the attack.

Two were five-starred, one had three stars, and two had one.

```
professorXXX: 3 stars/5. Refused to
come to my house even after I offered
her extra—she made me take out a room
in the most expensive hotel in town. I
guess because she's cute she's gotten away
with calling the shots before. Aside from
that, I can't complain too much—she worked
pretty hard to placate me and at least
at the Grand I didn't have to clean up
afterward.
```

mr _ kiss _ and _ tell: 1 star/5. Gave me a lot of attitude and wouldn't follow through on my requests.

top _ dog: 5 stars/5. As amazing as advertised. Gorgeous girl, sophisticated and fun. After a few preliminary dates I finally persuaded sweet Chloé to go with me to the Sundance Festival in Park City. She fit right in and could have been a starlet herself—people kept staring at her, trying to place her. At one point I caught James Franco flirting with her!!

playhard69: 1 star/5. TIME WASTER!!!! Made an appointment with her THREE MONTHS in advance and she STOOD ME UP. No call, no email. I guess this WHORE is too good for my money?

master _ P: 5 stars/5. ChloéChloéChloéChloéChloé. That is what you'll be saying over and over again as she works her magic.

Her eyes narrowed. Would the attacker be ballsy enough to review a girl he'd left for dead? She thought again of Mitch Bellamy, standing at that front desk, laughing with the receptionist. Yes. If he was the one who did it, he'd think it was his right. He'd think, since he'd gotten away with it, that the universe was clearly entitling him to use and throw away whomever he wanted.

"ProfessorXXX is obviously a local," she said softly. "He wanted Grace to come to his house. And Sundance is in January, so I'm thinking top_dog was just late in posting his review. Which leaves playhard69, master_P, and mr_kiss_and_tell." She leaned forward, resting her elbows on her knees. "Open up their profiles for me, will you?"

Mac clicked on playhard69. He hadn't included any personal information—no surprise there—but all of his reviews sprang up on the screen. In addition to Grace, he'd apparently sampled the wares of Larissa Grey, Angelica Starr, and Alexis van Dyne, all of whom worked in Neptune.

It gave Veronica an idea.

"We need to go through and flag any users who've reviewed women in multiple cities, and any users who've reviewed lots of women in San Diego."

Mac stared up at her. "You think Bellamy was crazy enough . . . ?"

"I don't know. Might be a long shot. It's not like every guy who hires an escort is going to leap right out of the sack and write a review, right? But if Bellamy's a serial offender, he's hired escorts before." She leaned toward Mac. "Maybe it doesn't matter that no one's reporting him. Maybe he's incriminating himself in his reviews."

They combed through the reviews. Fourteen of Grace's clients had supped from the erotic smorgasbord in multiple cities. Of them, only one of them had posted a review after the attack.

mr_kiss_and_tell.

The reviewer had patronized more than thirty high-end escorts. It was hard to pinpoint the exact dates; he could have waited weeks between when he saw a given girl and when he posted a review. But the majority of the girls worked out of cities in the western half of the United States: Boise, Albuquerque, Las Vegas, Salt Lake City, Seattle, L.A. All university towns with Division I teams—places a basketball coach would have a reason to visit.

"He has a type, that's for sure," she said, looking over the list. The girls were all "small," "slender," "petite." They were all very young, at least from what Mac and Veronica could see—most of their faces were obscured on their websites. All were high-end. And they all specialized in role-play.

```
    I have a full closet of fun costumes I
just can't wait to wear for you.

    Pretending to be someone I'm not really
turns me on!

    I'm eager to be the very girl you want.
```

Mac stared at a picture of a lithe brunette in a low-cut gown, a flute of champagne in one hand. "I just don't get how anyone could do it. Like, even if danger weren't an issue, there is no way I could let some rando get intimate with my lady parts."

Veronica didn't answer. It wasn't that Veronica could suddenly imagine going into the business herself, but Grace didn't feel foreign to her at all. Grace felt like someone who, in other circumstances, she might have been friends with.

Mr. Kiss and Tell's rankings were all across the board. He

gave most girls three or four stars out of five, critiquing their performances like a cross between Hugh Hefner and Simon Cowell. *Yvette had perfect breasts, full lips, and a toned body, but the sounds she made were distracting and ridiculous.* Or: *Delia was very sweet and obedient but I didn't care for her clothes. Why does everyone assume that just because I want a submissive that means I want leather and straps? That said, she had a great bedside manner.* A few girls, like Grace, had one star. Those reviews were even more critical: Tonya Vahn from L.A. *acted like a stuck-up bitch. Looked nothing like her picture.* One, a Nikki Valentine from Albuquerque wasn't properly groomed: *I could see her roots, her nails weren't done, she showed up in the trashiest dress I've ever seen. For $400 an hour I expect a princess, not a tramp.*

"What a charmer," Mac muttered.

"There's a reason he's paying for it," Veronica said. "Tomorrow we need to start searching the criminal databases in all of these cities. We'll look for open assault cases dating in the past four years and see if any of them match up. But I'm pretty sure Grace is right—if any of these women were attacked, most of them won't have reported it."

"So what are we going to do?"

"Can I see your computer for a minute?"

Mac handed over the laptop. Veronica opened up one of her private e-mail accounts and sat, thinking for a few minutes. Then she started to type.

```
    I'm writing in the hopes that you can
help me. I know you have a vested interest
in keeping your clients confidential, but
I'm currently investigating the rape of a
```

```
working girl here in southern California
and I think the man may have done it
before. I'm trying to establish a pattern of
abuse in the hopes that we can find a way
to stop him. I've enclosed a photo of the
suspect. If there's anything you remember
about him, please, call or e-mail.
```

It was a shot in the dark. If these women hadn't reported an abusive john to the cops, there was no reason for them to do so for a perfect stranger. But Grace had mentioned that there were forums where sex workers could warn each other about "bad dates." These women, at least some of them, looked out for one another. Veronica had to hope that the news that one of their own had been raped might move at least a few of them to reply.

Veronica and Mac sent the message to every girl Mr. Kiss and Tell had reviewed. A few of them had taken their websites down, apparently out of the business. A few of the e-mails bounced back immediately, the addresses no longer valid. But Veronica pictured the message winging its way across the country, popping up with little red *Urgent* flags in dozens of inboxes. Maybe landing in the right inbox. Maybe finding the woman who could help make their case against Mitch Bellamy.

CHAPTER THIRTY

"They're too long, man." Eli Navarro stood in front of the mirror outside the changing room, looking at his reflection. The slacks he'd tried on pooled at his feet. "You'd have to be seven feet tall for all this leg."

Keith smiled. They were in Brautigan's, a large department store in the Neptune Mall, trying to expand Eli's courtroom ensemble options. Light piano music tinkled from the speakers, and an obsequious sales clerk hovered near the doorway.

"They do that so you can get them sized. Turn around." Eli did. Keith nodded. "See, they fit everywhere else. We'll take them to a tailor, have them hemmed right up."

Eli shook his head slightly. "It's a lotta money to spend on pants that don't fit. And then you gotta spend more to get 'em fixed?"

"Trust me on this, Eli. It makes a difference." Keith crossed his arms over his chest and leaned back against a wood-paneled pillar. "When you have three million bucks you won't even remember what it was like to wear off-the-rack."

Eli smiled in spite of himself. "You're counting chickens, and they ain't hatched yet, Sheriff."

Weevil was the only person who still called Keith by his former title. It was strangely endearing. Keith had known the kid a long time, had watched him grow from a petty criminal to the head of the PCH Biker Gang. Hell, half the time Keith had been the one to arrest him. When he'd watched Eli pull his life together, it'd made him strangely proud. He'd been pulling for the guy then, and he still was today.

"Well, I happen to think we've got a good chance at making you a rich man."

Keith had managed a breakthrough in his search for witnesses. After weeks of pounding on doors, he'd found three more people willing to testify that evidence planted by Deputy Harlon had led to their wrongful convictions. From where he stood, the case against the department looked strong.

"It's not just gonna be fancy pants and new TVs and diamond studs, Sheriff," Eli said, padding back into the changing room and talking over the door. "I'm getting a house for Jade and Valentina. Even if they don't want me back I'm buying them a place. And I'm gonna send Valentina to one of them Mussolini schools, you know? Where they learn by doing crafts and playing games and stuff?"

"I think you mean Montessori."

"Yeah, that's the one." The door swung open, and Eli was back in his scuffed jeans and hoodie. "And I'm gonna invest. Find some way for my money to make money, you know?"

"But there's going be a *little* flash, right?" Keith leaned in conspiratorially. "I mean, you'll be able to afford one or two bad decisions."

Eli broke into a grin. "I have to admit I like the idea of gettin' a Segway, if only to see the looks on my PCH boys' faces when I roll up on it. Either that or an Xbox One. I've been wanting to get my hands on one of them since the new *Call of Duty* came out."

Keith handed him an armful of hangers. Pants, jackets, button-down shirts, and ties bulged from his arms. "Now let's pay for this and head to Ben & Jerry's. My treat—just don't tell Veronica. I'm supposed to be on a diet."

Keith paid for the clothes on his credit card. If Eli won, he'd pay him back; if not, Keith would consider it a donation to the Don't Re-elect Dan Lamb campaign.

They went down the escalator and were heading toward the mall exit when Keith heard a familiar-sounding voice called out from behind him.

"Keith? Keith Mars?"

He froze, Eli stopping short next to him. They were between Women's Shoes and Cosmetics, and the air was heavy with mingled perfumes. Slowly, he turned to face Marcia Langdon.

She was dressed in jeans and a blazer and she'd recently cut her hair. It now was too short for the severe bun she'd sported in her military photos but the new bob had an almost equally stiff and uncompromising look. Still it was a bit more stylish, and style counted in Neptune. You couldn't expect someone like Petra Landros or Celeste Kane—or any of the other moneyed women currently teetering around them, trying on too-high heels—to vote for a woman who looked like a samurai Ayn Rand.

"Marcia. It's been a while." Keith held out his hand, and she gave it a single, brisk up-and-down pump. "I didn't know you'd moved back to town until your election news came out."

"I've been back since February, but I've been keeping a low profile." The smile she gave him wasn't quite warm, but it was pleasant. "I *thought* I was retiring. But you know how it is. Hard to sit back and watch your hometown become synonymous with 'miscarriage of justice.'"

He put his hands in his pockets and studied her face. It was almost eerie; for a moment he could see the teenaged Marcia he'd known, superimposed over this older woman's face. The eyes and nose were the same, even if the crow's feet and the frown lines hung heavily around her features.

He gestured to his left. "This is my friend Eli."

"Mr. Navarro." She held out her hand to him. "I've been following your case with great interest."

"Yeah?" He glanced quizzically at Keith, and then turned back to Marcia. "Well, for my part, I hope you're able to run that asshole out of office."

To Keith's surprise, she grinned.

"Honestly, it was your case that made me decide to run," she said. "For months now I've been seething over this guy, but I didn't think I could do anything about it. But when you started speaking out, I thought . . . well, hell, it's worth a try, right?"

"Yeah. Yeah, it is." Eli shifted his weight.

She turned her gaze back to Keith. "And you. You do great work, Keith. I've read your books."

"Oh, those." He smiled self-deprecatingly. "Just a little something to make sure the bills get paid. PI work's kind of boom or bust, so I turned to the even-keeled and predictable world of publishing to round things out."

She laughed. "Well, I'm a fan. Anyway, I don't want to keep you. It was nice seeing you, Keith, really."

"Good luck, Marcia."

They stood for a moment, watching her disappear back into the shoe section. Several women around Marcia seemed to notice and recognize her, and one or two walked up to her to shake her hand.

"She seems nice." Eli said, glancing at him again as they started toward Ben & Jerry's.

Keith didn't answer right away.

The Langdon family had lived three doors down from Keith's tiny efficiency. Mr. Langdon, like many dads in the neighborhood, had vanished to parts unknown. Mrs. Langdon worked in a garment factory on the edge of town. Keith, who at the time had been a twenty-one-year-old newly hired deputy in the Neptune Sheriff's Department, remembered her as a soft-spoken woman with an expression that always appeared either anxious or frightened.

Keith often sat on his front porch to escape his gloomy apartment and quickly struck up a friendship of sorts with Marcia, who would walk by on her way to a 7-Eleven on the corner. With only four years separating them in age, they had plenty to talk about: the Padres, teachers, how much they both hated ABBA.

She was a different breed of cat than he'd been in high school. Keith had been a swingman between the gearhead and art-geek cliques. He'd also played bass for a local rock band that, infelicitously, played Springsteen and Warren Zevon covers at the exact moment punk rock was breaking. She was an avid JROTC member, socially maladroit, and a teacher's pet. But Keith had always respected her scathing honesty and uncompromising intensity.

Then there was Tauntaun. Bobby "Tauntaun" Langdon was enormous, the kind of looming presence forged in iron for offensive line play. He was two years older than Marcia, and his steamroller blocking had powered a Neptune ground game that took the team all the way to State his senior year. Even beyond his status as a sports hero, he was a good dude, the type you could count on to break up a fight or to offer you a ride to a party.

Until graduation, anyway. Post-high school life didn't agree with Tauntaun. He drifted, lost in the real world. Keith had only ever heard rumors, but not long after that, Tauntaun apparently fell in with a crew of guys who sold dime bags at the Boardwalk and broke into vacation homes to steal the hi-fis.

The summer after Marcia's senior year, Keith was called as a backup when two other deputies arrived at the Langdon's little apartment with a search warrant. He was just pulling up to the curb when they came out with fifteen kilos of coke that had been stacked neatly in Tauntaun's bedroom closet. Marcia's brother told them he'd been storing it for someone else, but when he wouldn't—or couldn't—name names, he took the fall.

It'd been Marcia who'd called the sheriff on him. Marcia who found the drugs while hanging her brother's clean laundry in his closet. Marcia who'd been humiliated every time the cops showed up at the duplex to haul Tauntaun in again, for vandalism or public intoxication or breaking and entering. The night of Tauntaun's arrest, the sound of breaking furniture and shouting echoed from the Langdon apartment. Keith heard later that Mrs. Langdon had kicked her out, claimed she never wanted to see her again. Marcia already had an ROTC scholarship at UCLA. She left Neptune and she didn't come back. Not for thirty-three years.

And Tauntaun? He'd been stabbed to death in the showers at San Quentin a few short years later.

As Keith and Eli made their way down the long corridors of the mall, sidestepping moms with strollers and slow-moving teenagers, he remembered Tauntaun's terrified face as the cop shoved him in the car. The whole thing had never sat easy with Keith, though it was hard to say why. It emerged at that trial that Tauntaun's IQ had tested at eighty-seven, but even Tauntaun had to know that storing a dozen bricks of coke in his room was a bad idea. He'd committed a crime, and he'd gotten caught. That was how it worked.

But who turned in family?

Maybe there was more to it. Maybe Marcia had tried to reason with her brother before turning him in. Maybe she thought it was for his own good. Either way, she *was* honest. And, most important, not Dan Lamb.

Weevil turned a quizzical look toward him as they got in line in front of the Ben & Jerry's.

"You all right, man? You look kind of . . . I don't know. Spooked."

Keith took a deep breath and smiled.

"Yeah, I'm all right." He pulled out his wallet as the smiling scooper called them forward for their order. "Just thinking what a good sheriff she's going to be."

CHAPTER THIRTY-ONE

The San Diego sky was bright and cloudless as Veronica turned down a quiet residential street, well behind the white Nissan that carried Bellamy and his sixteen-year-old daughter to his ex's house.

Her decision to start tailing him had essentially been an impulse, born of frustration and restlessness. The e-mails she'd sent to the call girls had been met with silence, and the alerts Mac had put on his credit cards and bank accounts had turned up nothing.

And so had her surveillance. The three previous times she'd tailed him that week he went straight from his apartment to the PSU campus and back again, stopping only for take-out or fast food. Once home, he didn't go out again. It wasn't entirely surprising. Bellamy was all about measured control—until, of course, he snapped. After being questioned by the San Diego police, it followed that he'd play the part of model citizen.

That afternoon, though, he'd broken his routine and taken his daughter to a used car dealership, where they walked through a lot filled with ten-year-old Toyotas. Bellamy had obviously thought he was going to make her day with the promise of her own wheels. From a few rows away,

Veronica had heard snatches of his eager words: ". . . know it's not flashy, but it'll be all yours!"

The girl had hung back the whole time, looking sullen and dispirited. Veronica couldn't tell if it was her dad's company that had her in this state, his taste in cars, or something else entirely. His ex had sole custody of both kids, and Bellamy had to request visitation on a case-by-case basis. While there was no evidence of abuse or neglect in the official documents, the arrangement struck Veronica as unusual.

Maybe she threatened to go public with something if he didn't give her the kids. She could have known about the prostitutes—or maybe she'd been his first victim.

Now he pulled up at the foot of a sloping yard, dryscaped to survive the SoCal droughts. In addition to the kids, his ex had won the house in the divorce, a stucco two-story with flower boxes in the windows, a grand step up from his two-bedroom rental in a drab apartment complex called Sunset Cove, which offered neither a sunset view nor proximity to a cove. *Hard to feel too sorry for the guy,* she thought. *Somehow he still manages to scrounge up enough cash to hire $500-per-hour call girls.*

Veronica passed him without slowing, then pulled up to the side of the road several blocks ahead, taking out her phone and pretending to make a call. In her side mirror, she watched as the morose-looking girl got out of the car and started up the driveway without pausing to hug her father good-bye. Bellamy stood awkwardly next to the car until his daughter disappeared through the door. Then he got in his car and started the engine.

Veronica checked the time on her phone. It was almost five thirty; she and Logan had plans to go to her father's for dinner that night. If she was going to be on time, she had to leave right now. She sighed, and put the car into drive. Just then, Bellamy sped up the street toward her. In her rearview mirror, she saw his light blue eyes narrow.

For a split second, she was sure he recognized her. But a moment later he blew past her, turned on his blinker, and cut left, no doubt going back to his apartment, stopping for something tragically unhealthy in a foil wrapper on the way.

By the time Veronica pulled up in front of Keith's house, she could smell the burgers cooking.

She and Keith had instituted the Daddy-Daughter Dinners when she first moved out of his house a few months earlier—a weekly night set aside for them to hang out and catch up. Even working in the same building, there were weeks when they barely saw each other. Since Logan's return he'd been a sincerely welcomed, if mildly awkward, addition.

When she opened the gate to the backyard, Pony scampered up to her, barking shrilly. She knelt down and ruffled the puppy's fur. Keith stood at the grill, wearing a Hawaiian shirt and shorts; Logan clutched a sweating glass of water at the patio table. He cast her a relieved look as she approached.

"Perfect timing. You missed all the cattle-slaughtering, butchering, and grilling—just in time to eat," said her father.

"I know better than to come between men and their blood rituals. I figured the whole meat-on-fire thing was a chance for you two to bond." She took Logan's water out of his hand and took a sip.

They settled around the table, the light starting to dim

over the yard. Keith piled his plate with salad, then passed the bowl around to Logan. "Dig in, guys."

"Three months on shore, and I have to tell you, real food hasn't gotten old yet," said Logan. He picked up his burger and eyed it appreciatively before taking an enormous bite. Then he closed his eyes and sighed with deep satisfaction.

"Those monosyllabic reviews are the ones you like to hear," Keith said, grinding pepper over his salad.

Veronica's mind began to wander as Keith and Logan made small talk. She was trying to decide whether she should drive back out to San Diego the next day. It was Saturday, so there wouldn't be basketball practice. Maybe Bellamy would break routine in a real way. *Then again, maybe he'll just sit around his apartment watching ESPN all day, and I'll be stuck in a parking lot watching his car bake in the sun.*

Logan's phone buzzed. He glanced down at the screen and frowned.

"Hey, this is a buddy of mine on the *Truman.* You guys mind if I grab this?"

"Go ahead," Keith said, smiling. Logan stood up from the table and went in through the sliding glass doors, already pressing the phone to his ear. Pony followed at his heels.

Keith looked at Veronica. "You're somewhere else tonight. What's up?"

She shook her head. "Sorry, Dad. This case is making me crazy."

She briefly summarized what she'd done since Bellamy's test results had come back. He listened, raising his eyebrows when she described The Erotic Critique, nodding with approval when she told him how she and Mac had combed through the reviewers and pinpointed Mr. Kiss and Tell.

"But it's been three days and none of the women have responded to my e-mail," she finished. "I've got no word from potential vics, no witnesses, and no other leads." She stabbed at her salad with her fork. "I've been following him, but he's not doing anything wrong that I can see. I don't know what else to do."

Keith leaned back in his chair and looked up thoughtfully. "Well, have you tried talking to Lamb?"

For a moment the only sound was a car backfiring somewhere in the neighborhood. She stared at her father in disbelief.

"*Lamb?* What's he going to do?"

"Well, the crime happened in his jurisdiction." Keith gave her a humorless smile. "He can request a search warrant."

Veronica snorted. "Sure. I'll just call my BFF Dan Lamb and ask him to do me a solid."

"Lamb knows this election depends on how good his stats look. He'll want this collar."

She set down her fork, suddenly not hungry. But her dad was right; she didn't have a lot of options. And Lamb might just be desperate enough in the midst of this election to listen to her.

She looked up at the sound of the glass doors sliding opening. "There you are. That was a long . . ."

She came up short at the sight of Logan's bone-white face. The jagged line of a single tear ran down one cheek and he bit at his lip, clearly trying to control his emotions. Instinctively, Veronica stood up from her seat, her skin going suddenly clammy.

For a moment he stood there, his phone still clutched in his hand. Then his eyes met hers.

"There was an accident," he said. "On the *Truman*."

CHAPTER THIRTY-TWO

Lieutenant Vincent "Bilbo" Malubay, twenty-nine, naval aviator, husband, and father, had gotten his call sign because of the weekly Dungeons and Dragons game he ran in the USS *Truman's* rec room. Apparently no one in the Navy was actually called "Maverick" or "Iceman"—real call signs were embarrassing, ridiculous, or patently disgusting. "Stewbeef," "Big Bird," "Purge." Logan's was simply "Mouth" for reasons Veronica took to be obvious.

"Bilbo" had brought a sack full of twenty-sided dice and a Monster Manual from home, and every Sunday he and a handful of other proud geeks would colonize one of the long folding tables to play. Logan had even played once, half ironically. "I was a *bard*," he told Veronica, smirking a little. "I spent the whole time writing limericks about the other characters."

"I bet they loved that." She squeezed his hand.

It was the following morning, and they were in line at the Delta ticket counter at the airport, waiting to check Logan into his flight for the funeral. Harried travelers moved in every direction, tired parents ushering their children toward security, college kids in hoodies and backpacks heading back to their campuses for the fall semester. Logan wore service khaki and a garrison cap that increased his already imposing height by two inches. People kept glancing at him out of the corners of their eyes as they passed along the busy concourse.

Late Thursday night, Bilbo had been on the return leg of a six-hour mission in the Persian Gulf. It was all routine. He'd made dozens of these nighttime landings, sometimes in fiercely pitching seas with the flight deck tilting back and forth beneath him. But this time something went wrong. Bilbo apparently miscalculated the angle of descent as he brought his Hornet in to land. He'd flown in too low and hit the ramp instead. The plane was turned into a white-hot mass of shredded metal, skidding violently across the flight deck.

Logan rubbed his eyes and kept them closed for a moment, and Veronica noticed how tired he looked. He'd barely slept since he'd gotten the call. When he reopened his eyes, they flashed with sudden anger. "It's not fair. Bilbo made that landing hundreds of times. He could park his bug on a dime. And then one mistake. One mistake with no margin of error."

It could have been you. It could just as easily have been you. The thought had an edge of giddy hysteria to it, the sense of a disaster narrowly averted. But she couldn't tell him that. Couldn't tell him that, in the six months he'd been gone, she'd looked up every fighter-class aircraft accident listed on Wikipedia. That she'd read, over and over, about G-LOC and midair collisions and the various malfunctions that could lead to a jet slamming to earth at four hundred miles an hour. She didn't tell him that there was a perverse sense of gratitude mixed in with her sympathy and her sadness. If it was that easy for a skilled pilot to destroy himself in the blink of an eye, she'd enjoyed several months blissfully ignorant of how close she always was to losing Logan.

"I wish you'd be there tonight," he said suddenly, opening his eyes. The words cut through her reverie. She squeezed his hand again.

"I just need one more day."

"You can't just make some calls from the hotel?"

"Lamb's not taking my calls and I need him to get a search warrant for Bellamy's computer and phone. I'll be on the first flight to Seattle tomorrow morning, I promise."

He didn't answer. His fingers felt limp and heavy in her hand. She moved closer, putting her arms around his waist and trying to ignore the guilt tightening in her chest.

"Come on. You know you'll be out drinking with your squadron tonight anyway. I'll be there tomorrow in time for the funeral."

"Veronica."

She looked up at him. For a few seconds he stood in silence, his mouth parted slightly as if trying to find the right words.

Then: "They want me to go back."

She frowned. "Go back where?"

"Aboard ship. They're short now." He ran one hand over his face. "You know, with Bilbo gone, they're shorthanded."

"Yeah, but . . ." Several people in the line looked her way. She realized her voice had gone shrill. When she spoke again, she concentrated on keeping it low. "Logan, you're on shore duty. That's supposed to last another five months, at least."

"I know. But they need me, Veronica."

"Wait." Her heartbeat felt uneven. The world tilted around her, unsteady. "Are they telling you that you *have* to go back? Is it an order?"

"No, but . . ."

"So you could choose not to."

"Veronica . . ."

"You could choose not to." She realized several people were looking at her again. She didn't care. "If you wanted, you could tell them no."

He put his hands on her shoulders and turned her to face him. "Look, I haven't decided for sure what I'm going to do, okay? But you have to understand—this is what the job *is*. I trained for this, I worked my ass off for this. I *chose* this life. You of all people should understand that."

She opened her mouth to answer. Before she could, the ticket agent called them forward. Logan stepped up to the counter, his ID outstretched.

He checked his bag, and they walked in strained, painful silence to the security checkpoint. When they got to the line, he hesitated for a second, his eyes meeting hers in what she realized was their first moment of real intimacy all day. She pressed her hand against his cheek; he took it in his and gently kissed it, holding it against his face for a moment before letting go.

"We'll talk after the funeral, okay?"

Then Logan took Veronica in his arms and kissed her forehead, sweet and simple. She forced a smile. "Okay."

Veronica arrived at the courthouse at eleven, her emotions frayed. A young female deputy sat at the front desk, her hair braided tightly behind her head. She gave Veronica a sour look when she came through the door. Her name tag said GANDIN.

Veronica stepped up to the desk. "I need to speak with the sheriff, if he's available. It's about a criminal investigation."

One smooth, over-plucked eyebrow lifted skeptically.

"You can fill out a report and leave it with me," said the deputy. "Or I can give you the CrimeStoppers tip line."

Veronica feigned consideration. "The tip line, you say? Interesting. And who *answers* that tip line?"

"It routes to one of the deputies on duty." The woman leaned on the counter. "Then they fill out a report, and leave it with me."

Veronica smiled tightly, leaning on the counter as well so she and the deputy were facing off. "The thing is, Deputy Gandin, my information is time sensitive. I don't have the luxury to wait for whatever elaborate filing scheme you use to move paper around this place. So if you wouldn't mind . . ."

"Veronica?"

She looked up to see Deputy Norris Clayton. He'd come in behind her from the lobby, a powerfully built man with a long, serious face. His uniform was snug across his chest, clean and pressed with almost military precision.

Veronica smiled. It still startled her a little to see Norris— one-time bully and reformed trench coat mafia don—in uniform.

"Hey, Deputy. How's the crime-and-punishment gig treating you?"

"Another day, another donut." Norris glanced at the

woman behind the desk and only then seemed to sense the tension in the air. He looked back at Veronica. "What's up?"

"Oh, you know. Crime solving."

A lopsided grin snuck in at the corners of Norris's mouth. Spotting the look on Gandin's face, he pressed his lips together to hide it.

"Come on back. I'll see if I can help."

Veronica gave Gandin a cool nod as she followed Norris through the gate.

"Don't mind her," he said as soon as they were out of earshot. "Brittany's a good cop. But Lamb has her stuck at that desk all day every day, filing paperwork and making coffee. County policy says he has to hire a few women, but that doesn't mean he to let them in the field. She's in a pretty constant state of fuck you."

Veronica's smile faded. She glanced back at the woman at the desk with a grudging sense of sympathy. "I guess I can't blame her for that."

"Yeah. Anyway, what's going on?"

She looked toward Lamb's closed office door. "Well, I need a search warrant and unfortunately Lamb is the only one who can get it for me. What are the chances he'll see me?"

Norris snorted. "You? Right now I'd say slim to none. His ass has been glowing red since that lawsuit was announced."

"That's all Weevil," Veronica protested. "I certainly didn't feed him that 'take the bastard down' quote."

He grimaced. "It doesn't matter. He sees you in here, I guarantee you he'll decide it's time for an early lunch."

"Norris, this guy I'm looking into—he's bad. Really bad," she said soberly.

He looked at her for a long moment. Then he heaved a sigh. "I can't make any promises, Veronica. He's probably gonna get a long running start and boot you out the door."

"That's fine. You can make a show of dragging me out if you have to."

Norris gave her another long look, and then, as if he couldn't help himself, shook his head and grinned.

A few minutes later, she stood in the hallway behind Lamb's door as Norris knocked.

"Yeah?" Lamb's voice was muffled from inside the office.

"Hey, Sheriff, I just got a tip on a case I think you ought to look at." For a moment there wasn't a sound. Veronica met Norris's eyes, questioning, and he shrugged.

"The Neptune Grand assault? From back in March?" he tried.

"Come in."

Norris pushed the door open and stepped through. Veronica held back for a moment, listening.

"Sorry to interrupt you, Sheriff. I've got some lady here who says she knows who did it."

"What the hell are you waiting for, Clayton? Send her in."

Veronica stepped into the doorway, jazz hands held aloft. "Ta-da!"

Instantly, a dark flush moved through Lamb's cheeks, his lips twisting into the kind of sneer most people reserved for shit on their shoes.

"You," he said, his voice low and venomous. It was with great self-control that she refrained from answering, *"Me!"*

"Look, Lamb . . ."

"Get. Her. *Out,*" he spat, biting down on each word as though he was ripping the sentence apart with his teeth.

"Listen to me for just a second!" She put her hands on his desk. "I have information on an open case. A big one."

"Like I'm going to trust Little Miss Frivolous Lawsuit." He turned to Norris. "She's a snake in the grass, Clayton. Anything she gives us is going to be poison. Get her out of here, and if she comes back, slap her with a false-reporting charge."

Norris hesitated. "You want me to take her report before I throw her out, Sheriff?"

"Fine." Veronica took a step back from Norris, holding up her hands in surrender. "I'll go. But do yourself a favor and run a luminol test in room 3031 in the Neptune Grand. I guarantee you, you'll find blood evidence there."

She turned to the door and made to leave. Lamb's voice came in a short, sharp bark behind her.

"Wait."

She stopped in her tracks, forcing the cynical smile off her face. When she turned, Lamb was leaning forward on one forearm, listening.

"I thought we already had DNA evidence in that case," he said.

"We do. And it's a match with my suspect. But he's claiming the sex was consensual." She hesitated. *He'll find out sooner or later anyway.* "The victim's a call girl. The San Diego PD took the guy in for questioning, but his lawyer had him out in less than an hour. He's saying she was fine when she left his room, that someone else attacked her after he'd already had consensual sex with her. Everyone knows he's lying but San Diego's not looking any deeper. Now, of course, the crime's in *your* jurisdiction, so you could prove the crime occurred in his room and get a warrant for his phone, his computer . . ."

"Whoa, whoa, whoa." Lamb shook his head. "You're out of your mind if you think I'm biting on that. A prostitute?"

"Who was *raped*," she said. "And strangled. And beaten so violently she had a two-week hospital stay."

A slow, ugly smile spread over Lamb's face.

"Yeah, but, I mean, if she's a prostitute, it's not rape so much as shoplifting, right?"

Norris stiffened beside her. For a moment Veronica couldn't draw a breath. She stared across the desk, her vision sharpening to a single point: Lamb's sneering face.

"A girl almost died, Lamb. And you know as well as I do that sexual predators don't stop until they're caught. When this guy ends up killing someone you consider worthy of justice—because he *will*—I'm going to make sure everyone knows you refused to investigate him."

She turned and walked out of his office, slamming the door behind her.

CHAPTER THIRTY-THREE

Tahoma National Cemetery was a lush green expanse about thirty miles south of Seattle. In the distance, Mt. Rainier loomed like the ghost of a mountain, pale and wreathed in wisps of cloud.

Veronica's taxi pulled into the parking lot twenty minutes before the service was scheduled to begin. She'd gotten the earliest flight she could out of Neptune but takeoff had been delayed, leaving her fidgety and irate during the three-hour trip. *I stayed behind on a fool's errand,* she'd thought, staring bleakly out the window. *Why did I think I could convince Lamb to do something even remotely helpful? Why didn't I just go with Logan? He needed me and, like always, I chose the job. I chose wrong.* At SeaTac International she'd changed in the bathroom, the black silk dress slightly wrinkled from her bag.

Now she stopped in the information center at the cemetery to get directions to the committal site, and took off walking as quickly as she could across the sprawling grounds. A harried flutter filled her chest. She'd never liked funerals. Not that any one does, of course, except maybe the mesh-and-lace-clad Oneiroi fans of the world. But even the *function* of a funeral—the "closure," the chance to mourn—didn't appeal to her. Perhaps it was because most of the people she'd lost had been taken from her, violently. Her strategy for honoring the dead had always been to take action—solve the mystery, punish the criminal. But what did you do when there was no one to punish? When there were no answers to find? How did you assimilate that kind of loss without losing your mind?

It took her ten minutes to find the right spot. Rows of white folding chairs were set up on a large stone patio. About a hundred people hovered around the area, many in Full Dress Blues—most of them officers, but a few enlisted seamen with their white Dixie-cup hats.

An enlarged photo of Bilbo rested on an easel. It depicted a boyish-looking Filipino man, his eyes lit by a smile. An American flag stood behind him—it was supposed to look formal, official, but Bilbo looked a split second away from laughing out loud.

Seated in front of the easel was a woman who had to be Bilbo's wife. Veronica couldn't see her face from where she sat, but a little boy, maybe two years old, stood in her lap, looking back at the gathered crowd with large, curious eyes. The woman's shoulders were stiff, her head facing forward. She didn't seem to notice anything going on around her, not even the people who leaned in to talk to her directly.

Veronica found an empty seat in the back row. Logan was a pallbearer, so she wouldn't see him until after the service.

"How did you know Vincent?"

Veronica glanced at the woman next to her. She was in her mid-twenties, snub-nosed and pale, with a swipe of coral lipstick across a wide but thin mouth. She was fanning herself surreptitiously with her program.

"Oh, I didn't. My boyfriend served with him on the *Truman*."

The woman smiled. A dimple popped out in her left cheek. "Nice to meet a fellow military girlfriend. Well, I'm a military *wife* now. I'm Cathy."

"Veronica." They shook hands. Cathy gave a soft sigh.

"It's just so sad, isn't it? I only met Vince once but I've gotten to be real close with Allison. My husband's currently deployed too. He's an operations officer on the USS *Henry Pritchett*."

They were barred from further conversation by the sound of choral music. The crowd got to its feet as the music began, turning to face the paved pathway behind them. A long white hearse had pulled up flush to the curb; behind it, six pallbearers in Full Dress Whites were silently sliding the flag-covered coffin out of the back. Veronica saw Logan among them, his face tight with emotion.

A senior officer stood beside the hearse, his spine ramrod straight. "Honor guard, ten-hut." His voice was deep and percussive. "Present arms."

Everyone in uniform saluted. Veronica's eyes darted around to the civilians in the crowd, trying to get a clue to what she should be doing. Most of them had their hands on their hearts, so she followed suit.

As the pallbearers began to carry their burden forward, Veronica couldn't help but wonder what was inside. What had been retrieved of Lieutenant Malubay after his plane had crumpled on the flight deck? Had his widow been given one last look? Had she been allowed to sit by his body, to touch his hand, his face? Or had there been nothing left to mourn?

Logan passed by so close she could have touched him. She'd never wanted to more in her life, but she kept her hand on her heart. She tried hard not to imagine an alternate universe in which it was Logan in that box.

Then the music was over, and the pallbearers placed the coffin on a long, low stand next to the smiling picture. The honor guard retreated to stand at the back as a black-robed chaplain took the podium. She closed her eyes as Logan passed her one more time. She was almost sure she caught a whiff of his aftershave, sandalwood and citrus.

"Today we gather to mourn the passing of Lieutenant Vincent Michael Malubay." The chaplain's voice was soft and gentle despite the powerful amplification. "A young man whose courage and conviction inspired those of us who were privileged to know him."

Next to her, Cathy rummaged in her purse for Kleenex, her mascara already running down her face. Intermittent, breathy sobs went up from all around the crowd. At the front, Allison remained motionless.

The chaplain's eulogy was short but eloquent and sincere. He listed Bilbo's achievements—his medals, his commendations, his outstanding flight record. Bilbo had hoped, one day, to join the Blue Angels.

"He wanted little Anthony to see him fly," said the chaplain, looking down at the boy in his mother's arms.

And then they were all standing again, this time for the three-volley salute. The riflemen moved in perfect synchronicity, their shots echoing across the cemetery. Logan and one of the other pallbearers returned to the casket. They picked up the flag at either end and began to fold it as a lone bugler began to play taps.

Veronica clutched her skirt in her fists. She watched Logan's hands moving with deliberate and solemn economy. She suddenly felt that she was seeing him more clearly than ever before, yet also at a thousand-mile remove. He knelt in front of Allison, taking her hand in his for a split second before giving her the folded flag.

Someone touched her arm. She looked up to see Cathy pointing up, and realized that everyone else was watching the sky. Four jets were moving across the clear-blue expanse, arranged in an uneven V. They flew for a minute in perfect formation, an unwavering constellation. Then, without warning, one cut sharply away from the group. The other three held their course. The fourth arced up and away, heading alone toward some other horizon.

That was the moment Allison Malubay started to wail. She threw back her head, still holding the flag, still clutching her son, and she screamed at the sky, her voice swallowed in the roar of the jets.

Afterward, Veronica stood awkwardly at the back of the crowd as the mourners quietly mingled. Logan had gone with the hearse to the gravesite. His eyes hadn't even flitted toward her as he stood at attention, waiting for the order to march behind the hearse. It was almost surreal to see him so formal. A part of her wanted to laugh. This was, after all, the guy who'd slouched his way in and out of detentions for four years.

But a part of her felt uneasy, watching him walk stiffly and in perfect unison with the other pallbearers.

Admit it, Veronica—it freaks you out to see him take this

so seriously. Freaks you out because you convinced yourself this
military thing was some fanciful rich-boy goof. But it's not. Not
even close.

She spied Cathy standing with four other women. One
of them had a young girl, about six, hugging her waist, and
another had a baby slung across her chest in a pouch. They
all carried oversized purses and wore low, sensible heels.
Cathy suddenly caught sight of her and waved. Veronica
approached them, feeling almost shy.

"Wasn't that the most beautiful ceremony?" Cathy asked.
"His parents wanted to do a Mass, but Allison insisted on an
outdoor service. She wanted to make sure he got his flyover."
She turned to the group. "This is Veronica. Veronica, that's
April, Lucia, Anne, and Jasmine."

They all nodded and murmured their greetings.

"I guess Allison will probably live up here full-time now,
don't you think?" Anne said.

"Well, her parents are here. They'll be able to help her
take care of Anthony." Cathy glanced at Veronica. "Vince
was stationed out of San Diego, but after Anthony was born,
Allison came home to Seattle to be near her family while he
was deployed. It's hard to be on your own when you've got a
little one."

"Tell me about it," said Jasmine, the woman with the
baby. She bounced up and down on the balls of her feet,
rocking her daughter in her arms. "My husband left just
before this one was born."

Veronica looked around the little group. All five wore
similar expressions—friendly, sad, resigned. "Are you all
Navy spouses?" she asked. They all nodded.

"So . . . how do you guys do it?" she blurted. "I mean, I

barely lasted our first six months apart. How do you do this for years?"

They exchanged glances, and she suddenly felt childish. Here she was, complaining about six months apart, when a woman had just lost her husband. But she had to know: How did they deal with the fear, the visions of planes falling out of the sky, the constant dread of casualty reports? How did they say good-bye again and again?

Cathy put a hand on Veronica's arm. "It's not easy. There's a lot of waiting. You have to put so much off. And not just the long-term stuff. Every day I think of a hundred things I want to say to Nate. I've started carrying a notebook to jot it all down in it, because I kept getting on the phone with him and forgetting everything."

The other women laughed. Veronica felt like crying.

Cathy seemed to notice. She glanced at her friends, then back to Veronica. "We look out for each other while our men are gone. That's a big part of it. Having the support of your sisters, finding people who know what you're going through. Well, you'll see."

Veronica saw Logan then, coming back up the walkway. He was alone, his spine erect, his shoulders square. Their eyes met. He didn't smile, but something in his face softened. Veronica gave an apologetic smile as she backed away from the women. "Excuse me. I have to go. Thank you. I . . ." She gave up, and turned away.

They met a few yards away from the crowd. She was afraid to touch him, not knowing if it would violate some kind of protocol. For a moment they just stood there, looking at each other in silence.

Her eyes fell to his service ribbons, a complicated, multicolored blur just above his heart. He'd explained once what each of them meant, but she couldn't remember any of that now. *His life is still a mystery to me in so many ways.* Bars of red and blue and green melted together as tears sprang to her eyes. Then she put her arms around him, protocol be damned. She pressed her face to his chest and closed her eyes.

She already knew that he'd decided to leave—knew before he opened his mouth to speak. But for one last minute, she could pretend that he was hers to keep. For one last minute, she held him, and let him hold her.

CHAPTER THIRTY-FOUR

"You know, I always thought you couldn't argue with results, but that seems to be just what my opponent is trying to do." Sheriff Dan Lamb looked out over the crowd, his eyes round with mock incredulity. Imbecilic guffaws and *woo!*s rose from the crowd.

Standing in the back of the auditorium, Veronica typed furiously into her phone: *Somehow his face looks even more punchable than usual today.*

It was the first Tuesday in September, and the Neptune League of Women Voters was sponsoring a debate between the incumbent sheriff and his challenger. Usually the only people who came out to observe local politics were the retired and the self-interested, but this evening, a healthy cross section of Neptune had come to hear what the candidates had to say. Petra Landros was there, along with an entourage of business owners representing the Chamber of Commerce. Inga Olofson, who'd been the office manager at the Sheriff's Department when Veronica was still a kid, sat in the front row next to her husband. There were a half-dozen off-duty deputies, including Norris. Keith and Cliff sat together in the first row, right in front of Lamb's podium.

What began as a solo cakewalk for Lamb now was one

of the most heated local elections in years. "Citizens for Dan Lamb" had bought up significant airtime. The latest ad opened with an old Super 8 clip of Marcia Langdon as a young soldier on an off-duty motorcycle cruise with several other muscular, short-haired Army women—one of whom sat behind Langdon, arms around her waist. The ad then cut to a screen grab from the home movie in which a heavily tattooed Weevil Navarro was Photoshopped onto the back of Langdon's bike in place of the mannish soldier. Dan Lamb himself supplied the closing line in voice-over: "My opponent likes to end her speeches by asking Neptune voters to 'Roll With Me.' Well, before we take her up on that, maybe we should ask ourselves: *Are we really her type?*"

Langdon had only her dignified bearing and speech to counter this slime barrage; her campaign war chest was half the size of Lamb's. But she had been doing a steady stream of interviews, and she showed up at town hall meetings all over the city—including, Veronica had noticed, the poorer neighborhoods. Three trade unions had endorsed her, and hordes of young and idealistic-looking people wearing her campaign T-shirt stood outside the supermarket, handing out voter-registration applications, making sure everyone who *would* vote for her *could*.

On the right side of the stage, Langdon stood behind her own podium, listening to Lamb with ill-concealed contempt.

"Since I've taken office," Lamb continued, "this department has successfully increased its arrest numbers by thirty percent. We've taken criminals off the streets and put them in jail where they belong. Street crime is lower than it's been in a decade. My opponent wants you to believe that's somehow a bad thing."

"General?" The moderator turned back to Langdon.

Instead of the military dress used in her PR photos, Langdon wore a cobalt blue suit. Somehow she looked like even more of a hard-ass than she did in uniform. She leaned into the mic. "Sheriff Lamb was caught on tape claiming he'd arrest and prosecute Logan Echolls for murdering Bonnie DeVille whether he was guilty or not, stating that the public perception of Echolls's guilt was enough for him. I'm afraid in his zeal to 'get results,' the incumbent has made a habit of taking shortcuts. Shortcuts that not only run the risk of putting innocent people in jail, but which severely compromise the public's trust in our law enforcement. I can't think of a more devastating way to undermine a department's effectiveness."

Veronica's phone vibrated in her hand. She looked down to see a reply from Leo: *Oh, snap.* She hid a grin. Leo was watching the debate as it live streamed, and the two of them had been texting back and forth throughout.

Lamb scowled. "Those quotes were taken out of context, as I've already explained. Our department has done more to clean up this town—"

"Clean it up for whom, Sheriff?" Langdon interrupted. "For the nearly forty people who claim your officers have planted evidence on them in the past three years? For the countless citizens I've spoken with who claim that officer response times exceed an *hour* in neighborhoods without a certain zip code? For the fifteen percent of Neptune residents who live under the poverty line, and who make up nearly eighty-five percent of your arrests?"

Applause broke out around the auditorium. Veronica saw Brittany Gandin, the deputy from the front desk, joining in. A few rows away, Petra Landros watched coolly, her face impossible to read. Lamb's eyes darted over the audience, his brow creased.

Her phone vibrated with another text message. *I don't know if you can see his face from where you're standing,* said Leo, *but I've got a good close-up. I think we just witnessed the moment Lamb realized he might actually lose.*

In addition to texting about the sheriff's race, Veronica had been keeping Leo updated on the Manning case, not that there was much to tell. She still hadn't heard back from any of the girls she'd e-mailed. She was starting to face the reality that the case might actually be over. That there might be no way to prove Bellamy had raped Grace Manning. The possibility kept her at the office till all hours of the night, most recently diving into the files "one last time" and combing through his credit card activity.

It also kept her from pursuing the pawnshop-wars case. She'd procrastinated so long the client had fired Mars Investigations, meaning they'd forfeited a two-grand base fee. Keith, fed up with the shop owner's incessant calls to the office, had kindly—and perhaps even sincerely—thanked Veronica. But she knew what she'd done: She'd let her obsession with her own pet case get in the way of supporting her partner.

Veronica knew as well that she ought to be spending more time at home before Logan deployed. But he'd been busy too, visiting doctors and dentists, lawyers and accountants. "It's hard to do any financial planning when you're in the middle of the ocean," he'd said. "Plus, I need a filling, and

Navy dentists operate from the *Little Shop of Horrors* school of patient care." Now he was on some kind of bromantic surf vacation with Dick Casablancas, leaving her surrounded by his half-packed boxes, trying to comfort a confused and agitated Pony, who seemed to have picked up on the tension hanging over the apartment.

Her overstressed, wandering mind clicked back into the moment as the debate grew even more intense. At the podium, Lamb was trying desperately to reassert control of the crowd. "Look, I've been in Neptune most of my life. I know the people here, and I know what makes them tick." He pounded a fist on the podium. "My brother died in service to this town."

The room went quiet again. Regardless of how you felt about Lamb, nobody was about to disrespect a fallen officer. Veronica had heard that Dan Lamb had campaigned on his dead brother's back four years earlier, invoking his name as if they were Kennedys.

"I ran for office in part to honor his memory. And if I didn't think I'd succeeded, I wouldn't be standing up here again asking for your vote. I've made this city a safer place to live. I've been in the trenches. And I've done it for Donny."

The moderator turned to Langdon. "General, do you have a response?"

The slight twist in Langdon's lips straightened out to a long, thin line. She looked down at her notes and then up into the crowd.

"Any loss to our law enforcement community is a great tragedy. I never knew Sheriff Don Lamb, but I have no doubt he was a capable, valiant officer."

It seemed a bit too crass to text Leo an all-caps *LOL* in

response to this. Don Lamb had been a malignant jackass, but he *had* died in the line of duty. Besides, Leo would be thinking the same thing she was. He'd actually *worked* for the guy.

"Yet it would be a discredit to the memory of all the men and women who have given their lives for this town if we allow this department to be seen as a mercenary and corrupt organization. If I am elected, I'll make ethics and accountability my top priorities as we move forward. I'll make sure that justice is available to everyone in Neptune, no matter what they've got in their bank account. Thank you very much."

DROP THE MIC, Veronica typed into her phone. *LANGDON OUT.*

Twenty minutes later, as the auditorium cleared, Veronica met up with Keith and Cliff in the beige linoleum hallway outside. She grinned.

"You'd think I'd be tired of seeing that man publicly humiliated. But it just keeps getting sweeter and sweeter."

Cliff didn't smile. He rubbed his jaw, an uneasy look on his face. "Let's not gloat *too* much."

"Come on, Cliff, you know what they say—if you're tired of schadenfreude, you're tired of life." Veronica punched him lightly on the shoulder.

Cliff shook his head. "He looked scared. And a scared Lamb is a dangerous Lamb."

A door opened down the hallway. Marcia Langdon emerged, trailed by a small entourage, on her way to a meet-and-greet on the green outside the rec center.

She was shorter than Veronica had thought, maybe five-foot-seven or -eight, and her movements were brisk and economical.

"Keith! I'm glad you could make it." It was the first time Veronica had seen her smile. She shook Keith's hand, then glanced at a young man taking notes in her entourage. Marcia turned to look at Veronica. Her eyes were piercing, measuring, and Veronica found herself straightening a bit under her gaze.

"And this must be the storied Veronica." Her palm was cool and dry in Veronica's. "I've been following your career with great interest."

"Believe me. The feeling is mutual," Veronica said.

"General?" One of her advisors glanced at his watch. She nodded.

"You'll have to excuse me, but I hope we meet again soon."

"Can't we just vote now?" Veronica said as the front door shut behind Langdon. "I mean, who says we have to keep Lamb around for the next two months?"

"The town charter, I think," Keith said. "Something about 'term lengths' and 'election laws.'"

"C'mon, I'm sure that was meant as a *suggestion* more than a hard-and-fast *rule*," she persisted.

"Look at that law degree at work!" Cliff said. He opened his mouth to say more when the auditorium door swung open again. Dan Lamb pushed through, glowering heavily. Petra Landros was at his side.

An ugly flush crept across his face. "Mars. McCormack." He gave them a humorless smile.

"Sheriff," Cliff acknowledged.

Lamb's smile broadened. It didn't touch his eyes. "I hear I have you to thank for Navarro's publicity stunt."

"That's probably your best bit of detective work all year.

Score one for your *results* column." Veronica made an exaggerated *check* motion in the air.

"Enjoy the moment," Lamb advised, running a hand over his slicked-back hair. "You'll never win."

"Oh, maybe not," Keith said, a bit of lightness still in his voice. "But when we're all in court next month, when you're getting your butt pounded by the lawyers, when you're sitting there in mute awe as you see all the evidence stacking up against you . . ." He paused, his eyes not moving from Lamb's. When he spoke again, his voice was as cool and hard as Langdon's. "Just remember: That's all for Jerry Sacks."

Lamb's flush deepened. He opened his mouth to respond, but Petra steered him deftly through the door before he could.

Cliff and Keith were still looking at him when Veronica's phone vibrated. *Probably Leo, wanting to know if he missed anything good after the live feed ended.* She glanced down at the screen.

It wasn't a text message, though; it was an e-mail alert.

RE: FORMER CLIENT, POSSIBLY VIOLENT

It was a reply to the e-mail she'd sent to the escorts.

```
    hi miss mars—I received your message a
few weeks ago and have been going back and
forth on whether or not I should reply.
discretion and confidentiality are very
important in my field as you must know and I
have built a career on keeping my clients'
secrets. but I can't in good conscience keep
my silence when it seems like this behavior
is escalating.
```

I do remember this client. I remember because I had to cancel all my clients for a week and a half after so the bruises would fade. no I don't know his real name but he said his name was bobby, and he had a room at the san jose hilton. he told me on the phone he wanted me to act like a concubine, very submissive and demure. I arrived at the hotel and at first it was fine. we had sex once, which was what he'd paid for. because there were still a few minutes on the clock he asked if we could go again. I told him it would cost an extra $200. that was when he lost it. he grabbed me by the neck and pushed me against the wall. I struggled as hard as I could but he's a big guy. at some point I lost consciousness. when I came to he was having sex with me. I didn't fight back anymore as I was afraid for my life. when he was finished, he left me on the floor and went to take a shower. I got up and left.

I would prefer not to deal with cops if at all possible or to go public with this information, because my livelihood is at stake. but if there's any other way I can help you, I will. good luck. sincerely, bethany rose

CHAPTER THIRTY-FIVE

Veronica went straight home from the rec center. She'd read the e-mail over again at every red light, filled with equal parts of revulsion and triumph. *Not that I like having my direst preconceptions about humanity confirmed or anything. But I was right.* Finally she had proof that Bellamy was, in fact, Mr. Kiss and Tell.

Once in her apartment, she pulled up his profile on The Erotic Critique, looking for Bethany Rose's review.

```
    1 star/5. It's a real turn-off when I
have to haggle over every nickel and dime.
I guess that's pretty close to the actual
Girlfriend Experience, right? But seriously,
an hour is an hour. If I've paid you for
an hour, you owe me sixty minutes of your
time.
```

Bellamy had gotten cocky. He'd gotten away with rape at least twice, and then he'd gone a step further and smeared his victims online. She could imagine that, in his mind, the fact that he hadn't been caught or punished was like a mandate from heaven, a kind of tacit approval of his behavior.

That was how psychopaths worked, how escalation happened.

"Loose lips sink ships, Mr. Kiss and Tell," she murmured. "Who else have you been talking about?"

She started to comb through the other single-stars, jotting their names on a whiteboard she'd pulled out of the broom closet, along with their home city and the date of the review. Aside from Grace, there were four other one-star reviews. Nikki Valentine, the girl whose grooming he'd criticized, had been reviewed in March 2012. In April 2013 he'd reviewed Bethany Rose, and then in December he'd posted two at once: a "Tonya Vahn" in L.A. who "acted like a stuck-up bitch and looked nothing like her picture" and a "Madelyn Chase" in Vegas who "didn't follow directions at all."

The last two girls seemed to be either out of the business—or perhaps had changed their working names—as their websites had been taken down. Veronica noted that on the whiteboard as well.

No one but Bethany Rose had responded to her e-mail, and it seemed reasonable to assume no one else would.

Veronica held her phone for a moment. Then she dialed the number listed on The Erotic Critique for Tonya Vahn. The number had been disconnected.

She tried Madelyn's next. A robotic voice mail recording answered: "Leave a message after the beep."

"Madelyn, hi." She gave a nervous giggle into the phone. "My name's Angie. Oh my gosh, this is so awkward, I've never done this before but, um, my boyfriend's thirtieth birthday is coming up, and I was looking to celebrate in a, uh, special way. I was calling to find out if you ever work with couples. Call me back at this number. Thanks!"

She rerecorded her own voice mail message in "Angie's" chirpy falsetto. *Alter egos all around.* Then she glanced at the clock; it was just after nine.

"What time do you think escorts man the phones, Pony?"

The dog cocked her head to the side and wagged at the sound of her voice. Veronica scratched behind her ears, then dialed the number listed on Nikki Valentine's profile, ready to record another message. She was startled when it was picked up on the third ring.

"Hello?"

Veronica's fingers twitched slightly around the phone. "Nikki, please listen. A friend of mine, a working girl, was recently raped, and I think the same guy may have assaulted you sometime in the winter of 2011 or spring of 2012. Please, I'm not a cop. I'm not interested in getting you in trouble. I just want to try to get some answers and I need your help."

The line went silent. Veronica held her breath, listening. For a moment she thought Nikki had hung up on her. Then she heard a tiny, soft *snick*. The sound of a cigarette lighter, followed by a swift exhale.

"No one's ever raped me on the job."

Veronica cradled the phone against her ear like it was something delicate, like if she clutched it too hard she'd lose this one slender thread.

"If I sent you a picture, could you tell me if you recognize this guy?"

"I don't dish about my clients."

"This guy's a psycho, Nikki."

There was another pause.

"Send me the picture."

Quickly, Veronica paused the call and texted her the

headshot of Bellamy from PSU's basketball website. When Nikki came back to the phone, Veronica was surprised to hear her laughing, a low, humorless chuckle.

"*This* piece of shit. Yeah, I remember him. He thought he was going to get rough with me. He pushed me against the wall, got one punch in, chipped my tooth. Then I called for my boyfriend." There was the little *kiss* noise of her taking another drag on her cigarette. "He could barely walk when Marty was done with him. I'm kind of shocked he tried it again with someone else."

Veronica sat up straight. The basketball trip to Tucson, when the players had seen Bellamy's injuries. "Wait—was this the night of February third?"

"I don't know. It was about two years ago."

"Did you ever report it to anyone? The cops, or—"

"Riiight." Nikki interrupted, drawing out the word. "You think I'd still be working if I talked to cops? No, after Marty beat the shit out of him I figured it was over and done with."

"Can I ask you a logistical question?"

"Shoot."

Veronica put her forearms on her desk. "How did your boyfriend get there so quick? Was he somewhere listening?"

"Yeah. When I do outcall, he hangs out in the hallway in case I scream for him."

"That doesn't get people suspicious? Hotel staff, other guests?"

"You'd be surprised how little anyone cares what's going on in the next room over." The girl sounded weary, almost disgusted. "If anyone talks to him, he just says he's waiting for a friend. If you act like you're supposed to be there, people generally don't ask too many questions."

Fair enough. It was a strategy Veronica had used many times.

"Did he do anything else besides hit you?"

"Nope. I showed up to the room, he gave me a once-over and decided to be mean. Some guys are just looking for an excuse. He had a problem with everything I did. Kept calling me a stupid bitch. Whatever, it's his dollar—and it's not like that was the first time I've been called names—but he just got madder and madder, like he was deliberately working himself up. He got in my face and told me I looked like a whore, hit me, and that was it."

Veronica was silent for a moment, thinking.

"Anything else? I've kinda got to clear the line here," Nikki said.

"Should I assume you don't want to give an official statement about this?" The girl just snorted. Veronica sighed. "Okay. Okay, thanks, Nikki. You've helped a lot."

"I hope your friend's okay." There was a soft click as she hung up.

Veronica swiveled in her chair. Bellamy had learned from his mistake. He'd discovered what happened when he gave a girl a chance to scream. So he'd started choking them, at first just to keep them quiet, but then perhaps he realized he actually *liked* that part. Liked to strangle them, liked to hurt them.

Her reverie was interrupted by the phone cutting through the silence. Her screen displayed a number with a Vegas area code.

"This is Angie," she sang into the receiver.

"Hi, Angie, this is Isabella." The voice was young, a throaty purr. "I'm returning your call?"

Veronica frowned, changing the phone to the other ear. "I'm sorry, who?"

"You called for Madelyn but she's not with the agency anymore. I thought I'd give you a call back and see if we couldn't set anything up instead."

Her heart picked up speed. "Madelyn's not with the agency?"

"If you're looking for a three-way . . ."

"Did something happen to her? Do you know where she is now?"

Isabella was quiet for a moment. "Just a minute."

The line went on hold. Veronica waited. It was almost three minutes before Isabella came back.

"Who is this?" she asked.

"My name is Veronica Mars. I'm not a cop. I'm a private investigator. I'm trying to find proof that a suspect has been raping and assaulting high-end escorts all over the country. I think Madelyn may have had an encounter with him."

"I'm not talking about this on the phone," Isabella said. "Can you get to Vegas?"

Veronica leaned back in her chair. "Maybe. Do you know Madelyn Chase?"

"Stay at the Mercury tomorrow night. Call me back at this number and leave your room number once you're there."

"Did something happen to Madelyn, Isabella?" Veronica asked urgently.

But the girl had already hung up the phone.

CHAPTER THIRTY-SIX

"Pony! Drop it. Drop it!"

Veronica knelt down next to the puppy, trying to wrestle her favorite boot out of the dog's mouth. It was the morning after her conversation with Isabella, and Veronica's suitcase was open across the bed, half packed with clothes. The hard-shell case of her snub-nosed .38 Special was just visible from under a folded pair of jeans.

Pony gave a little grunt of exertion, her hindquarters waving back and forth with excitement as she tugged on the boot. Veronica sighed and stopped pulling. The struggle was just getting tooth marks all over the leather. She rested her chin on her hand and looked the dog in the eye. "Why don't you go chew up Daddy's things? He has a bomber jacket just begging for some puncture marks."

"I heard that." Logan's voice came from the hallway. She straightened up as he poked his head in the door. His cheeks were pink, his hair streaked from the sun. He leaned against the door frame and smiled.

"You're home. I didn't hear the door." She stood up and went to kiss him on the cheek.

"It's my advanced military training," he said. He wove back and forth in a shadow-boxing stance. "They teach you to move like a *panther*."

"Oh yeah? Is there a lot of call for stealth in the cockpit of a fifty-million-dollar fighter jet?"

"The SEALs aren't the only ones with moves." He leaned down to pet Pony, who licked his chin. "How're my girls?"

"Well, one of us peed in your shoe. And the other barked all morning," she said. "How was the trip? Were there some gnarly waves?"

"There were indeed." He noticed the suitcase and frowned. "What's up? You going somewhere?"

"Just for one night. I have to fly out to Vegas for a case. But I should be back Thursday afternoon, barring anything unforeseen." She put her arms around his neck.

That was when she saw the manila folder he was holding. "What's all that?"

"My paperwork. To get back on the *Truman*." He opened the envelope and slid out a stack of papers. "I'm going to get it in the mail this afternoon."

Without thinking, she let go of him. He raised his eyebrows at her, his smile turning both wry and wistful. "Okay. Let me have it. Again. Give me your best Columbia Law School try."

"I'm out of ideas," she said, trying to keep her tone light. "Unless you think a rendition of 'Billy Don't Be A Hero' will work."

"Nothing's going to happen to me. These guys we're fighting, they don't have anything that can take down a Hornet."

"You do realize I *just* went to a military funeral, don't you?" She stared up at him, her spine bristling with a sudden surge of anger. "And there are Wikipedia pages about every single aviation accident in naval history?"

His face darkened. "Come on, Veronica. I don't do this to

you. The stuff you do is at least as risky as what I do. I mean, you're off to Vegas to do God knows what. You work crazy hours, you deal with dangerous people. I don't like it, but I've learned to accept that it's the price of admission."

Her cheeks flushed. "How long have you been holding on to *that* argument?"

"Well, it is the obvious one."

She raised her hands. "Look, I'm not saying you don't have the right to do exactly what you've made up your mind to do. I'm just saying, don't act like it's nothing. Don't act like you have to do it. Don't act like it's just another day at work. It's a big deal, Logan. You could be hurt. I could—" She suddenly came up short. She'd been about to say *I could lose you*; instead, she bit her tongue.

Veronica took a deep breath and glanced down at her watch.

"Look, I have to go, I can't miss my flight. We can talk about this later."

"Later, right." Logan sighed.

She took him in, guilt forming in her chest as she realized how few *laters* they had left. But she had to find out what Isabella knew.

Just like he has to go back and join his squadron, she told herself. Because, for better or worse, that was the way they were both wired.

CHAPTER THIRTY-SEVEN

The Mercury Resort and Casino was one of the newest hotels on the Strip, a sprawling, thirty-three floor behemoth. It boasted five different restaurants, a nightclub, forty high-end shops, a full-service day spa, and the world's longest waterslide—the Quicksilver, a long, knotted tube that stretched from the eighteenth floor of the hotel down to an amoeba-shaped pool below. It was a pleasure dome that would likely have disappointed S.T. Coleridge but was right in the wheelhouse of a Baton Rouge dermatologist with money to burn.

Veronica stood for a moment outside her $300-per-night room. A few feet away, a small black table held a towering ikebana arrangement, a cluster of plum branches and irises arcing out at surreal angles. She glanced around, then carefully set a tiny wireless nanny cam just behind the vase. It was synced to her phone, and showed a clear shot of her own door.

Then she went into the room and dialed Isabella's number. She got the girl's voice mail. "Hi, this is Isabella. Do leave me a message."

"Um, hi. I'm at the Mercury, room 347. It's Veronica."

Congratulations, Veronica. You've just ordered your first call girl.

Then she settled in to wait.

No one could accuse the Mercury of blandness. Thick amethyst carpet covered the floor of her room. The walls were papered in an elaborate gray filigree, the curtains and bedspread shiny white. But there was a tiny tear along the base of the velvet armchair, exposing just a centimeter of yellowed foam cushion beneath. In Vegas, the veneer of glamor was bright but thin. You didn't have to look that hard to see the darker realities that lurked beneath the surface.

Isabella hadn't specified a time for their meeting, and Veronica hadn't thought to ask. An hour ticked by, then another. Every time she heard footsteps she whipped out her phone and checked the camera. The only people she saw were other tourists heading back to their rooms.

She thought about calling the agency again, but if their phone call was any indication, Isabella wasn't the kind of person who'd respond well to being hounded. So Veronica kept waiting, too on edge to turn on the TV or open the *New Yorker* she'd brought to read on the plane.

Maybe she got cold feet. Or maybe someone stopped her from coming. The thought sent a stab of cold through Veronica's stomach. She'd gleaned from her research that a lot of escort agencies were scarcely better than pimps, bullying and manipulating the girls in their employ. What if someone had decided to silence her?

When a soft knock came at the door she jumped and looked down at her phone. The screen was black. Someone outside the door had turned the nanny cam facedown.

She stood on her toes and stared through the peephole. There, in front of her door, was Isabella. Unlike the escorts in other cities, the Vegas girls tended to show their faces on their websites; both Isabella and Madelyn Chase had been fully visible when Veronica looked them up. Isabella was abundantly curvy; she bore a passing resemblance to a young Monica Bellucci, if Monica had the word "goddess" tattooed along the curve of one full breast.

Veronica opened the door.

"Isabella . . ." She stopped as an enormous man shouldered around from behind the door and into the room. Isabella stepped in behind him and quickly shut the door.

". . . and friend," Veronica finished lamely. The man was at least six-five, cleanly bald, and unsmiling. A black sports coat strained to contain his bulk. His head was massive, his features broad and stony, as if he'd been rough-chiseled from a boulder. Gold hoops glinted from his ears. Veronica took a few steps back as he advanced into the room. She bumped into the bed and lost her balance. Suddenly, the man's brawny arm shot around her shoulder. She tensed for a moment, then she realized he'd reached out to keep her from falling.

"Careful there." His voice was a bass rumble. Her breath came back to her all at once, a sharp stab in her lungs. She gently detached herself from his arm.

"I didn't know to expect an entourage. I would have ordered us a cheese platter. Some Bellinis. Maybe some hookers. Make a party of it," Veronica said, looking from Isabella to the giant.

"Oh, funny. She's funny, Sweet Pea." Isabella leaned against the wall, a cool, haughty tilt to her chin. She reached into her purse and pulled out an engraved cigarette case.

"I think this is a non-smoking room," Veronica said.

Isabella lit her cigarette and exhaled a long stream of smoke in Veronica's direction. "Guess they might hit you with a $200 upcharge then. They're thieves."

Veronica wondered, fleetingly, if she'd been somehow set up. If the plan had been to rob her, or worse. She thought about the gun in the holster at the small of her back. It didn't seem the right time to go for it, though—not yet. She forced an expression of calm as Sweet Pea walked quickly to the bathroom, turned on the light, and looked around. Then he came back into the bedroom.

Isabella raised her cigarette to her lips again, exhaling in a long, cool stream overhead. "I read about you. After the Bonnie DeVille thing. You're shorter than I expected."

"Yeah? You're more people than I expected," Veronica said, glancing at Sweet Pea. "So neither of us got what we were counting on."

Sweet Pea spoke. "Couldn't be helped. You call us up out of the blue, asking about missing girls, I got to be involved."

That got her attention. "Missing? Madelyn Chase is missing?"

Sweet Pea and Isabella exchanged a quick glance before he spoke again.

"Since December of last year."

A sudden sick feeling came over Veronica. She stared at Sweet Pea, trying to see if this was some kind of con. His expression didn't falter.

"You didn't know that?" Isabella broke in. She sounded almost angry.

Veronica shook her head. "No, I . . . I don't know anything about Madelyn. That's why I'm here."

Sweet Pea pulled a chair out from under the desk and offered it to Isabella. She shook her head impatiently, so he sat down himself.

"So what is it you *do* know?" he asked.

Veronica crossed her arms over her chest.

"I know the confidentiality issues in the PI business are probably similar to those in the escort business," she said. "You know I can't just tell you what I'm investigating."

Isabella pushed off the wall, jabbing at the air with her cigarette. "You knew *something* happened to Maddy, and you'd better start talking, or I'm—"

"Hey." Though Sweet Pea's voice wasn't loud, it filled the room. He gave Isabella a meaningful look. "Everyone in here wants information, okay?" He turned back to Veronica. "How about you tell us what you came out here to find, and we'll see where it takes us?"

Veronica sat down slowly on the edge of the bed. *I guess I can give them a version of the truth. Tit for tat.* "A woman I know in Neptune was assaulted by a client in March. She's an escort. I'm trying to help her prove it was a rape. I'm sure you know all the reasons why that's tough to prove." She glanced at Isabella, who was slouching back against the wall again. "I'm trying to find other victims. If I can show this is a pattern I can force the issue. The cops won't be able to ignore it, then."

Isabella gave an angry snort. Sweet Pea frowned.

"And what makes you think the same guy did something to Madelyn?" he asked.

She hesitated. Isabella, at the very least, had googled her. And something told her Sweet Pea was smarter than most in his line of work. If she said too much she'd risk them tracing the same set of clues she'd found. She didn't know what they'd do with that information and she couldn't afford a loose cannon.

"Can you tell me a little more about Madelyn's disappearance?" she deflected. "Is anyone looking for her?"

"What do you think *we're* doing?" Isabella went to the

corner sink and filled a cup with water. She threw her cigarette in and placed it on the counter. When she turned back she seemed calmer.

"I meant the cops."

"Oh, I *talked* to the cops," Isabella interrupted. "They don't give a shit. They have her picture in a file somewhere, but they're not doing anything to find her." She sat down on the edge of the bed, across from Veronica. Her eyes were dark, almost black—restless and sharp. "Maddy and I were friends. I want to know what happened to her."

"When exactly did she go missing?"

"December sixth, 2012," Isabella said promptly. "It was a Friday. We met for drinks at Emerald's at around nine. I had a date at eleven at the Four Seasons. She wasn't prebooked that night, and she was debating whether or not to go work the floors."

"Work the floors?" Veronica asked.

"Yeah, sometimes we hang out at the casinos, talk up guys, see who's spending money and who's making money. It sucks, though, because you're hoofing it all over the Strip, and a lot of times you strike out or waste a lot of time with a guy who turns out to be a cheapskate. We only do it if it's been a slow couple weeks. She was thinking about heading home and taking a night off. But a few minutes before I took off, she got a call. A client." Isabella smoothed out the tassels on one of the pillows, her brow crinkled. "She agreed to meet him at midnight. I left right after that. That was the last I ever saw her."

"When did you try to contact her again?" Veronica asked. "And how long was it before you realized something was wrong?"

"I texted her the next morning. She never answered back. That was a little weird, but not raise-the-alarms kinda weird. Our schedules are so crazy, sometimes we're not in contact for weeks at a time. But a few nights later she had a big client on the books—one of her regulars, a guy she'd never stand up without good reason—and she didn't show. That's when we knew something was up."

Veronica furrowed her brow. "She went alone to meet this last-minute client, the one she knew nothing about?" She gave Sweet Pea a sidelong look. "Is that how it normally works in your agency?"

Sweet Pea's expression didn't falter. "We usually *do* send someone out with the girls, especially if they're seeing someone new. Mad called in that night, asked for someone to come around, but we didn't have no one free. She still wanted to take the job. Well, good luck telling one of these hos what to do, you know what I'm sayin'?" Isabella snorted again, but this time with more humor than anger. "I ain't no pimp. The girls, they're independent contractors. We just do booking and security. So she went ahead on her own." His knuckles tightened almost reflexively. "But you're right. It was a lapse. And I don't like lapses."

Somehow, his businesslike demeanor was even more terrifying than if he'd raged or snarled. Veronica suddenly had no doubt that this was a man who'd hurt people, methodically, dispassionately.

"Did you know anything about the client?" she asked. "Where he was staying, who he was?"

"He said his name was Mike and he was staying here, at the Mercury. She was supposed to text Sweet Pea the room number but she never did. She could be a flake like that," Isabella said.

Veronica didn't answer for a moment. It was all too easy to imagine Madelyn Chase arriving at Bellamy's room, forgetting to check in before she knocked. Figuring she could text them from the bathroom once she got in and saw if the guy was okay or not. Never quite getting the chance—because Bellamy had learned to strike quickly if something set him off.

"Did you check her house, contact her family?"

"Maddy wasn't in touch with her family," Isabella said. "I got the feeling they were assholes. She grew up in West Texas but she told me she ran away when she was sixteen. And yeah, I went to her condo. I had a key—I used to take care of her cat when she was out of town. Anyway, she wasn't there, but all her stuff was. There wasn't any sign that she'd packed up and left. And Taffy was there—she loved that fucking cat. She wouldn't have left her behind without arranging for someone to take care of her."

"I'm assuming Madelyn Chase wasn't her real name?"

Isabella shook her head. "Of course not. I've got no idea what her birth name was, though. The name on her condo was Molly Christensen, but that turned out to be a fake." She rolled her eyes. "The cops got a lot more interested in finding her when they realized she'd committed identity fraud."

"This guy you're looking into. He hurt a lot of girls?" Sweet Pea asked in an almost offhanded way, like he was asking about the weather.

Veronica hesitated. "Three for sure. Four if I can prove he did something to Madelyn."

He nodded slowly. "Gonna be straight with you, because you seem like you don't mess around." He crossed his large hands in his lap. "I think you know as well as we do that the cops ain't gonna touch this guy. Let's say you find a girl who'll testify, which I wouldn't put money on. That don't mean you'll find a cop who'll take it seriously, or a lawyer, or a judge, or a jury. But there *are* other options." The guy didn't do anything ominous when he said it—didn't crack his knuckles or punch his fist—but the words sent a chill down Veronica's spine nonetheless.

"Options?"

He gave a little shrug. "You know. Maybe you give me this guy's information. Then you head on back to your nice little 'burb on the beach, and I make sure the right people look into the matter."

The air in the room became dense, weighted down by the silence. She could feel Isabella's eyes on her, sharp and searching. She thought back to Dan Lamb's sneering face when she'd taken the case to him. Would it make any difference if she found another victim—if she found a dozen victims? These girls lived in a world that only tenuously overlapped with society at large. The law offered them no protection. They were disposable.

Veronica took a deep breath.

"Thanks, Sweet Pea. But I'm going to keep doing this my way."

His jaw tightened slightly, but he didn't argue with her.

"Suit yourself," he said. He stood up and went to the little writing desk, opened the top drawer. He took out a notepad and jotted something down. Then he ripped off the page and handed it to her.

"My cell," he said. "In case you change your mind."

For a moment she thought about protesting, handing it back, throwing it away. *That's not how I do things,* she'd say. *Dirty as this world is, I've got to stay clean.*

But she didn't. Instead, she folded the piece of paper and slid it in her purse.

"In case I change my mind," she echoed.

CHAPTER THIRTY-EIGHT

It was a Tuesday morning, the light still low over the east hills. The beach was almost empty, save a few surfers hauling their boards out of the water. Salt and the mildly rotten smell of seaweed hung on the air. Veronica and Logan sat on an old plaid bed sheet, watching as Pony played in the surf. Logan was in Service Khaki, his shirt and pants almost the same color as the sand beneath them. His cap sat on top of their cooler, his shoes and socks stowed neatly nearby. He was due back on base at noon. From there, they'd fly him out, first through Norfolk, then through Italy, and then— the final leg—back to the *Truman*, which was somewhere in the Arabian Sea.

The remnants of their breakfast picnic littered the blanket around them—plastic tubs of fruit, quiche Lorraine, chocolate croissants, and mugs of hot coffee. Veronica had barely eaten, picking at her food, but Logan had sampled everything and gone back for seconds. "Real food's about to be a thing of my past," he'd said, his mouth full of pineapple and blueberries. "Gotta savor it while I can."

They watched as Pony charged and retreated from the surf, her body writhing with excitement. She'd almost doubled in size since the day they got her. Now she was too big to sit in Logan's lap. It didn't stop her from trying—Veronica had at least three pictures of the dog awkwardly splayed over him. One was now her desktop wallpaper.

"How am I going to raise Pony without you?" she asked. "You know what happens to puppies who don't have a strong masculine figure around. She'll grow up with daddy issues."

It wasn't meant to be a real argument; she'd let those go the day he'd mailed his paperwork. She'd bottled up all the things she'd been feeling—resentment, fear, grief—and forced herself to smile and pretend everything was normal. He'd be leaving, whether she liked it or not. It didn't do her any good to fill their last days together with fights.

And they say Veronica Mars doesn't know how to pick her battles, she thought wryly. Well, she still had plenty of windmills at which to tilt. In the weeks since her trip to Vegas, she'd been stuck, unable to gain any more traction against Bellamy. She'd e-mailed Bethany Rose again, asking if she'd consider filing a police report, but she'd never heard back. She'd sent another e-mail to Tonya Vahn, the girl whose phone had been disconnected, and begged her to call with any information. Strike two.

Without another witness who'd go on record, there was nothing else she could do. Nothing but watch Mitch Bellamy, and wait, hoping they got a break before he tried to hurt someone else.

At least Mac is still monitoring his accounts so we'll know if he does try something. That's some comfort. And I always have Sweet Pea's number—not that I'll use it. But she thought about it sometimes, taking it out of her wallet and holding it up. Imagining the no-niceties dimension in which she could casually sic a very large, very businesslike man to take care of cases she couldn't prove in court.

Between that and Logan's preparations to leave, she'd felt uncharacteristically helpless. She'd started jogging in the mornings, just for something to do. She'd run along the beach and weave through the neighborhood, trying to make herself too tired to care. So far it wasn't working, but she'd shaved a few seconds off her mile. And she'd started to follow the election coverage feverishly. She read every article she could get her hands on about Marcia Langdon, obsessed over poll updates and projected voting patterns. She'd helped with Keith's caseload a few times that week to free him up to work on the trial preparations. It wasn't much, but it was easier than all this *waiting*.

Voices of the Navy wives at the funeral echoed in her mind like a Greek chorus. *We try to look out for each other. Well, you'll see.* It didn't make her feel better. She didn't want to *be* in their club. Didn't want to learn how to be apart from the one person she longed to see every day.

"Veronica."

She snapped back into the moment and looked over at Logan. He was watching the ocean, his eyes intent on the waves, his brow slightly furrowed.

"You know we can do this, right?" he said.

She wanted to say *yes*. To reassure him, to keep their morning simple. She had a feeling that was what Cathy and the other Navy wives would do. But she couldn't seem to make herself speak.

"Well, that's not reassuring," he murmured, turning to look at her.

She hugged her knees to her chest. "Logan, all of this is

still new to me. This coming and going, the cycle of losing you and then getting you back, only to lose you all over again."

"You're not *losing* me, Veronica." He ran his hand through his hair. "You know, I'm not leaving you."

"But you're not staying either."

For a moment, they sat in silence. Veronica's shoulders were tight, her fingernails cutting into her palms. When Logan spoke again, his voice was low. She looked up to meet his eyes. They were serious and sad.

"Look, Veronica, I know you're pissed that I'm going back early." She blinked, surprised. He smirked. "Sorry—you're not that good an actor. And I come from a family of bad actors so I should know. Anyway, you have a right to be pissed. I get it. But this isn't about you. It kills me to leave you. I hate it. But I have to, because this is who I am. You just don't know what this job means to me."

"So tell me."

He ran his hand over his face. For a few long minutes he seemed to be gathering his thoughts.

"You were gone for nine years, so all you got to see was the 'after' picture. The 'before'—let's just say it wasn't so nice. I was hitting the bottle pretty hard. And some other stuff too, bad stuff." He laughed humorlessly. "You know how it is around here. As long as you call it 'partying' it's all okay. But it was getting pretty out of control. Even Dick was worried, and that should tell you something." He shook his head. "There's stuff I barely remember. Like, once I wandered into a woman's house, thinking it was Dick's. She found me passed out on the sofa. I was lucky she didn't call the cops. But the thing is, I didn't even *care*. That was the worst of it."

Something clenched around Veronica's heart, a tightness that tore into her like claws. But she held her tongue.

"Everything just felt pointless and stupid. I remember being out on my surfboard one morning and sitting there for the longest time. I'd paddled out as far as I could, and the waves were amazing, but I couldn't make myself stand up. I thought about just rolling off the board and letting myself drift. Seeing if I could drown without too much effort." He looked up at the sky. "I guess it's no big shocker. Another Hollywood brat who can't handle his shit."

Veronica inhaled sharply. She'd been at Stanford by then—trying her best to forget everything she'd left behind her. Trying to forget Logan. While she'd been complaining about all-nighters and turgid academic prose, he'd been casually, calmly thinking about ending his own life.

Logan continued. "It went on like that for a couple of years, worse and worse. And Veronica, it would have *killed* me. Without a doubt, it would have killed me, if not for Dr. Galway. I don't know if you remember him; he was a history professor at Hearst. He showed up at the hospital after my second OD. I'd already dropped out of Hearst by then, but I guess for some reason I had made an impression on him. Turns out, he used to be a flyboy himself. He was the one who told me I was made for this. He checked me into a detox and rehab program and made sure I stuck with it. Afterward he helped me reenroll at Hearst, then he made some calls to get me into OCS."

Logan scooped up a handful of sand and let it trickle through his fingers. "After that, it was like things just snapped into focus for me. For the first time in my life I had something that seemed worth working for. Something with actual, you know, *purpose*."

He laughed, embarrassed by his own earnestness.

"Sorry—lamest recruiting script ever. Take Two: *I just wanted the badass flight suit and a chance to reduce architectural treasures of the ancient world to smoking rubble.*"

"Now that's the man who won my heart," Veronica said, gently rubbing his back.

"Look, you've known me a long time," Logan said, the urgency returning to his voice. "I'm living proof it's possible to have total freedom—to be indulged and deferred to by everyone around you—yet feel utterly worthless. You can't imagine that feeling, Veronica, because you've never spent a day being worthless in your life. But for me it was like . . . a revelation."

He took her hand and looked at her steadily. "So please understand, this isn't some asinine death wish. This is what saved my life."

Her eyes blurred, and she was half surprised to find tears running down her cheeks. For a moment she couldn't think, couldn't process; all she could do was hear his words echoing over and over. *Drown without too much effort. Second OD.* She felt his hand squeeze hers, and she squeezed back.

A warm, wet ball of fur suddenly collided into her. Pony ran back and forth across their blanket, tracking sand everywhere. Veronica pointed her finger at the puppy.

"Sit," she said.

Pony licked her finger, then bounced in circles around them. Veronica looked at Logan.

"You see? She's already acting out. It's a cry for help." She wiped her eyes quickly, and ruffled the fur on the puppy's neck.

Then she took a deep breath. "Acceptance has never

been one of my strong suits. But I'm trying, Logan. I just need some time."

"That I can give you," he said. He slid an arm around her waist. "I've gotten good at waiting for things."

"Who knew you'd be the patient one?" She rested her forehead against his.

They sat that way for a few minutes, looking into each other's eyes. And for that brief moment, nothing that'd come before or after mattered. The sound of gulls and waves surrounded them, the puppy leaned against Veronica's leg, and she and Logan were just where they were supposed to be: side by side, at the edge of the world.

CHAPTER THIRTY-NINE

"What do you think? More cheese? Less cheese? Different cheese?"

Keith held up a measuring cup of shredded mozzarella and looked inquiringly at Veronica across the kitchen island. She was slicing tomatoes but paused mid chop to look up with one raised brow.

"When is the answer *ever* less cheese?"

"Fair point." He dumped the entire cup into the mixing bowl and started to stir.

It was Wednesday night, the first "Daddy-Daughter Dinner" since Logan's departure a week earlier. Keith hadn't seen Veronica much in the past week. Ostensibly, she'd been out of the office, busy with a few minor cases, but Keith knew she was struggling to keep her feelings about Logan hidden and controlled.

She'd always thought she was good at that. He never had the heart to tell her he could see right through it.

At least there was plenty to keep her busy. She'd started on a few new cases, picking up the slack so he could focus on Eli's upcoming trial. Now Keith's part in the preparations was more or less over. He'd found all the witnesses he could and convinced several to testify, looking into their cases to select the most credible for the witness stand. In the meantime, he'd put security measures in place, installing cameras and panic buttons at both Eli's and Lisa's places, showing them what to inspect on their cars before getting in, in case of sabotage. Lisa had been unfazed by the entire process but Eli was openly unnerved.

"For real? You think someone might try to take me out?"

Keith had held out his scarred arms at his sides as if to say, "Exhibit A." "Do you really think a meth head hit Sacks's car in January?"

The trial was three weeks away now, and Keith's nerves were on edge. He realized he was waiting for some shoe to drop—but how? Lamb probably wouldn't have the stones to do anything overtly violent given all the publicity, but he wasn't about to roll over and give up. The thought made him uneasy.

Keith refocused his attention on the lasagna. With artful delicacy he sprinkled the last bit of mozzarella over the lasagna pan and looked at his work. An odd little flicker moved in his chest. "Your grandma made the best lasagna. I've never been able to get the sauce quite right."

Veronica put down the knife and rested her chin against her fist. "You know, you've been weirdly nostalgic lately. Is this just the ravages of time at work, or is something wrong?"

"Hey, a grown man can miss his mommy without shame."

"Yeah, he can, but it's not just Grandma. You've been talking about high school and racing your '78 GTO in the streets of Omaha. I'm just waiting for the day you pull a Werther's Original out of your pocket and try to give it to Pony."

Keith put on a Grandpa Simpson voice and bent over. "That reminds me of the time I went to Hampton, which is what they called Hampstead in those days, so I tied an onion to my belt, which was the style at the time. . . ."

She threw a towel at him. "All right, wise guy, deflect away. Just remember, I was a psych major. I can see right through your emotional repression."

Then that makes two of us, doesn't it? The thought made him smile. *Mars and Mars, always trying to believe they're the best spy in the room, when they know each other's tells by heart.*

"Okay, Dr. Mars. Maybe I have been waxing a little nostalgic." He shrugged. "I guess it's partly seeing Marcia again. Most of the people I knew back then have moved on. Both my parents are dead. Not a lot of people to talk with about ye olden days."

"So were you guys friends?" She took a carrot from the veggie platter and crunched it between her teeth. "I mean, it's kind of funny. You both ended up cops, and you lived, what, three houses from each other?"

He hesitated. Friends. He'd been expecting a question like that for a while, but he still didn't know how to answer it. To buy a little time, he scooped up Pony, who'd gotten so big he had to bend his knees to lift her.

"No," he finally said. "Not friends. But I liked her. She wasn't exactly a laugh riot, but she had a *very* dry wit. She was a little bit prickly and didn't take any crap."

"A woman after my own heart," Veronica said.

Somehow, the idea made his jaw tighten. It wasn't a bad comparison, really; Marcia *had* been smart, driven, and ambitious. All the things he'd loved in his daughter. All the things he'd tried to raise her to be. But he shook his head.

"She could also be uncompromising and a little judgmental. But that was thirty-five years ago. We were both kids. I don't really know what she's like now, other than that she's got a glorious military record and talks a great game on the stump."

"You think she'll do a good job?"

He shrugged. "I don't know. She's been in CID for a long time and that's a tough gig, so I'm sure she can handle herself. And she can't possibly do any worse than Lamb."

"True dat."

He was bent over the oven, about to slide the lasagna in, when both of their phones chimed at once. Veronica grabbed hers first.

"It's Cliff," she said. He shut the oven door and straightened up to see her frown. "He says, 'Channel Four, stat.'"

The vague paranoia that'd been lingering inside him for weeks suddenly spiked into full-blown anxiety. He lunged for the remote and turned on the little kitchen set. Visions of car crashes or "accidental" falls darted through his head, Lisa or Eli lying in pools of blood.

But when the picture appeared on Channel Four, his heart seemed to calcify in his chest.

Weevil stood at a podium in front of the courthouse, wearing the slacks and jacket Keith had bought him. Camera flashes lit his face in erratic bursts. He leaned forward to speak into the microphone in a serious tone.

"You know, I'm just a regular guy, and all these fancy lawyers had me all turned around. This lawsuit-crazy society we're living in makes us think we can solve all our problems by suing somebody instead of just sitting down and talking it out, you know?"

Keith groaned out loud and plunked down into a chair.

Out of the corner of his eye, he saw Veronica doing likewise on one of the island stools. He stared at the screen, scarcely able to believe what he was seeing and hearing.

"I mean, the truth of the matter is that mistakes were made in my case. But after talking at great length with Sheriff Lamb, I just don't believe that's evidence of some kind of *institutional* problem," Weevil said. "I'm satisfied that the sheriff is gonna make this right so that no one has to go through this again."

"You fucking weasel," Veronica hissed.

"Mr. Navarro, how much are you settling for?" a reporter shouted.

He leaned in. "I'm afraid I can't discuss the terms."

That was when Keith remembered the remote in his hand, and turned off the TV.

"That fucking *weasel*!" Veronica repeated. "After everything we've done for him. After everything we've been through to get him out of this mess . . ."

"Language," Keith said. His voice sounded faraway to him, muted and strange. He turned to look at her.

"But, Dad, he . . . we . . ." she sputtered. "You almost died trying to get to the bottom of what happened to Weevil. You've spent months building this case. You of all people should be furious."

"And I am. Believe me, I am," he said, speaking with controlled intensity. "But there's nothing we can do about it right now, Veronica. So we might as well sit down and have a nice dinner, the way we planned. We're not going to strike any blows against Lamb by starving ourselves."

"Against Lamb? Oh, no. When I get my hands on Weevil . . ."

He took a deep breath. "Honey, let's just drop it. We've barely seen each other in weeks. There's half a season of *True Detective* on the DVR for us to get through, and in forty minutes we've got six thousand calories of molten cheese and Italian sausage coming out of the oven." He put an arm around her shoulder. "It's Daddy-Daughter Dinner night. I don't want these people to take that away from us too."

Keith tried to sound gentle, but he couldn't quite keep the bitterness out of his voice. Because he'd been waiting, braced for a dirty fight, but he'd never expected this. Never expected Eli Navarro to bail. A dull, sick feeling was spreading through him. Veronica looked up at her father, her eyes still fierce, but when she saw his face she softened, clearly worried.

"Okay. Come on, let's go sit down."

She led him toward the door to the living room. Then she paused, Pony bumping into her shins.

"You know, I've always thought *your* sauce was about perfect," she said. She squeezed him around the waist, and then held open the door for him to pass.

CHAPTER FORTY

Pan Valley was, like Neptune, a small town in unincorporated Balboa County. The similarities ended there. Fifteen miles inland, Pan Valley had no beachfront property, no tourist industry, no movie star residents, and no booming tech company to put it on the map. It was a blue-collar enclave, a dusty stretch of modest houses and postage-stamp yards.

Jade Navarro's mother, Rita, was a retired schoolteacher who lived in a neat yellow rambler near Pan High. An avid gardener, she filled her yard with lilac bushes and clusters of black-eyed Susans. Finches and swallows splashed and primped in a stone birdbath, and a pair of plastic rabbits wearing sun hats looked out from the shade of a honeysuckle bush.

Veronica pulled up in front of the house on Thursday morning, the day after the settlement was announced. She knew immediately that Weevil was there; his motorcycle was parked in the driveway. For a moment she sat in the car and watched.

What's the plan here, Veronica? You can't just charge into his mother-in-law's house and tear him a new one, however much you'd like to. Besides, it's not like you can change his mind. The papers have already been signed.

But she wanted answers. He owed her that much, at least, after everything they'd been through together. She got out of her car and shut the door.

Weevil appeared on the front porch. His shoulders had a sheepish curve, his hands buried in the pockets of his jeans. He met her at the foot of the steps.

"Whatever you got to say to me, I don't want Valentina to hear it. So can we please do this out here?"

Veronica's lips twisted downward. "What, you don't want your daughter to find out you're a sellout? You're not *ashamed*, are you, Weevil?" He looked down, but she continued, relentless. "I mean, it's not like you'd want her to believe in justice in a town like Neptune. Better that she finds out how things really work early on. Everything's for sale, right? Everything's got a price."

"You wanna get off your high horse for a minute?" Weevil's eyes sparked angrily. "I get it, okay? Sorry I can't live up to your high moral standard. But I didn't have much choice."

"You always have a choice," she spat. "You fight until you see you're beaten, and then you keep on fighting."

"I hate to tell you, but I ain't in on your crusade, okay? What I wanted all along was to get my life back. To get my family back. You know what it's like to have people counting on you and to let them down?" He stared her hard in the face. "Well, maybe you don't. So let me tell you. You feel helpless. Lower than dirt. I can't stand that, okay? I can't stand knowing someone else is paying for my daughter's clothes because I can't. I'd rather get shot again than feel that way."

"The money you would have won at trial . . ."

"There wasn't gonna *be* any money from that trial." Weevil ran his hand over his head. "Be real, V—Lamb and his cronies are buddy-buddy with every judge in this town. I didn't stand a chance."

"We had your back, Weevil! Me and my dad. Cliff. Lisa. And we had Lamb on his heels. He was scared, for good reason. Those judges you talk about—it's not Lamb they're obedient to, it's power. And he was losing it with every embarrassing news story, every witness we turned up, every voter who suddenly felt like they had a real shot at booting him out of office."

His eyes flickered back to the ground. "I know. And I'm sorry. I really am. Especially for letting your dad down. He's been better to me than I deserve, and I gotta live with that. But that trial could've stretched on for months—months that would have taken me out of work." He looked up again, a pleading expression in his eyes. "Now I can buy Jade a house. I can pay off my debts, maybe seed a new garage or something. Get my life back on track."

Veronica didn't answer. Anger still stiffened her spine, and her blood felt hot and heavy in her body. There didn't seem anything more to say.

Suddenly, Valentina appeared on the porch behind Weevil. She wore a purple sweat suit with puppies printed across the front.

"*Ponies* is starting, Daddy! C'mon, you're gonna miss the song!" she said imperiously. Then she saw Veronica and went suddenly shy, popping her index finger in her mouth and huddling behind her father's legs. Veronica tried to smile at her. Valentina just stared.

"I'll be right there, baby. Go back inside and sing it for

me real loud." Weevil didn't break eye contact with Veronica as he said it. Valentina hesitated, then ran back to the door.

"We done? I got to see a toddler about a talking unicorn," he said.

She gave him another long, disgusted look. "Oh, we're done. Have a great morning, Weevil. I'll see you around."

He seemed about to say something else. Then he gave a little shrug, and turned his back on her. A moment later he was gone.

She got in her car and slammed the door, seething. Excuses. Everyone always had so many *excuses*. And yet she'd been the one who'd told him he had to go back to Jade, had to take care of his kid.

What would you have done, Veronica? Would you have taken the money, for your family, for the people you loved? Or would you have kept on fighting, even when losing seemed more and more likely? Even if it meant hurting people who relied on you?

She didn't want to think about it. There was no answer that didn't make her feel like an asshole.

Veronica suddenly felt her phone vibrating in her pocket and pulled it out. She didn't recognize the number.

"Hello?" She leaned back against the driver's seat, the key dangling in the ignition.

The voice on the other end was high, babyish, and shot up at the end in a superfluous questioning tone. She thought for a moment it belonged to an actual child.

"Um . . . hi. My name's Rachel. Rachel Fahy. I'm trying to get in touch with Veronica Mars?"

"This is Veronica."

"Oh. Oh, um, hi. You sent me an e-mail. About the guy who raped me?"

Not a child. A victim. Veronica's fingers went slack for a split second, and she fumbled the phone. Grabbing it, she clutched it hard in her hand.

"Are you Tonya? Tonya Vahn?"

"Um, yes. That was my working name. One of them, anyway."

Tonya Vahn. The girl from Los Angeles, the fifth low-rated escort from Bellamy's reviews. The one who "looked nothing like her picture."

"You said this guy raped you?" Veronica said, keeping her voice low. "Can you tell me what happened?"

The girl's voice caught on the other end of the line.

"Sorry. It's still really hard to talk about this."

"That's okay. Take your time."

"I've been in therapy for the better part of a year, trying to sort this all out. My therapist said I should call you. She said it might help."

Veronica didn't say anything. She just waited.

"It was in October of last year . . ."

The story Rachel Fahy told her was by now familiar. She'd gotten the call late in the evening. She'd agreed to a last-minute, unscreened date for an extra two hundred more than her usual fee. He'd asked her, as usual, to be "demure." He wanted her to serve him, to keep her eyes down, and speak in a whisper. She worked incall, from a small studio apartment in Hollywood that she used for clients, and he arrived precisely on time. Rachel described a "middle-aged man, white, thin on top, very tall, and kind of heavy." According to her, he didn't seem happy to see her. "The first thing he said was that I was 'fatter' than I looked in the pictures," she said. Here, for the first time, a note of anger entered her voice. "I'd gained a few pounds I guess, but it wasn't a big deal."

It would have been a big deal to a guy looking for any excuse to hurt someone, Veronica thought. *It would have been a big deal to a guy who, by that time, had a ritual he had to see through.*

At first, Rachel had tried to placate him. She'd tried to stay in character, contritely apologizing for her appearance, begging him to forgive her. But when he didn't stop the verbal abuse, she had the temerity to suggest he find a different girl.

Veronica tried to conjure up an image of Rachel. Like Grace's, her website had been taken down; but the cached site Mac found had shown a young woman with a ballerina's build—long legs, prominent clavicle, all willowy, delicate lines. She imagined that body slightly rounder, fuller. She imagined that body taking a step backward, moving back toward the door, fed up with this man and his surly, domineering attitude.

That was when his meaty hand shot out and grabbed her by the throat.

From there it was the same story as Bethany Rose's and Grace Manning's. He choked her, raped her, and beat her. Then he left her there, alone and bleeding on the floor of her apartment.

"I couldn't walk for three days. I just pulled myself into the bed and curled up in a ball and stayed there until I felt like I could move again."

"You didn't call anyone? The cops, the hospital?"

"No."

Veronica felt a pang of disappointment. Of course she hadn't reported it. If she had, Bellamy's DNA would've been in the system and pinged as a match for the swab Veronica took.

"But you remember his face clearly? You could ID him?"

"Yeah. I could. The picture you sent, that was him. I'll never forget."

Veronica closed her eyes. The car was starting to get warm, the sun cutting straight through the windshield. Did this change anything? Another working girl, this one with no DNA evidence, no documented physical evidence at all, wouldn't win a case. But it might be enough to get a search warrant.

"Would you be willing to testify that this guy assaulted you, Rachel?"

There was a short pause before the girl spoke again. "I don't know. I, uh, didn't report it because I didn't want everyone to know what I was doing. I don't want to embarrass my family. They don't know. They still don't know. But that guy—what he did to me . . ."

The girl's voice dissolved into tears. Veronica's throat tightened in sympathy. She bit hard on the inside of her cheek, trying to keep steady. Something in her gut told her it was best to stay silent, that this girl was working through what she needed to on her own time.

Minutes passed. Rachel Fahy took several deep, gulping breaths. She was still crying, but she finally was able to speak through it.

"He ruined my life. I can barely leave my apartment, I'm scared of everything and everyone. I had to drop out of school. I was taking these pills for a while, and they helped, until they didn't, and then they made everything worse. I'm used up. I'm twenty-three and I'm all used up." She gasped as if in pain. "Yeah, okay. I'll testify. I'll do whatever you need me to do."

Veronica straightened her spine almost unconsciously, squaring off her shoulders. She talked a few more minutes with Rachel, arranging the details. Then she hung up the phone and sat for a moment, collecting herself before picking up the phone one more time and calling Leo.

He didn't even say hello. "Let me guess—you need a favor."

"Is that any way to talk to an old friend who's about to set you up for the collar of your life?"

"Hm, I feel like I've heard that promise before. I think I'm still chafed from that last once-in-a-lifetime opportunity."

Veronica moved the phone to her other ear. "I just heard from another one of Bellamy's victims. She's going to make a statement with LAPD tomorrow morning. You think that might be enough to get a warrant?"

"Yeah, it should be. This one actually remembers the attack?"

"Vividly. She's willing to ID Bellamy."

"I'll put in a call, see if LAPD can expedite the paperwork. I'll give you a call tomorrow."

"You're the best, Leo."

She hung up the phone again. Then, finally, she started the car, and pulled away from the curb.

It's probably too much to hope that Bellamy kept mementos of his attacks, but maybe there's something on his computer, in his phone. Maybe there's something that'll help us connect the dots.

But that would take some luck. And so far at least, luck hadn't been on their side.

of every call, almost like their patter had to warm up for a few minutes before they found the right rhythms.

"Anyway, he spends half his shift looking for the stuff, and he comes back up to the flight deck all excited, and he says to Shepard, 'This boat needs some organization. You ever think about alphabetizing the different kinds of grease, so it's easier to find?' I'd just taken a swig of water. Sprayed it right out my nose."

Veronica smiled. "Ah, classic. What will you young comic prodigies think of next? Have you tried calling the kitchen and asking if their refrigerator's running?"

"First of all, it's called the *galley*, and second of all, you don't want to mess with the cooks. They're already crazy." He gave a lopsided grin. "Anyway, we've all been through it. It's a rite of passage."

"I'm glad it's not just frat boys and Hell's Angels that get all the fun of hazing," she said.

Even missing Logan as much as she did, she couldn't keep her mind from wandering. She was expecting a call from Leo. He'd promised to give her an update. The San Diego cops had gotten a warrant to search Bellamy's place on Tuesday, but it took time to process a crime scene, especially if there was a computer involved. She tried to stay focused. *There's time to worry about the case later. You don't know when you'll talk to Logan again.*

"How's Po?" Logan craned his neck, making as if he were straining to see her. "I thought she'd be wearing a saddle by now."

Veronica picked up the laptop and angled it down so that he could see the puppy. He cooed her name, and she turned in excited circles.

CHAPTER FORTY-ONE

"So we've got this kid running all over the boat asking everyone he meets for 'relative bearing grease.' And of course everyone knows what that means—I mean, it's one of the oldest gags in the book—so they're all just stringing him along, telling him stuff like, 'Oh, yeah, I think they have some over in Maintenance.' 'Oh, sorry, we're out, so you'll have to go down to Supplies.'"

It was Friday, a week since Veronica had gotten the call from Rachel Fahy, and she sat at her kitchen counter, Skyping with Logan. It was early evening, and she had the windows propped open so she could hear the low thrum of the ocean a quarter mile away. Pony—now as tall as Veronica's knee—was sitting at her feet, looking alert and excited at the sound of Logan's voice. Table lamps gently lit the room and Neko Case streamed at low volume from the iPod dock.

It was just after six a.m. in the Persian Gulf, and Logan had already been awake for a few hours. He was wearing workout gear; after he logged off he was going to the gym to do a few miles on the treadmill before his shift started. Veronica took in his face greedily. It had been hard to find times when both of them could talk in the weeks since he'd left. She felt awkward, almost shy, for the first few minutes

"Sit," he said.

Pony sat.

"Damn! I still haven't been able to convince her that I wield the same authority you do," Veronica complained. "Pony, sit."

Pony barked, wiggled her butt, and ran around the living room. Veronica gave Logan an exasperated look.

"You see? Without you, it's chaos around here."

"It's the delicious, fetishistic thrill of military discipline," he said. "Isn't it, Pony . . . isn't it, my sweet little kinkster?"

The little dog frolicked toward his voice, whining softly. He smiled.

"Hey, listen, I gotta go in a second here," he said. "My time's almost up. You sure everything's okay?"

"Me? Yeah, I'm fine. Why?"

"I don't know. You seem a little out of it."

She felt her cheeks get warm. "Sorry. I've just got a lot on my mind, I guess. Maybe I need some of that *severe* military discipline too." She tried to make it sound light and flirty, but the words fell flat.

He gave her a worried look, but before he could say anything else, the screen went dark. They'd lost their connection.

She sat numbly in front of the computer for another few moments. Sometimes this happened, and he was able to get right back on and call her again just to say good-bye. Sometimes he wasn't. It was always jarring, frustrating, even scary. It was just one more thing she had to live with if they were going to make it.

She stood up and stretched. Then she looked down at Pony, who seemed to be waiting for more commands.

"Sit," she said. Pony wagged, her butt nowhere near the earth. Veronica sighed and knelt to pet her.

"I miss him too," she said.

She sighed again and glanced at her phone. Still blank. Impulsively, she pulled up Leo's contact info and hit Call.

"Hey. Sorry, I know you've probably been waiting to hear from me," Leo said when he picked up.

"With bated breath," she said. It was strange how much easier it was to talk to Leo than Logan right now. *Is it, though? We're working this case together. That's all it is.* Still, her voice got a little jauntier as she realized it. "What you got for me, D'Amato?"

"Sorry, Veronica, but we're coming up empty. There wasn't any evidence in that house—that we could find anyway."

The news stung. She drew in her breath a little. "There had to be *something*."

"I don't think so. That house was clean. Bellamy didn't even have any garden-variety pervert stuff around—no porn, no weird toys, no squicky pictures. And I just got the report back from the computer guy. He hasn't been able to turn up anything incriminating on Bellamy's hard drive."

She closed her eyes. The search warrant had been her last big shot. If they didn't have any physical evidence it was literally Bellamy's word—the word of a well-known, well-liked college basketball coach—against those of a handful of prostitutes who'd either lied to or avoided the cops entirely.

He's going to get away with it. Unless . . .

"Veronica? What are you thinking?" Leo asked. He sounded slightly worried.

"I've got to go. I've got some work to do," she said vaguely. "Call you tomorrow, Leo. I might very well need your help."

"With what? Veronica, what's—"

"See you, buddy. I owe you one." She hung up before he could say anything else.

Veronica sat for a moment, staring out into mid-distance. Then she pulled up the Pacific Southwest basketball schedule and skimmed over the upcoming games: *Seattle, Eugene, Las Vegas* . . . And there it was.

The scrap of paper was still tucked into her wallet, slightly crumpled but still legible. She grabbed one of her burner phones out of her bag—she always kept one or two handy, just in case—and dialed.

It only rang once before the baritone voice answered. "Yeah?"

"Sweet Pea. This is Veronica. The woman who was asking about Madelyn."

"I remember," he said matter-of-factly.

"I've got some information for you."

"Yeah?"

Her fingers tightened around the phone. She took a deep breath.

"Yeah. It looks like the man you asked me about is going to be in Vegas again in a few weeks. And I know exactly where he'll be."

CHAPTER FORTY-TWO

The Stardust Restaurant was a high-ceilinged, glittering cavern a floor above the Mercury Resort's casino. The walls were covered in purple velvet, and the Deco-style chandeliers were hung with multicolored crystals, sending tiny pinpricks of purple, red, blue, and green light dancing all over the room. The tables were crowded with late diners. It was after ten, but the Strip was just warming up.

Veronica sipped her Merlot and glanced around the room. Across the table from her sat a man with heavy, horn-rimmed glasses and a full black beard, cutting continental-style into his filet mignon. He looked almost professorial in a tweed jacket. It was all she could do to keep from laughing.

"What?" Leo asked. "What's so funny?"

"Just, you know, the whole effect." She stroked her own chin. "You grew that in a few weeks?"

"Hey, the D'Amatos are a hairy people."

She caught a glimpse of herself in the mirror behind Leo's head. She was every bit as disguised as Leo was: Her hair was tucked under a wavy brunette wig, and she'd caked on pink blush and dark lipstick that aged her by at least five years. It wouldn't fool anyone looking very closely, but no casual observer would be able to identify them either.

Maybe it was overkill but she hadn't wanted to run the risk of anyone in the hotel recognizing them.

It was the end of October—two weeks after the fruitless search of Bellamy's apartment, and two months since Veronica had last been at the Mercury. Veronica and Leo had been on the road since ten a.m.; he'd picked her up at her apartment in his vintage Mustang, and they'd cut across the desert with the top down. This time he wasn't along as Leo D'Amato, SDPD Detective; he was along as Leo D'Amato, heavily bearded private citizen.

"So, are we doing dessert, or . . ." She raised an eyebrow meaningfully. He grinned.

"You minx," he said. "Let's go upstairs."

As they passed through the casino they had to weave carefully between middle-aged women with fanny packs and sweaty, red-faced men. A few statuesque women in sequins drifted through the crowd like sea creatures, and Veronica wondered fleetingly if they were escorts.

They took the elevator up the tower to their room and locked the door securely behind them. She kicked off her shoes and took the wig off her head. It'd been hot underneath; her scalp was sweaty, her hair mussed. She sat on the edge of the bed, putting her laptop on her knees and opening it.

"Well, Coach D, as college hoops excitement builds here at SportsCrime Central, let's check in with Kestrels' coach Mitch Bellamy, who seems to have his own unique pregame ritual," she said, channeling Greg Gumbel.

The grainy image from a video camera suddenly filled her screen. It showed a room just like theirs, down to the purple bedspread and the strange geometric paintings on the walls.

Lying on his back, propped up against a half-dozen pillows, lay Mitch Bellamy.

"Looks like he's still alone," she said.

Leo shrugged off his jacket and sat down next to her. "What time did he check in?"

She checked the text Mac had sent her that evening. "Nine thirty-five. After dinner with the team, I'm guessing."

The Pacific Southwest Kestrels were in Vegas for a pre-season Invitational. That afternoon, they'd been slaughtered by the Oregon Ducks. Veronica and Leo had watched it on the hotel TV, resting from the long drive. Zabka had stormed the sidelines, purple in the face. But every time the camera showed Bellamy he looked calmly focused. It made Veronica bristle. She still remembered his mad fury when he'd found her in his office.

So it's just women you let loose on. Just women you think you can brutalize, she'd thought.

The team wasn't staying at the Mercury. They were set up at Caesars, along with all the other teams playing in the tournament. Bellamy had a room over there too, but a little over a week ago, Mac had discovered that he'd secured a second room at the Mercury—the same hotel where he'd met with Madelyn Chase almost a year ago—on his personal credit card.

That could mean only one thing—he was planning to "order in," and didn't want to risk the university finding out.

She watched Bellamy flip through channels on his TV. Every so often he glanced at the clock, his fingers tapping impatiently. He sighed heavily. When a knock finally came at his door, he jumped up from the bed.

"About fucking time."

Veronica felt Leo tense next to her as Bellamy lumbered across the hotel room. The camera was angled to catch most of the room—it'd been tucked behind a strategically draped curtain valence near the ceiling—but the small hallway leading to the door was cut off from view. For a moment all they had was audio.

The door opened. Bellamy's voice came, low and surly. "You're late."

A female voice answered. "Sorry, baby. I got here as quick as I could."

A short pause, and then Bellamy's voice again: "You're Morgan?"

"I can be." Her voice was teasing, somehow simultaneously insolent and sensual.

"What does that—"

"Can we discuss this in your room? I don't like to linger too long in doorways, you know?"

Veronica was willing to bet Bellamy hated being interrupted almost as much as he hated tardiness in his prostitutes. But after a moment, the door shut, and both of them moved back into view.

The girl was tall and amply curvy with full, voluptuous features. She wore a form-fitting cocktail dress and high silvery heels, and her thick, dark hair was pinned up behind her head. She stood with her legs slightly parted, leaning on one hip.

She glanced around the room approvingly. "This is nice. Real nice room." Then she turned to face Bellamy. "I'm sorry, baby, Morgan's not coming tonight. She got in a car accident on the way. She's okay, don't worry, but her car is totaled. She called me begging to come and see if there was any way you'd take me, instead. I'm Kenzie."

Veronica saw Bellamy's hands twitch, ever so slightly. She gave a grimly satisfied smile. Bellamy had gotten predictable through all his attacks. He didn't react well to having his fantasy interfered with; didn't like girls going off script. "Morgan," the girl he'd asked for, had been much more his usual type—delicate, slender, fine-boned. Getting someone else, specifically an Amazon with a centerfold body and a brassy attitude, was as off script as it got.

The girl seemed to sense his indecision. She put a hand on his forearm. "I won't disappoint you." Her voice was softer, suggestive.

He moved his arm away from her touch. "Fine." He looked her up and down. "Go get cleaned up. Wipe off that lipstick, it's fucking tacky. Then come on out and let me see you again, and I'll decide if I'm going to keep you."

She smiled coyly. "I'm pretty sure once you see what I've got you're not going to want to trade me in." She went into the bathroom, and Bellamy moved agitatedly around the room for a few minutes, plumping pillows, straightening things on the dresser top.

A moment later, the bathroom door clicked open. The girl stepped out. She'd changed into a short, tight chemise. Her hair was loose around her shoulders, her lipstick wiped away. Across the arc of one breast was the narrow line of a tattoo. It was hard to make it out in the video camera, but Veronica knew what it said: GODDESS.

"Like it?" the girl asked, pirouetting slowly in front of him.

"Don't look at me!" Bellamy snapped. He stabbed his index finger at her chest. "God, why do so many of you bitches ruin yourselves with all this tattoo crap? It just makes you look like a cheap whore."

"Whore? Sure. Cheap? No." She gave a cool smile, not flinching as his finger prodded her flesh. "And talking mean costs you extra, so you should be a little nicer unless you want this to get expensive in a hurry."

Veronica thought for just a moment that the video feed had frozen. Bellamy stood stock-still, as if trying to process what he'd just heard. "Kenzie" put her hands on her hips, Wonder Woman style.

Veronica had a split second to admire the woman's solid brass ovaries before Bellamy's hands shot out and grabbed at her throat.

The brunette deftly dodged out of his reach, her reflexes faster than Veronica would have guessed. She caught a glimpse of Bellamy's shocked face as he came up empty. Then his face contorted in pain as the woman drove her knee forcefully between his legs. He crumpled to his knees, clutching his crotch, and she kicked him again, this time in the face.

He was still curled up on the floor when she stepped over his body and went to unlatch the door. Her heels were soft in the carpet. The door opened and an enormous, hulking mass of a man entered the room. The shoulders of his sports coat strained to contain him. Like many big men in the security field, Sweet Pea moved gracefully, almost silently.

"Hello, Mr. Kiss and Tell," he said. His voice was a soft croon. He had a brisk, professional expression on his face as he looked the other man over. Veronica realized that he was sizing him up.

"Who the fuck are you?" Bellamy groaned. He struggled to push himself up. His face was flushed, a ribbon of blood trickling from one nostril.

Sweet Pea shrugged out of his jacket and handed it to the girl. He rolled his sleeves up. Veronica wondered in passing what he'd told the real Morgan, the girl Bellamy had ordered; the plan had been for Sweet Pea to intercept her in the lobby, pay her for her time, and send her away.

"Friend of Madelyn Chase. I bet you remember her. You met her just down the hall from this room, what, 'bout a year ago?" Bellamy's look turned to one of dawning horror. Sweet Pea nodded, as if his suspicions had just been confirmed. "Got some questions for you about her."

He glanced up at the girl who'd let him in. "You want to wait in the lobby, sweetheart?"

Isabella looked directly at Bellamy, the smile spreading wider across her face. She sat in a chair, crossing her legs and resting her hands on her knee.

"Oh, don't mind me," she said. "I like to watch."

CHAPTER FORTY-THREE

The following night, Veronica and Leo stepped out of the Mercury, and found themselves in the lights and noise at the heart of the Strip.

Drunken tourists staggered up and down the street, sipping on foot-tall frozen drinks. To the south she could see the Luxor's spotlight piercing up through the murky sky; north was the Stratosphere's glowing protrusion. Every inch in between flashed, sang, glittered, and roared. They made their way toward the corner, maneuvering past a crowd of tourists buying official *CSI* merchandise at a sidewalk kiosk. Just past the crush they had to wedge through a gauntlet of card-snappers. Veronica didn't glance right or left, but Leo looked startled as one persistent guy shoved a card right into his hand. Veronica pushed him forward, and as they came out the other side, he looked down at what he'd been given. Blushing red, he fumbled and dropped it.

"What the hell?" he asked, staring back at the crowd behind them.

Veronica bent down to pick up the card. It showed a girl with large fake breasts, her nipples covered with Photoshop stars. CALL MAI, said the print along the top. AT YOUR DOOR IN 20 MINUTES.

"Pretty ballsy," he said, frowning at the men who were still shoving their cards at everyone who passed them.

"They're out of your jurisdiction, Detective," she said. "Besides, we've got an appointment. Let's stay on track."

He made a face, then shrugged and followed her. She threw away the card in a trash can as she passed.

Desert Bluffs was Vegas's newest golf course, open just a few months. Tucked behind the Mercury, it was a stretch of green fringed with palms and acacia trees that boasted eighteen holes, a half-dozen water features, and the biggest sand trap in North America. Leo and Veronica arrived at the clubhouse a few minutes before ten. Two people were waiting for them, a man and a woman.

Leo was back in a suit and tie, his beard gone. Today he was back to being Detective Leo D'Amato. As far as the SDPD was concerned, he'd been in the middle of a long weekend in Vegas, using a few hard-earned days of vacation to play the slots and watch Cirque du Soleil when Veronica's tip came in. Convenient, because he'd be able to assist the Las Vegas police with their investigation, which seemed to be connected to the rape case he'd *just* been looking into back in San Diego.

"And a good thing too," he'd told his CO when he'd taken the call. "I already lost my shirt at the craps table. Time to get back to work."

He shook hands with the woman first. "Detective Garcia. Thanks so much for your help." She was in her mid-forties, threads of gray weaving through her short dark hair. She was dressed for manual labor in heavy canvas work pants and boots. "This is Veronica Mars, the PI I told you about on the phone."

"Pleasure to meet you, D'Amato. Mars. This is the property manager, Kevin Cornell." She gestured to the man, sallow and slender in an English-cut suit. He cast Leo a fretful look.

"How long do you think this'll take? Our earliest tee off tomorrow is at eight thirty. If we could just get this taken care of before then . . ."

Garcia laughed. "I keep trying to explain to him that this golf course is now a crime scene, but he doesn't seem to get it. No one's teeing off at eight thirty, Kevin."

"We'll try to be as efficient as we can," Leo said. "But Detective Garcia's right. You'll probably need to cancel tomorrow's clients. At least those before noon."

Cornell gave a feeble little groan, but didn't argue.

"The dogs definitely reacted out there, but we haven't been able to pinpoint the exact spot," Garcia said to Veronica and Leo. "It looks like it could be a long night."

They all climbed into a golf cart, Cornell at the wheel, and took off into the darkness, headed toward the seventh hole.

The ride was dreamlike, surreal. The cart's rising and falling movements as it passed over rolling terrain felt like a night flight in a glider. Straight ahead was an even darker horizontal swathe formed by a row of trees. Above them the lights of the Strip pulsed like the aurora borealis.

Even by night it was obvious the course was incredibly lush. Man-made lakes spread out on either side of them, dense with cattails. The grass looked velvet-soft. *All in the middle of a desert,* Veronica thought. *Water crisis be damned.*

Floodlights came into view ahead, a few people moving around beneath them. The sand trap, nicknamed "the Little

Mojave," stretched out across twenty-five thousand square feet of the green, just surpassing "Hell's Half Acre" at New Jersey's Pine Valley as the new standard-bearer for sand trap grandiosity.

"How exactly did you get this lead again?" Garcia turned to glance at them in the backseat.

Leo glanced at Veronica. Veronica gave a brisk smile.

"Can we call it an anonymous informant and leave it at that?"

Garcia grinned. "I'm a Vegas cop, honey. That's how *most* of our work gets done."

They pulled up just outside a perimeter of police tape, then ducked underneath it. Four people in coveralls were digging, scraping, and sifting. Cornell covered his eyes and moaned.

"Relax, Mr. Cornell." Veronica smiled brightly. "You'll be able to put it right. I'm pretty sure this is what hospitality insurance was made for."

Garcia handed Leo a shovel. Veronica picked up another from a small pile of implements. Silently, they got started.

The work was slow. They didn't know how deep to dig, so forensics had been loath to bring out a bulldozer. Something that big could accidentally destroy evidence. But the trap was over a half-acre wide, a sprawling area to explore by hand. The dogs had helped to narrow the search, but not by much.

Veronica's back ached, her hands starting to blister from the shovel. She thought about what she'd learned the night before, after she'd turned off the video at the point when Sweet Pea shed his coat and advanced on Bellamy. Plausible deniability had something to do with her decision not to watch, but mostly she just didn't want to see what came next. She'd gone down to the bar, back in her wig, and met Sweet Pea an hour and a half later. He'd taken a seat on a stool next to her and ordered a Coke.

"I'd have thought you'd be ready for a drink after all that," she said, not glancing at him.

"Not me. I'm eight years sober." He took a sip. Then he turned to face Veronica and told her what she needed to know, his voice soft but distinct: "The Little Mojave."

She was surprised at how unruffled he looked. His jacket was neat and crisp, and there was no blood or sweat, no smell of iron, no bruises. You would have thought he'd come straight from the office.

"What?"

"The Little Mojave. It's a sand trap on the Desert Bluffs golf course. It was under construction in December, back when Maddy went missing."

Veronica had been surprised to feel her heart sink. She'd known since first meeting with Sweet Pea and Isabella that Madelyn Chase—or Molly Christensen, or whoever she really was—was most likely dead. But hearing it stated so matter-of-factly made her shoulders sag.

"And Bellamy . . ."

"He's en route to the ER. Iz told the front desk she'd heard screaming from the room. I saw an ambulance pull up about five minutes ago."

The thought should have chilled her, but it didn't. She'd made her choice. She'd known exactly what the result would be.

Sometimes, that was the job.

It was just after three a.m. when Garcia let out a shout.

The rest of the team hurried toward her. Veronica moved slowly, setting down her shovel. There was no hurry. Not anymore.

A partially mummified foot protruded from the layer of soil below the sand.

They'd finally found Madelyn Chase.

CHAPTER FORTY-FOUR

Veronica stepped into Miki's Diner, just after the lunch rush. Dick Dale's sixties surf rock played over the speakers, the rampaging tempos and twanging guitars an uneasy match for the afternoon quiet. The tables were mostly empty. Veronica lingered in the doorway for a moment, waiting.

Then she caught sight of the person she'd come to meet: Grace Manning, dressed in the diner's boxy pink uniform, her ticket pad tucked in her breast pocket.

Grace looked up at her and gave a little wave, motioning for her to take a seat wherever. "I'll be there in a sec. Just got to clock out for my break." She was already untying her apron, draping it over one arm. Veronica took a seat under the fiberglass statue of a cartoon surfer on a cresting wave, the same one she'd sat in with Keith while waiting for the verdict in Weevil's case. She slipped out of her jacket and placed it on the seat beside her.

Grace hadn't been able to make tuition that fall. She'd dropped out of Hearst, picking up as many shifts as she could at the diner. Veronica had only heard about it that morning, when she called Grace to tell her they'd busted Bellamy. She'd been so busy with the details of the case that she hadn't thought to ask the girl about school. Grace, prickly and private, hadn't offered the information until now. The news triggered a pang of dismay. Veronica and Keith had spent years on the brink of poverty but they'd always been able to make ends meet. She'd never been faced with a reality like Grace's—a world in which she had no money and, even worse, no family.

"Hey!" A moment later, Grace appeared at the side of the booth. She set a tray on the edge of the table; it held two cups of coffee and two pieces of pie. "On the house," she said. "One of the perks of working here."

"Thanks." Veronica looked the girl over. She'd expected to see Grace looking more hostile than ever, assumed she'd take the loss of her education hard. But she actually seemed, if not deliriously happy, at least amiable. Her cheeks were fuller than they'd been the last time they'd met. Her demeanor was calmer, less high-strung. "How're you doing, Grace?"

Grace sat down across from her. "Well, my feet hurt, and some klutz spilled orange juice on me first thing this morning, but I'm doing okay." She poured two creamers into her coffee and stirred with brisk, delicate movements. Then, in a slow, measured voice she asked, "So . . . this guy. He's in jail?"

"Not yet. Right now he's in the hospital. But as soon as they can move him, yeah, he's going to jail."

"In the hospital?" Grace frowned.

Veronica took a sip of coffee. "Yeah, I guess someone roughed him up pretty good. The cops formally arrested him at the hospital but the shape he's in—they won't be able to take him in for at least another week or so."

"Roughed him up" is probably an understatement, Veronica

thought. Sweet Pea's fastidious attentions had left Bellamy with two broken fingers, four broken ribs, a ruptured spleen, and a collapsed lung. Veronica was glad there was no one to ask if she felt at all bad about her role in the confession. She generally didn't like violence, but she felt that Bellamy had earned a special exception.

Apparently she wasn't alone in this judgment. A cold smile spread across Grace's face as she cradled her mug between her hands.

"It's hard to say just what'll happen next," Veronica continued. "They're still looking at the evidence. But the victim we found in the sand trap had strands of hair on her that match Bellamy's."

The body had belonged to eighteen-year-old Kimberly Weir of Odessa, Texas—otherwise known as Madelyn Chase. The scraps of human skin under her fingernails were still at the lab, but Veronica had a feeling they'd match Bellamy's DNA too. Between that, Rachel Fahy's testimony, and the semen sample they'd found on Grace, the prosecutors would have a strong case for conviction.

"So it's not really over," Grace said, looking down.

Veronica placed her hand over Grace's. "It's never really over."

For a moment, they sat in silence. But there was more to say. Veronica steeled herself and continued. "I have to warn you, Grace, it's possible you'll face public exposure when this goes to trial. Technically, they're supposed to keep victims anonymous; in practice it doesn't always work that way."

The girl nodded. "I know. I figured." She gave a little shrug. "I told Lizzie on the phone the other night. She's in New York now—she's a chef, did I tell you?" She laughed softly. "I hadn't told her any of it. I don't know why. She's the only member of my family I've ever been able to talk to. Well . . . her and Meg." Her voice dropped slightly when she said her oldest sister's name. "Anyway, I guess I was embarrassed. Not just about the job, but about . . . about the attack. I didn't want her to have to know what'd happened to me. I know that's stupid."

Veronica thought about how long she'd kept her own secret. She'd never told her father about the night at Shelly Pomroy's party; a part of her had wanted to protect him from that knowledge. "It's not stupid. But I'm glad you told her. It's a lot to go through on your own."

Grace nodded. "It wasn't a fun conversation. But she knows the whole thing now, and she's the only person left whose opinion I cared about. It was good for me too. I was starting to feel myself get just a bit too casual about lying. Too inattentive to the point where selling a necessary lie turns into . . . losing yourself in the part." She smiled ruefully. "Kind of an occupational hazard for me, I guess. But, Veronica, I still cringe when I remember how fucking sanctimonious my performance was when I looked you right in the eye and falsely accused a man I'd never even met."

"Well, Grace, I know a lot about your family history," said Veronica. "Compelling lies were a constant theme. All things considered, I'd say your grip on reality is remarkably strong."

"Hey! Speaking of . . ." Grace gave another sudden, savage grin. "I am totally relishing the idea of my parents finding out what I used to do for a living. I'd love to see my mom's face. But I already know exactly what they'd say." She leaned forward, a wild, zealous gleam entering her eyes. "*And the*

*daughter of any priest, if she profane herself by playing the
whore, she profaneth her father: she shall be burnt with fire.'"*

"Nice," said Veronica, offhand. "I'd have gone with ston-
ing, myself."

"That's for witches," Grace said. "But if you're feeling left
out, I'm pretty sure they've been praying for your demise too.
At least since Faith went missing." She set her mug down
and looked up at Veronica, her expression suddenly hard to
read. "Veronica?"

"Yeah?"

"Would you tell me if you knew where she was? Faith, I
mean?"

Veronica hesitated. She'd made a promise, a long time
ago. She'd kept her silence for years. But now Grace watched
her with hopeful, desperate eyes—this girl with almost no
one in her life, with a mattress on the floor, a legacy of
trauma and loneliness and fear she was only now coming to
terms with.

"All I know," she said, "is that Duncan renamed her Lilly."

Grace bit the corner of her lip. For just a second Veronica
thought she might be about to cry. But then she nodded, and
picked up her fork.

"Anyway," Grace said, an abrupt signal to change the
subject. "I'm working here five days a week now. More or
less full-time, depending on how many hours they have for
me. It's not so bad."

"I'm sorry. About, you know . . . Hearst. I can't believe
they wouldn't find you any aid."

Grace shrugged. "It's all right." She speared a bite of pie
on the end of her fork. "I mean, don't get me wrong—I don't
see this as some kind of awesome character-building situa-

tion that God has favored me with. But I'm not going to let it stop me. Either I'll find the money to go back to school, or I'll figure out a different way to get where I want to go. Hell with it, maybe I'll just go straight to New York or London, and Hearst College can just go fuck itself."

"Hear, hear," Veronica said, lifting her mug in a toast. They clinked ceramic lightly over the table.

Grace's face softened. She looked down at her pie, her lower lip sticking out in a thoughtful pout. When she looked back up, her face was pink.

"How often do people say thank you to you?"

Veronica swallowed her mouthful of coffee and cleared her throat. "'Thank you' ranks just below 'You ruined my life' and just above 'When I get my hands on you.'"

"I mean, if you hadn't kept at it, the Grand would've settled, and I'd still be at Hearst. I don't know exactly why I'm grateful to you and your stupid integrity," Grace said wryly. Then she smiled. "But Veronica . . . thank you."

Veronica wasn't sure what to say. She held the girl's gaze for another moment, then Grace smiled, shrugged, and headed back toward the kitchen. Veronica took another bite of pie. And as she delighted in the sugary goodness, she had an epiphany. She knew in that moment she'd never be rich. Veronica found comfort in being jaded. She could imagine no greater shame than to have her emotions manipulated. To get played. So why did this "thank you" from a girl who'd lied to her, who'd tried to game the system, mean more to her than the big check from a corporate client that had been wholly in the right? *Figure that one out,* she thought, *and maybe I can help my kids understand why their mom resigned herself to a lifetime of truck-stop pie and coffee—just like Granddad.*

CHAPTER FORTY-FIVE

"Honey, could you take the nachos? I need to get these stuffed mushrooms into the oven."

Veronica took the tray from Keith's outstretched hand. "You got it."

It was a week after Veronica's return from Vegas, and they were in her dad's kitchen, putting the finishing touches on an array of party snacks that could've fed the Union Army at Gettysburg. Plates of veggies, mini quiches, and chips and dip sprawled haphazardly across every surface. It was election day, and Keith had put out an open invite to anyone who needed a little emotional support while the votes came in. Now he crouched over the stove in an apron that said "Kiss the Cop," fumbling with a pan of breadcrumb-and-Asiago-filled cremini mushrooms.

Veronica pushed through the kitchen door. The living room and dining room were full to bursting with friends and neighbors. There were plenty of familiar old faces—retired deputies, friends Keith still had in the fire and EMT departments. A few of their neighbors from their old apartment. Inga waved at her from where she sat in her father's armchair. Lisa stood in the doorway, sharing a plate of strawberries and Gouda with her wife, Lindsay. Mac and Wallace sat on the sofa, eyes glued to the election reports, Mac absently stroking Pony's ears as she watched.

The dining room table was already brimming with cheese platters, wine bottles, veggie dip, and a tower of chocolate cupcakes Veronica had baked that afternoon. She made room for the nachos and had just set them down when Cliff sidled up to her.

"How's it looking?" she asked, moving aside as he picked up a paper plate. He shrugged.

"Still too close. It could be a long night."

The polls had closed three hours earlier, and while a lot of the ballots had already been called, the sheriff's race was far too tight to project a winner. She sighed.

"Well, at least we've got enough food to survive tonight's scheduled apocalypse."

"That's cheerful. Any word from our friend, Judas?"

Veronica gave him an admonishing look. "Dad invited him to stop by tonight, no hard feelings, but I doubt he'll show. He seemed pretty ashamed when I talked to him."

"I tell you what. If Lamb loses tonight, I will forgive and forget. No harm, no foul." Cliff popped a cherry tomato in his mouth.

She smiled. "And if he wins?"

"Four more years of Lamb would be plenty punishment for all of us," Cliff said. "*And* I won't invite Eli to my birthday party."

Veronica watched Cliff lope back into the living room, his plate laden down with food. She hadn't forgiven Weevil, per se. But earlier that week he'd texted her a simple photo, no accompanying words. It showed Jade and Valentina burying him to his neck in the sand on the beach, all of them laughing.

His voice came back to her suddenly. *You know what it's like to have people counting on you and to let them down?* What *would* she do to take care of the people who counted on her? How far would she compromise? She thought about Bellamy, handcuffed to his bed at the hospital. She thought about Grace's expression at the diner when she told her he'd be charged for his crimes. She was less able to answer the question than ever.

A knock came at the front door. Veronica shook off her reverie, and went to get it. Leo stood on the porch, wearing a black leather jacket over his shirt and tie. He held a bottle of wine. They hadn't seen each other since Sunday, on the long drive back to Neptune. Then, they'd both been keyed up from their discovery, jittery and sad and excited all at once. They hadn't talked much, but at a rest stop just outside Joshua Tree State Park they'd sat at a picnic table and eaten burgers and greasy french fries. The sky was a stark, steely blue over the desert, the landscape as dry and saturated as autumn leaves. *The east coast can keep its fall colors,* she thought. *We've got landscape of our own.*

"You know, Veronica, we're really good together." Leo spoke suddenly in the midst of the silence. Veronica felt her cheeks burn, remembering the shared kisses of a decade before. She'd be lying if she denied feeling Leo's affection for her as they'd worked on the case. She'd be telling herself a worse lie if she refused to admit that she enjoyed it. But the dirty little secret, the one that pained her in the wee hours when she couldn't sleep, was that she felt something similar for Leo.

Until this moment, she'd buried it deep. It was not unlike the way she'd turned off the camera when Sweet Pea went to work on Bellamy. She was anxious to maintain plausible deniability. Leo was here. He hadn't chosen to leave her. Her dad adored him. Keith didn't have to figure out a way to "develop a healthy relationship" with him. Veronica's feelings became jumbled, and she was just trying to figure out how to articulate them. *I'm with Logan, and I love him more than I thought I could love a man, and we have an opportunity to be happy in spite of everything and I can't throw all that away for something more convenient.* But then she realized that Leo was still talking. "You ever think about going legit? You'd have to start on a beat, but you'd make detective in no time. The academy's testing in December."

She smiled then. Her confused thoughts went still. She was certain she was blushing, something her dad often compared to a Halley's Comet sighting. There were already so many complications to her life; why did her brain seem so eager to invent more?

"Me? On the force?" She laughed. "Can you imagine me reporting to a CO? Come on, D'Amato. I'm a loose cannon. A cowboy cop. A maverick. Besides, just because I'm not legit doesn't mean we can't work together. I think this arrangement worked out pretty well for both of us. And I'm not sure Detective Veronica Mars, SDPD, would've been quite so willing to play fast and loose with the criminal element."

"Really? Because I'm pretty sure Detective Veronica Mars would be plenty willing. And that might be a problem." He grinned. "But fair enough." He grabbed one of her fries and dipped it in the ketchup. "Let me know if you ever start dreaming of a pension and actual benefits. It's not all bad, playing by the rules."

Now she opened her dad's front door wider to let him in.

"Sorry I'm late," he said to the group. "We win yet?"

"Not yet. But we haven't lost yet either. Thanks for coming."

"Hey, thanks for having me. Nice spread." He waved at Mac and Wallace as he entered, setting the wine bottle on the table just as Keith burst out of the kitchen with his mushrooms.

"Detective!" he said, spying Leo. "Welcome, welcome. Hope you brought your appetite."

"I never leave home without it, sir," Leo said, grinning.

Keith slapped Leo on the shoulder and went into the living room to offer the hors d'oeuvres around. Leo turned back to Veronica, looking suddenly more serious. "How you doing?"

"I'm doing all right. Apart from the fact that we're about to get four more years of Lamb, I mean."

"Yeah, well. That just means you'll have four more years to give him hell." His eyes sparkled.

A hubbub rose up in the living room, overridden by Lisa's authoritative "Shhhhh!" Veronica hurried to the doorway to see what was happening.

On the screen, a stiff-haired Martina Vasquez stood on the steps outside of the courthouse, microphone in hand. "It seems we're only a few moments away from hearing the results from the Balboa County sheriff's race. And if you're wondering why we haven't projected a winner it's because, so far, no clear leader had emerged when the last precinct results came in. But the head of elections just informed us that they've finished counting the ballots and are preparing their announcement."

Inga had her hands over her mouth, her eyes wide. On the sofa, Mac pulled her knees to her chest in a protective hug.

"No whammy, no whammy, no whammy," said Keith. Nobody laughed as they stared at the screen.

The newscaster seemed to be listening to something for a moment. Veronica's knuckles were white as she clutched the doorjamb, braced for the news.

"These numbers are subject to final certification, of course, but it appears that political newcomer Marcia Langdon has edged ahead—largely on the strength of votes from precincts in the predominantly minority Eastside. We're projecting she will win the race by fewer than two hundred votes."

The room erupted. Wallace leapt from the sofa, doing a modified touchdown dance in the middle of the living room. Lisa threw her arms around Cliff, then turned and kissed her wife. Drinks were exultantly chugged, pots and pans were pounded with ladles, and Pony bolted maniacally around the room on an interspecies contact high.

Veronica stared at the TV. Marcia Langdon was coming out to the podium to deliver her acceptance speech, surrounded by falling balloons and cheering supporters. Even her victory smile was grim; she waved at the crowd with a satisfied, no-nonsense set to her chin. For a moment Veronica let herself imagine what it could be like, this world without Lamb. Would Langdon be able to whip a long-corrupt department into shape? Would the wealthy of Neptune tolerate a sheriff who didn't pander to their every need? Or would they just find another way to get what they wanted anyway?

She took a flute of champagne from the platter Keith was passing around, lifted her glass, and toasted the new order. Surely things couldn't get worse.

Veronica drove home a few hours later, after helping Keith make a dent in the mess. Pony was asleep in the back of the car, one enormous paw dangling over the side of the seat.

The celebration had gone on far later than anyone had planned. They'd opened a bottle of champagne that Cliff had brought, just in case. Inga got giggly after her third glass. Keith proposed a toast. "To Marcia," he'd said, holding up his red plastic cup. "To our new sheriff."

Cliff raised his cup in assent and hoarsely added, "And to the citizens of Neptune, for voting her riveted-on, steel-plated ass *in!*" The group had shared a final *Hear, hear!* and clapped their PVC chalices together.

So Lamb was out. Veronica entertained the thought that perhaps she'd been wrong; maybe things *could* change in Neptune, slowly and against the tide. She wasn't sure what kind of sheriff Langdon would be, but at least she'd be different. That was a start.

Other than that, things were set to get back to normal—or what passed for it in her life. In a few weeks she planned to drive to Tucson to spend her first Thanksgiving with her little brother. She wouldn't see him for Christmas. That she reserved for Keith, forever and always. But Lianne had found a used guitar, and Veronica had arranged for him to take weekly lessons with a local teacher.

She'd have to start finding more paid gigs. Some would be with people she didn't respect or like. Some would be seedy, dirty, and as crooked as Neptune's black heart. But some of them? Some would matter.

First things first, though. Tonight she had a date.

She pulled into the parking lot of her complex. Pony was on her feet the moment they parked, wagging wildly. Upstairs, she turned on the lamps and checked her reflection. Then she opened her computer.

She didn't have to think about all the time she and Logan spent apart, all the distance their lives might put between them. Not tonight, anyway. Right now, all she had to think of was him. The fact that he was alive. The fact that he was doing something that made him proud and strong. The fact that she loved him. In this moment, that was enough.

The computer chimed. She clicked Accept, and Logan's face appeared on-screen. His eyes lit up at the sight of her.

"I wasn't sure if you'd make it," he said.

She smiled.

"I'm here," she said.